THE GHOSTS OF
RAYNHAM HALL

The first novel in The Watchers of Time series

S G Taylor

ISBN: 1983545988
ISBN 13: 9781983545986
Library of Congress Control Number: 2018900359
CreateSpace Independent Publishing Platform
North Charleston, South Carolina

For Dannie, Andrew, and Christian
My Talismans

TABLE OF CONTENTS

Let us go in together,
And still your fingers on your lips, I pray.
The time is out of joint—O cursèd spite,
That ever I was born to set it right!
Nay, come, let's go together.

Hamlet Act 1, scene 5

1

THE GHOST BOY

“There are no such things as ghosts!” said Grandpa George in a singsong voice as he tucked Andrew and Christian into their beds. “Nothing but figments of the imagination. Stuff and nonsense.” He pulled a silly face, and his big blue eyes sparkled brighter than ever through the thick lenses of his gold-framed glasses.

“But Ethan said he saw a small ghost boy,” Andrew insisted, his little face earnest in the bedroom light.

“Ghosts are as real as flying pigs. Have you seen any of *them* around here lately?” Grandpa George’s face contorted in exaggeration. He put his hand above his eyes and pretended to look out the window like an old sea captain looking for dry land. “Nope, nothing out there!”

“But Camille said the reason adults don’t see ghosts is because they only come out at night to scare kids.” Christian hated being frightened. He disliked nothing more than eerie music in movies and loud surprises, like fireworks banging on the Fourth of July.

“Ha!” chortled Grandpa George, his eyebrows bouncing like dancing caterpillars. “Those children are filling your heads with hogwash.” The old man tutted to himself.

But as Andrew looked at his grandfather’s face, he could tell there was something Grandpa George was holding back. Only someone who knew Grandpa George very well could have spotted the all-too-brief expression. His lip twitched, he raised one eyebrow sharply, and he cast a sideways glance at Christian and Andrew, as if he didn't want them to see his eyes in case they were giving away the truth. Although Andrew didn't believe Grandpa George way lying, he did believe his grandfather wasn't quite telling him the truth.

Andrew leaned as close as he could to Grandpa George, hunting for clues in his grandfather's face. "So you're telling me there are no such things as ghosts?"

"Poppycock!" said Grandpa George without blinking. His face had returned to its normal appearance.

Andrew laughed. "People don't say 'poppycock' anymore."

"They do in England," said Grandpa George.

"But we live in America," Christian replied.

"I know that!" Grandpa George faked being indignant and put his hands on his hips. "But don't forget, I came from England."

"How could we ever forget!" Andrew said. "You remind us every day."

Grandpa George was a tall, portly man. He had a tuft of gray hair that crept in a semicircle around the sides of his bald head. Despite his age, Grandpa George was still a very powerful-looking man. His hands were as large as bear paws and his fingers were as strong as grappling hooks. He stood on stout legs, and his chest was as broad as a kitchen table. But there was a softness to him also. Grandpa George never raised his voice, and he didn't anger easily. Instead, he always spoke kindly and was incredibly polite to everyone. And there was nothing quite like the sound of Grandpa George laughing. It reminded the boys of birthday parties.

"It's late. You'd better get to sleep or you'll wake up all tired and grumpy. Don't worry about silly things like ghosts. They don't exist. Nothing but a waste of the imagination. You should think of something nice before you go to sleep."

"But Grandpa," said Andrew, trying desperately to get to the truth, "if there are no such things as ghosts, why are there so many ghost stories?"

Grandpa George huffed to himself and sat down on Christian's bed, which creaked and dipped gently under the old man's weight.

"All those stories," said Andrew, gaining confidence, "of ghosts, and vampires, and werewolves, and trolls. Are you telling me there's no truth in any of them?"

"You do have a point," Grandpa George conceded. "There are a lot of stories about things that go bump in the night. But that's all they are: stories." As Grandpa George finished talking, Andrew saw it again: a sign in his face indicating Grandpa George wasn't quite telling the truth. Only this time, Andrew was sure of it.

"But if some stories are true, why aren't ghost stories?" Christian asked.

Grandpa George laughed loudly, filling the bedroom like a booming drum. He crossed his arms in front of him and jutted out his chin. "Because ghosts don't exist and ghost stories are written to scare naughty boys so they'll be good for their grandpas!"

Getting up from Christian's bed he patted each of the boys on their head, then turned off the table light and shuffled toward the door.

"Are you sure there are no such things as ghosts?" Andrew called, his small, round eyes peering intently through the dark.

"*Really* sure?" Christian insisted, tilting his head to see his grandfather.

"I'm confident," Grandpa George said, looking back at them with a smile. "They're the stuff of books and silly folklore. Now go to sleep. It's late."

With that, he turned away and walked downstairs, the sound of his heavy footsteps receding as he went.

"Do you believe him?" whispered Andrew as soon as he knew Grandpa George was out of earshot.

"I guess so," Christian replied.

Both boys sat up in their bed. It was impossible to know they were brothers simply by looking at them. Andrew Redmond was tall and willowy, with dark hair and olive-colored skin. He had inquisitive eyes that were always brimming with questions. Christian Redmond was fair-haired. He had a bridge of freckles that crossed his nose, running from cheek to cheek. He loved to solve puzzles and always had a book in his hand. Christian was eleven months younger than Andrew, but the two brothers stood nearly as tall as one another. Christian was stocky and looked like his grandfather, whereas Andrew's slenderness came more from his mother's side of the family.

"I don't believe him," Andrew said. "He's hiding something."

"Why would he do that?" Christian protested.

"I don't know. I just feel there's something he's not telling us."

"But Grandpa never concealed anything from us before."

"I guess not," Andrew said, agreeing reluctantly. "But I'm sure there's something he's not telling us."

The boys looked at each other. They had shared the same bedroom for as long as either of them could remember. They did everything together whenever they could. They played on the same soccer team, went to the same school, and sometimes even finished one another's sentences.

"What made you ask Grandpa about the ghost boy?" asked Christian.

"The rumors," Andrew said. "I wanted to know if he knew anything about them."

Andrew remembered how, earlier in the week, stories about the ghost boy had begun to float around school like bits of old paper blown by the wind. Andrew's friend Ethan had told David about the ghost boy while playing on the basketball courts two weeks ago. Later, David told Chloe, and then Chloe told Alison, James, and Chase. Soon, children all over school were huddling in packs and whispering among themselves about ghosts. The rumors grew ever more fantastical with each retelling.

Christian opened a book about a guinea pig detective who hunted werewolves. The night-light between the brothers' beds shone dimly as he thumbed through a few pages and then stopped. He stared intensely at a picture of the small hero, who was dressed in a cloak and was wearing a deerstalker. The hero shook a little fist at a huge man-shaped monster with a wolf's head. Christian wanted to turn on the table light, but he knew it was late and Grandpa George, or, worse, his mom and dad, would expect them to be asleep by now. So he struggled in the half-light, squinting to read as best he could.

"What did Ethan say that got you so spooked?" asked Christian, without taking his eyes from his book. "You didn't tell me everything about the ghost."

Andrew paused before speaking. "Well . . . Ethan saw a strange-looking boy in his backyard one night last week when he went to take out the garbage."

"What was strange about him?" Christian said. He put down the book and shuffled across his bed to get closer to his brother.

Andrew smiled. He enjoyed telling stories to Christian. Nothing gave him greater pleasure than making his brother laugh or scaring him silly.

"Ethan said the strange boy was *shining*," said Andrew, carefully pronouncing every word.

"What do you mean 'shining'?" asked Christian. "Was he carrying a flashlight or something?"

"Shining," Andrew whispered, "like a ghostly spirit."

"No way," Christian said, pulling back from his brother. The hair on the back of his neck stood up, and he felt a little shiver go down his arms and legs.

"But the strangest thing," Andrew continued, "is that Ethan said the ghost boy just disappeared right in front of him, as if by magic."

"Are you kidding me?" Christian's eyes grew to the size of small saucers.

"He was there one minute and gone the next," Andrew said, clicking his fingers.

The boys sat quietly in their beds, feeling the warmth of the blankets lying against their bodies. The dim night-light cast deep shadows on their faces and exaggerated their features, making them look like little goblins in the dark. The room felt eerily quiet, as if it were scared by the ghost stories. Neither boy knew quite what to say next.

"Ghosts can't be real," said Christian, shaking his head and trying to convince himself.

"I guess you're right," Andrew said, pulling the sheets closer to him. "There are no such things as ghosts."

Suddenly, they heard a massive crash. A heavy book about dinosaurs had slipped off Andrew's bed and crashed to the floor. Both boys jumped in surprise, their hearts rushing into their mouths.

"Jeez!" Christian exclaimed. "That scared the life out of me."

"Me too," Andrew said.

They both began to laugh uncontrollably. The tension eased. The boys were safe at home, in bed, warm, well fed, and sleepy. Nothing could be going wrong in the world. Grandpa George was downstairs reading, or, more likely, sleeping, with a book rising and falling on his broad chest as he snored. *Ghosts are just a figment of the imagination,* thought Andrew. *They're just stuff and nonsense, as Grandpa George says. How can we be so silly?*

From the living room, the deep, soft voice of the children's grandfather filled the house then rose to the second floor: "Time to go to sleep, boys!"

"Feel the wrath of The Grandpa," Christian joked, placing both hands on his cheeks and feigning fear.

Turning off the night-light, Andrew lay down and stared at the blank ceiling. Christian did the same.

"I'm going to find that ghost boy," Andrew said, in a clear, determined voice.

"Can I help you?" Christian asked, turning to look at his brother excitedly.

"I was hoping you would say that," Andrew said. He smiled to himself before drifting off to sleep.

2

THE PLAN

When Andrew woke up, he was relieved to see it was a beautiful summer's morning in the town of Oyster Bay. That night, he had dreamt about the shimmering ghost boy. But he had also seen something else in his dreams. Something that had been chasing him. A dark, gloomy man with big teeth and orange eyes.

The sun was slowly beginning to crest the steeple of St. Dominic's Church, and although the morning still was early, all signs pointed to a sweltering, hot day. Birds were chorusing: chickadees, blue jays, and cardinals, their sweet melodies dancing between the trees like dueling echoes. The grass and leaves bloomed a fresh, lush, summer green. Down by the bay, the water, still cold to the touch, lapped invitingly against the pebble beach at Theodore Roosevelt Memorial Park. People were beginning to start their mornings, and they breathed the sweet, fresh scent of a day full of hope and optimism.

From the house next to Andrew and Christian's came the sounds of Michael Young practicing his trombone. He slowly fumbled up and down scales and then hesitantly played "When the Saints Go Marching In." Across the street, a neighbor's dog barked. Someone, somewhere, was mowing a backyard. Next door, two older boys played basketball, bumping into one another as they tried to dribble the ball to the net, laughing and cheering whenever one of them scored.

Andrew and Christian climbed slowly out of bed and sleepily plodded downstairs, where they heard Grandpa George cooking in the kitchen. They were both glad today wasn't a school day.

"Are you okay?" Christian could see that Andrew wasn't his usual self.

"I think so." Andrew sighed. "Had a bad dream is all."

"About what?" Christian asked.

"About a ghost trying to eat me," Andrew said, with a wry smile. "Would you believe it?"

"All that talk last night spooked you," Christian said.

"I guess," Andrew replied. "But I'm still going to find that ghost boy."

"I knew you'd say that," Christian said, seeing the determination in Andrew's eyes. "And I'm still going to help you!"

Andrew gave his brother a playful punch on the arm, and they skipped down the hallway to the kitchen.

Breakfast time in Andrew and Christian's house was always hectic, especially on the weekends. Grandpa George liked to cook a big breakfast on Saturdays. The boys watched as he shuffled around the kitchen, cooking bacon, breaking eggs, and mixing pancake batter. Pancakes were a favorite of Christian's.

The boys sat next to one another at the countertop, on their usual stools. They sipped from large glasses of milk and then compared milk mustaches while they waited for their grandfather to finish cooking. From where they were sitting, Andrew and Christian could clearly see their parents. Mr. and Mrs. Redmond drank coffee in the family room and stared intently at their laptops. If Andrew didn't know any differently, he would have thought his parents' brains had been sucked dry by work zombies. The harsh, white glow of the computer screens shone in his parents' eyes as they gazed vacantly at facts and figures on spreadsheets.

Andrew and Christian's parents loved to work. If they weren't working, they were talking about work, thinking about work, or simply being excited about work. Andrew believed they even dreamt about work. When Mr. and Mrs. Redmond were with their friends, all they would do was talk about work while they drank huge glasses of wine and regularly checked their phones for email. At times, Mr. and Mrs. Redmond would leave for days on end to meet clients, traveling to Chicago, Boston, or San Francisco. Not that Andrew and Christian worried about it all that much; after all, they had Grandpa George to look after them.

But there were times when Andrew wondered if his parents even knew he and Christian existed. They would be so caught up in work they would hardly speak to him; instead, they would sit for hours on end taking calls and working on their laptops. He couldn't help but feel forgotten, as if he and his brother were an afterthought. Andrew still loved his mom and dad just about more than anything else in the world. But some days he felt as if he were an inconvenience, like having to do homework after a long day at school.

Grandpa George served breakfast and sat down at the counter-top beside Andrew and Christian. "So," he said, in between bites of a piece of lightly buttered toast. "It's a beautiful day out there. The sun is shining, the day is young. We should all do something together. Something fun. What do you think, my beautiful boys?"

"Sounds great," Christian said, as he eagerly forked large bites of pancake into his mouth.

"What are you thinking?" Andrew asked.

"Dunno. A walk to the park, perhaps?" Grandpa George replied. "Finish it up with some ice cream. What do you think?" The old man winked at his grandsons.

"Sounds good to me!" both boys exclaimed.

No one was quite sure how old Grandpa George was. He never told anyone. Andrew guessed his grandfather was well past seventy, but he often acted much younger. Andrew loved to listen to Grandpa George's stories about how he had come to America when he was a young man and worked in construction. "It was the only thing I could do," Grandpa George said, shrugging his shoulders. "But I got good at it—so good, I never had to do it anymore." Grandpa George would wink when he told Andrew and Christian this story, as if he were letting them in on a deep secret, but he never fully explained himself, and Andrew thought better than to ask.

Grandpa George turned to the boys' parents. "And what about you, Mum and Dad? Do you care to join the fun?" Grandpa George already knew the answer but thought it polite to ask anyway.

"Too busy," said Mr. and Mrs. Redmond together, without looking up from their laptops, their fingers typing frantically on the keyboards. "We have work to do."

The boys watched as their mom and dad began a short conversation between themselves:

"Did you get the name of that client?" Mom said to Dad. "It's crucial."

"I'll look him up," Dad said to Mom. "Here he is. Now would you look at that? This could be a good deal!"

Grandpa George shook his head slowly, disappointed in their reaction. He looked at the two boys with an apologetic expression, but Andrew and Christian just shrugged their shoulders. Then, they all began to laugh. It had become a bit of an inside joke that Andrew and Christian's parents were a lost cause when it came to participating in any activity that involved having fun.

"Seems like your mom and dad have got an exciting deal on the horizon." Grandpa George arched his caterpillar eyebrows.

"They always do," said Andrew, in a resigned voice.

"So!" Grandpa George boomed in such a way that his voice grabbed everyone's attention. He was in a good mood and was excited to get the day started. "Let's get ready to have some fun. Last one dressed is a rotten egg."

The boys scrambled from their seats, raced down the hallway, bumping each other playfully, and then skipped up the stairs. And as their parents continued to talk to one another over their laptops, Grandpa George slowly sauntered after Andrew and Christian with a big grin on his face.

"How are we going to find the ghost boy?" Christian asked.

Andrew and Christian were sitting on the swings at the park by the harbor, slowly rising forward and ebbing backward, in the bright sunshine. This was their favorite park in all of Oyster Bay. Tall masts of clean white boats were moored in the bay. Seagulls rode the ocean breezes, hovering over the water and crying to one another. The boys could smell the pungent seaweed that fragranced the air, and, across the water, in the distance, they saw the outline of the houses on Center Island.

The morning had quickly grown into noon, and the boys had spent the day in the playground. Grandpa George sat on a bench not too far away, reading the newspaper and thinking his way through the crossword. Every now and then he would raise his head to the sky in deep thought, count on his fingers, and then hunch over to complete a clue. Doing the crossword was one of Grandpa George's favorite morning treats, and his mood for the day would be largely determined by whether or not he was able to complete it.

"It's not as if we know where to find a ghost, and we can't just go and hang out in Ethan's backyard waiting for it," Christian continued. "His parents might get mad at us or think we're crazy."

The boys were determined to do everything they could to find the ghost boy. The problem was, they didn't know quite where to start. Christian racked his brains trying to think of a solution. He knew how to solve the most intricate math problems or spell the most complicated words at school, but ghost hunting wasn't on the curriculum.

"Well," Andrew said, with the cautious voice of a conspirator as he leaned closer to his brother, "Ethan wasn't the only person to see the ghost." The boys stopped swinging and now sat motionless, as close to one another as possible.

"What do you mean?" Christian asked, surprised.

"I heard someone else talking about seeing a strange ghost boy. The same strange ghost boy that seemed to glow in the dark." Suspense hung on every word that Andrew spoke.

"Who told you that?" Christian's eyes were a mile wide, eager to learn more.

"Riley," Andrew announced. "Apparently she saw something strange down by Raynham Hall when she went grocery shopping with her mom last week."

"Where's Raynham Hall?" Christian asked.

"You know," Andrew said, "that ancient house opposite the supermarket."

"Didn't we go there with Boy Scouts?"

"No," Andrew replied, "that was Sagamore Hill. This is the other old house that's a museum."

"What did she see?" Christian was anxious to know everything Andrew had to say.

"Riley told me she saw a strange-looking boy who seemed to glow in the dark," Andrew said. "He was standing by Raynham Hall, and Riley thought he was just one of the kids who worked at the museum." He stopped for a moment to let the tension build. Seeing Christian almost about to burst with excitement, he continued: "That is, until he suddenly disappeared. And that got her spooked."

"Ethan only lives a block away from Raynham Hall," Christian said, in slow comprehension as the pieces of the puzzle began to slot into place.

"Exactly," Andrew replied, a knowing smile on his face. "It's a bit too much of a coincidence, isn't it?" Andrew's inquisitive eyes burned brightly. "Do you think the two could be connected?"

"I guess," Christian said, shrugging his shoulders.

A brief silence fell between them as they sat still on the swings. Both boys looked over at their grandfather holding the newspaper, pen in hand. He was staring at the sky, looking for inspiration, counting on his fingers again, shaking his head and mumbling to himself.

"Raynham Hall is really old," remarked Andrew.

"It's ancient," Christian agreed.

"Perhaps it's haunted?" Andrew said, in conclusion.

On a tall street lamp in the parking lot, a crow started cawing. Its piercing call filled the harbor.

Andrew looked up. The crow was staring at him, or so it seemed. It twitched its black head from side to side, as if trying to get a better look at Andrew. Then it started to caw again, but this time it cawed much faster. "Caw, caw, caw!" the crow wildly screeched, but it sounded to Andrew as if the crow were laughing, "Ha, ha, ha!"

"So how do we go about finding a ghost in the middle of Raynham Hall?" Christian looked at his brother perplexed. "Do you know how crazy that sounds?"

"Well," Andrew said, momentarily breaking his gaze from the crow to look at his brother. "Ethan said he saw the shining ghost boy two weeks ago today. Riley said she saw something weird a week ago today, exactly a week after Ethan."

"So you're saying that if the ghost boy is going to appear anywhere at all, then it will be today at Raynham Hall?" Christian asked, hopefully.

The crow began to caw again. It jumped up and down on the lamppost, bobbing its head maniacally, and this time Andrew was confident the crow was laughing at him. "Ha, ha, ha!" it screeched repeatedly. "Ha, ha, ha!" The crow pointed its long, shiny beak at Andrew and stared at him with small, black, beady eyes. Andrew stared right back, refusing to blink, and, after what seemed like a long time, the crow stopped bobbing and stood motionless. It eyed Andrew in eerie silence and then—spreading its big, black wings—flew off toward Center Island. Its laughing caw faded away across the bay.

Andrew watched it go, and a shudder ran up his back and down his arms.

"So, a ghost? Today? At Raynham Hall?" Christian asked.

"What?" Andrew said. He was still thinking about the crow and was wondering why it had laughed at him.

"I don't know," Andrew eventually stuttered, turning back to Christian, "but it seems more than just a coincidence that a ghost is seen on the same day of the week, exactly one week apart, at Raynham Hall. And I think if we're going to have any chance at all seeing something, it will be tonight."

On the bench near the playground, Grandpa George started laughing to himself. Then, taking his pen, he started filling out a piece of the crossword. "Of course!" he said to himself. "How could I have been such a Silly Billy?" He seemed content, sitting in the sun, finding the answers to his puzzle.

"We're going to need a plan if we want to get out tonight," Christian said. "You know Mom and Dad won't notice, but we have to say something to stop Grandpa George from worrying."

"Working on it," said Andrew.

Neither boy wanted to deceive their grandfather, but they both knew that without a plausible excuse, getting out of the house would be impossible.

Grandpa George looked up with a satisfied smirk on his face as he put the lid on his pen. "Boys!" he called. "I'm going back to the house. It's getting too hot for an old man like me, and I'm slowly boiling like a lobster. Are you coming home or do you want to stay down here a little bit longer?" He stood up and put the folded newspaper under his arm. He seemed happy with himself; the boys knew he had completed the crossword puzzle.

"We'll stay a little bit longer, if that's okay." Christian replied.

"Of course it is young man," Grandpa George said. "I'd rather you were out here than inside playing those silly video games." He looked at the boys with kindness, then walked over to them and ruffled their hair. "My boys," he said. "My beautiful boys."

"Grandpa, have you ever been to Raynham Hall?" Christian asked, without thinking about it. As soon as he'd asked the question, Christian wondered if he'd said the right thing.

Grandpa George looked at Christian with a surprised expression. "Yes, I've been there. It's very nice indeed. Why do you ask, son?"

Andrew gently nudged Christian forward, as if to say, "You started this, so now you need to finish it."

"Well, some kids were saying they sometimes see some strange things there, and I wanted to know if you knew anything about it?"

"Are we talking about ghosts again?" Grandpa George said, with a huge smile on his face. "I thought we agreed there were no such things." He thrust his hands into the pockets of his shorts and peered quizzically at Christian and Andrew.

"But if there *were* such things as ghosts," said Christian, in an almost confident voice, "then perhaps they would be there. We think it could be haunted."

"Yes," Andrew said, "really haunted!"

The boys watched as Grandpa George thought about what they had said for a few seconds. His caterpillar eyebrows raised in contemplation, and then he began to smile, as if he'd just solved one of his crossword puzzle clues.

"Do you want to go to Raynham Hall and have a look around?" he asked, leaning down toward them.

"Can we?" Andrew returned, surprised. He hadn't thought their grandfather would even suggest such a thing.

"Of course we can. It's a museum nowadays, and it's open most of the time." The old man looked at his watch. It was a quarter past one in the afternoon. "It should be open, so let's take a walk over there and have a look around."

"Nailed it!" Christian said, with a huge grin. He was excited at the prospect of visiting Raynham Hall.

"What are we waiting for? Let's go!" Grandpa George said, chuckling. "Follow me!"

3

A VISIT TO RAYNHAM HALL

Raynham Hall is as old as the town of Oyster Bay itself. It's a small, white, saltbox house with broad wooden clapboards and a black, shingle roof. Nine small windows poke through the facade, and a red brick path leads to the front door. The old house stands on a modest plot of land, edged with a white picket fence and a small, neat garden. Two large oak trees stand proudly in front of Raynham Hall, their stretched branches and broad leaves obscuring the house from view, as if trying to keep it secret.

Andrew and Christian followed their grandfather. They walked past the train station and turned up Spring Street, then turned onto West Main Street. Grandpa George took long, purposeful strides, slapping the newspaper rhythmically against his leg as he walked. The boys did their best to keep up with his pace, walking and jogging gently behind him. Both boys were excited their grandfather had agreed to take them to see the old haunted house.

Their parents must have driven the boys past Raynham Hall countless times, but somehow they had never really noticed it before. As they now stood in front of the white, saltbox house, Christian was amazed how small and beautiful it was. *A relic from another time,* he thought.

Grandpa George opened the gate in the white picket fence then walked up the brick path to the stout front door. It was painted stark white, with a black, iron handle and a shining brass door knocker shaped like an eagle. At the top of the door loomed two windows made of antique glass, warped so much that each looked like the concave bottom of a murky wine bottle.

"Those windows remind me of Grandpa George's glasses," Christian said.

"Shh!" Andrew urged.

"I heard that!" Grandpa George said, with a smile on his face.

The boys looked at each other and sniggered. Grandpa George ignored them and knocked on the door.

They waited. The sun beamed high in the sky, and they could see that Grandpa George was sweating. He didn't like the heat very much, saying he preferred the cool, fresh air of autumn.

Still, no one answered the door. Grandpa George and the children were becoming a little impatient.

"Strange," said Grandpa George.

He knocked again, a little harder.

Still nothing.

The boys began to feel anxious, believing they wouldn't get to explore the house and search for clues about the ghost boy's whereabouts.

"Maybe there's no one home." Grandpa George huffed to himself. "It should be open." He checked his watch again and then looked at the museum sign attached to the wall.

Open 1 P.M. – 5 P.M. Closed Mondays.

Grandpa George was about to knock again when a loud *click!* echoed and the dead bolt was pulled back. It seemed a long time before the door slowly opened.

"Hello!" said a cheerful elderly woman. She was wearing a red and white dress with puffy sleeves, and a full, round petticoat. The dress seemed to date from the colonial period. Andrew had seen pictures of women wearing such dresses when he had learned about the War of Independence and General George Washington at school.

"Sorry about that. I was upstairs," the elderly woman said, out of breath. "Takes me a little longer to get down the stairs these days."

"No problem." Grandpa George smiled. "I know all about old age." He rubbed his hip in sympathy.

The elderly lady nodded. "Come in," she welcomed, "come in." She opened the door wide to let everyone enter.

Grandpa George and the boys walked into a narrow corridor. On each side of them, entrances led into small, square rooms. Looking directly ahead, they could see a passageway leading to the back of the house.

The air was silent in Raynham Hall. The street noise was muted, and, despite the searing sun, the entryway was cool. An old smell, like the odor of one of Grandpa George's history books, faintly permeated the air. Andrew wondered how Raynham Hall had survived. The old museum was so different from every other house he had seen.

"Have you ever been here before?" The elderly lady put on a friendly smile. She looked at Grandpa George and the boys for an answer.

Grandpa George cleared his throat. "Some time ago," he muttered. "Quite some time ago, actually."

The elderly woman nodded again. "And how about you boys?" She looked at them with intense, mouse-brown eyes.

"This is our first time," Andrew said.

"Oh good!" the elderly woman replied, clasping her hands. "This is a lovely place. It's full of incredible history. Feel free to look around. I'm here if you have any questions." She smiled at the boys again and then walked toward the back of the house, leaving them to explore its musty interior alone.

"Wow!" Andrew said. "This place is old."

"Older than Grandpa George," Christian quipped, in a voice just loud enough for his grandfather to hear.

"I heard that!" said Grandpa George. "This house is over two hundred and fifty years old—and I'm not quite there yet." He grinned at the boys, his blue eyes beaming large through his glasses.

Andrew and Christian began looking around the house, trying to find clues about the ghost boy. *Any* clues at all. The house seemed narrow and compact, and all the passageways were dark. Only a slither of light entered the rooms from the tiny antique windows, and the clapboard floors creaked as they walked.

A fireplace stood front and center in each small room. "No forced-air heating or air conditioning in those days," said Grandpa George. "You had to make a fire to keep warm." Simple decorations adorned the walls: a display of spoons, an elegant mirror, and an old rifle in one room. A walnut-brown writing desk, a chest, and a commanding grandfather clock in another room.

They wandered from room to room, searching every unusual, dust-covered object and every dark, murky corner of the house for clues.

"What do you think, boys?" Grandpa George asked.

"It's so small," Christian said.

"Well, people didn't need big houses back then."

"So, when did you last come here, Grandpa?" Andrew asked.

"Many, many years ago," Grandpa George said, wistfully. "And it hasn't changed a bit since the last time I was here. Everything seems the same. I wonder...." He began to lose himself in thought then left the boys to walk upstairs. The steps creaked under his weight, and the boys heard his distinct footfalls, pacing the bedrooms above them.

The boys walked to the back of the house and entered the kitchen. A huge cast-iron range stood along one wall. Tin pails were stacked on the floor. Pots and pans hung from the walls. A wooden table and four chairs sat in the middle of the kitchen, and some pretend food lay in a bowl, depicting how the table would have been arranged when Raynham Hall was in use.

As they drew close to the pantry, Christian stopped short, as if someone had pulled him sharply backward. He felt the room go dark, and a tingle rushed up his body, like cold water.

"Do you feel that?" Christian stammered.

"What?" Andrew said. "I don't feel anything."

Christian felt a freezing breath blowing on him, and fields of goose bumps sprouted along his arms and neck. He shuddered in surprise and started rubbing himself to get warm.

Andrew was surprised to see his brother shivering. "Are you okay?" he asked.

"Kind of," Christian said, his mouth chattering. "Don't you feel cold? I'm absolutely *freezing*." He looked intently at his brother.

"No," Andrew said. "It's still pretty warm in here."

The next instant, Christian began to feel normal again. He felt the warmth rush back to his fingers and hands, as if he had been covered by a large duvet. Christian was confused. One minute he was hot, the next freezing—and then he was suddenly warm again.

"Are you sure you're okay?" Andrew asked.

"That was *really* strange," Christian replied.

"Did you know that Raynham Hall played a significant role during the War of Independence?"

Christian and Andrew jumped. The elderly woman had suddenly reappeared. She smiled quietly and clasped her hands in front of her.

"No," said Andrew, trying his hardest not to let on that she had scared him half to death.

"Yes, indeed, it did. From seventeen seventy-six to seventeen eighty-three, this house protected one of General Washington's most valuable spies, a critical member of the Culper Spy Ring. The spy ring helped Washington win the War of Independence." The elderly woman smiled again and tilted her head to one side.

"Really?" Christian asked.

Both boys looked at her, enthralled.

"Indeed," the elderly lady said once more. "He lived here. In this very house. His secret agent code name was Culper Junior. And he had a special secret agent number. Seven twenty-three. But his real name was Robert Townsend. And the Townsend family owned this house for over two hundred years."

Andrew saw that the elderly lady was getting excited.

"When war broke out, this house was taken over by the British, and the British colonel, John Simcoe, used it as his headquarters. A good part of Simcoe's battalion, the Queen's Rangers, was camped here in Oyster Bay, in a place called Fort Hill, which is by where the fire station is now on South Street. There were over three hundred men here. You couldn't move for Redcoats—that's what the Americans called the British soldiers back then."

"I never knew that," Andrew said, surprised.

"Well, that's the good thing about life." The elderly lady grinned. "You get to learn something new every day!

"And there's something else," she continued, stepping closer to whisper to the boys. "Another big secret."

"What's that?" Christian asked. He watched as the fine lines on the woman's face crinkled as she smiled. Her small brown eyes seemed electrified, and she wrung her hands, as if washing them with soap.

"This house is haunted!"

Both boys nearly fell backward, as if they had been pushed.

"Haunted?" Grandpa George said. He had come down the stairs with one of his eyebrows raised.

"Our grandpa doesn't believe in ghosts," Andrew said, gathering himself. "He says it's all a load of hocus-pocus."

The elderly woman laughed as Grandpa George came to stand beside them. He stared skeptically at the elderly lady, wondering if she could be trusted.

"Well, it's said that the house has ghosts from many different eras," the elderly lady continued, ignoring Grandpa George. "But the most frequent ghost seen around here is Sally Townsend's."

"Are you kidding me?" Christian was astonished. "So, there's a real ghost?"

"Indeed," the elderly woman said, smiling kindly. "Some people say this is one of the most haunted houses on Long Island." She paused for effect, searching the boys' faces for any hint of fear, but instead saw only an eagerness to learn more. "Some people say Raynham Hall is like the Grand Central Station for ghostly activity."

The elderly lady enjoyed the suspense for a moment before continuing.

"You know, sometimes I hear strange things, like footsteps up-stairs, or doors opening and closing in the kitchen when nobody is here."

Grandpa George huffed. His hand slowly cupped his chin in thought, but, uncharacteristically, said nothing.

Then, Christian asked, "What about a ghost of a small boy? Have you ever seen that?"

The elderly lady looked at Christian thoughtfully. "You know, I've not heard of any ghosts of small children. All the ghosts I know of are adults."

Christian stared at the elderly lady, considering her words. Suddenly, from the kitchen, loud creaking rose off the floorboards, as if someone were in the room, cooking dinner. Everyone stood still and listened—even Grandpa George.

"There's one of them now," said the elderly woman. "They're just letting us know they're listening to us." She started giggling to her-self. "Oh my, they must like you boys. Generally, they only come out when I'm here alone!"

The boys instinctively moved closer to Grandpa George, as if for protection. Christian held onto the old man's arm.

"Aren't you scared?" Andrew looked at the elderly lady.

"What for?" The elderly lady looked confused. "There's nothing to fear. They won't hurt me. They're like my friends. They keep me company when the house is empty."

The floorboards upstairs then began to creak, as if someone were pacing in one of the bedrooms, and the elderly lady giggled to herself again. "They seem really excited," she said.

"Well, I'm sure we've taken up too much of your time as it is," Grandpa George said. He looked anxious, and one of his caterpillar eyebrows stood raised in concern. "Come on boys, it's time for us to leave."

"Going already?" The elderly woman seemed upset. She rushed to the front door, almost blocking them from leaving.

Grandpa George blurted, "Afraid so. It's time for us to go. It's late."

He marched to the door, and for a moment, Christian thought the elderly woman was going to try and block his exit. But at the last second, she stepped aside. Grandpa George opened the front door, letting sunlight flood into the dim hallway.

As Grandpa George stepped outside, the boys said "thank you" to the elderly woman in a single voice then followed their grandfather outside.

"Have a beautiful day," the elderly woman said. "Come back and see us again soon." She gave them a broad smile, a quick fluttering wave, and then gently closed the door.

Grandpa George quickly strode along the brick pathway, toward the sidewalk. The boys could see that he was flustered.

"Are you okay, Grandpa?" Andrew asked. "You seem a little out of sorts."

"I'm okay. Not a problem," Grandpa George said, slapping his newspaper against his leg. However, the expression on his face said otherwise.

The sun had grown hotter. The air had become dense and more humid. Andrew could feel beads of sweat under his T-shirt. Christian felt like he needed more sunscreen.

"What do you think?" Christian asked. "Do you still believe there are no such things as ghosts?"

Grandpa George remained quiet for a little while as he thought about what to say next. Then, he let out a big sigh and said, "I only said there were no such things as ghosts so you wouldn't get scared." He looked at Andrew and Christian carefully. "But in truth, there are many strange things in this world which are difficult to explain, and I don't have an answer for all the weird things that happen."

The boys were flabbergasted. They looked at Grandpa George as if he had just stepped off a spaceship from Mars.

"So, there *are* such things as ghosts?" Christian cried.

"Perhaps," Grandpa George acknowledged, under his breath.

"Really?" Andrew looked at his grandfather and could tell he was telling the truth.

"If you can call them ghosts." Grandpa George seemed unwilling to say anything more, and the boys knew better than to ask. He stood silently, slapping the newspaper against his leg, staring past Raynham Hall as if he were trying to remember something long forgotten . . .

Christian looked back at the house and saw the elderly lady at one small window. He saw her smile at him; then, the curtain slipped back into place as she disappeared into the darkness of the house.

Christian shuddered. The freezing cold he had felt in the kitchen was not a figment of his imagination. It was real to him, like snow.

There was something unusual about Raynham Hall. He could sense it, but he couldn't explain it.

"I'm going back home," Grandpa George said, breaking the silence. "It's getting far too hot for an old man like me, and I have some things I have to do. Are you coming?"

The boys looked at one another. "Can we come back later?" Andrew asked. "I thought we would go down to the park again for a little while longer."

"Fair enough," Grandpa George said. He began fishing in his pockets for something. "Here's a little bit of allowance for you." He handed Andrew ten dollars. "You can go and buy yourselves some water or a snack if you get hungry. But don't go wasting it on sticky candy. That will rot your teeth. And I want you back at the house in two hours. I'll have dinner ready, so don't be late."

"We won't," the boys said together.

Grandpa George kissed them both on the tops of their heads then turned to start the short walk home.

Christian was excited. "Got any excuses to tell Grandpa George why we're ghost hunting tonight?"

"Yes," said Andrew, smiling to himself. "I know just the thing."

4

STRANGE ENCOUNTERS

It was hot as the boys stood alone outside Raynham Hall. An elderly couple walked their dog, who stopped and sniffed a lamp-post before trotting on its way.

"So, what's the big idea to escape the house tonight?" Christian asked.

"We're going to see the girls," Andrew said. "Time to get Alysse and Jacklyn involved. They'll cover for us."

"Awesome idea," Christian said. "Grandpa George won't mind us hanging out with our cousins. It will give him some quiet time to read his books!"

The two boys wondered what to do next. "Let's go and have a look around the gardens," Christian said. "Maybe there's a clue that will help us find the ghost boy."

"Sounds good," Andrew said.

The gardens of Raynham Hall were small and compact. Borders were crammed with blue and purple hydrangea, their heavy flowers drooping in the summer heat. Trees and shrubs mingled cozily with one another, and differently colored flowers bloomed haphazardly in patches of unmatched hues. A large, green lawn took up most of the space; it spread before the boys like an emerald tablecloth.

The boys started to investigate. They kicked bushes and lifted tree branches. They peered into the dark corners of the garden, using sticks to poke the dirt. They weren't quite sure what they were looking for. Any clue would do, if it lead them to the ghost boy.

"Well, well, well," said a deep sonorous voice, as smooth as oozing honey. "What do we have here?"

Andrew and Christian looked up. A tall, slender gentleman stood in front of them. He was old—perhaps a little older than their grandfather. His hair was graying, and his skin was wrinkled around his eyes, around his neck, and around his hands. He was wearing a well-fitted seersucker suit, a white shirt, and a pert bow tie. His shoes were brightly polished. In his hands he held a long walking cane, capped by an ivory pommel and shaped in the form of a wolf's head.

As he stood just inside the fence, the man looked at Andrew and Christian intently. His black eyes showed no emotion.

"Two young pups doing some gardening, it seems," the man said, with a forced smile. He leaned deliberately on the cane. "But what, exactly, are you doing?"

"We're just looking around," Christian blurted innocently. "We're not doing anything wrong."

"I didn't say you were."

The man walked closer. He stood less than twenty paces from the boys. Christian couldn't help but look at the pommel of the man's cane. The ivory wolf's head wore a calm expression as it looked at Christian.

"Don't worry, little boy. I didn't mean to scare you." The man looked at the boys and asked, "So what are your names?"

"I'm Andrew, and this is my brother, Christian."

Christian felt uneasy, as if something about the man's demeanor or his strange, sudden appearance in the gardens were not quite right. But he couldn't quite put his finger on it. He had always been told to be wary of strangers. Now, he moved a little closer to Andrew, scared of what might happen next.

" 'Andrew' and 'Christian.' What charming names you have to match the fine young gentlemen you are." The man smiled unconvincingly at the boys, and his eyes turned even blacker than before.

"Let me introduce myself. My name is Mr. Baines." As he spoke, Mr. Baines placed his hand on his chest. Christian noticed a gold signet ring on the man's pinky finger. He stared at the ring quietly: it had another silhouette of a wolf's head.

"Nice to meet you," Andrew stammered, not quite sure what else to say.

Mr. Baines reached out his skinny fingers and in turn shook the boys' hands. Andrew was surprised to feel how cold Mr. Baines's hand was. It was as if he had touched frozen flesh.

"What a *lovely* day it is. And what a *beautiful* town. Do you live around here?" Mr. Baines looked at the boys inquisitively.

"Yes," said Andrew. "We live just around the corner. Off South Street."

"I see," said Mr. Baines. He paused for a moment. "And have you lived in this charming town your entire life?"

The boys looked at one another in surprise. Neither was quite sure why Mr. Baines would ask such a question.

"I guess so." Christian shrugged. That same moment, he took another look at the wolf's head cane. Gone were the calm, ivory eyes. Instead, the wolf's expression was angry, its mouth snarling sharp teeth.

Christian shuddered. He could hardly believe his eyes. *How could that have happened?* he asked himself. *It's impossible!*

"And do you know about this house?" Mr. Baines glanced at Raynham Hall.

"We've just been inside for the first time," Andrew said. "It's very old."

"Indeed it is," said Mr. Baines. "It has lots of hidden secrets. Secrets from the past that have been kept in this house for hundreds of years. *Dark* secrets…*Powerful* secrets…Can *you* keep a secret, Andrew?"

Andrew looked at Mr. Baines. "Yes," he said, cautiously.

"Good. Good."

Mr. Baines twiddled his cane, and Christian could see that the wolf's head was no longer angry. He shook his head, as if trying to rid himself of a dream.

"Well," said Mr. Baines, "I wish I could stand around and chat all day, but I have some important business to attend to." He smiled again at the boys. "Now, don't get into any mischief. You know what they say: the devil makes work for idle hands!"

Mr. Baines strode off. The boys watched him leave. They heard the clicking of his cane as it tapped against the sidewalk. The tapping grew fainter and fainter as he disappeared toward East Main Street.

The boys stared at each other in bewilderment. Then, they began to laugh.

"Do we know that guy?" Andrew said, raising an eyebrow.

"I don't think so," Christian answered, "but he does seem vaguely familiar."

"He does," Andrew said. "It's as if we've met him before, but I just can't remember where."

"Or when," Christian said. "Did you see his walking stick? It seemed to change. One minute the wolf was smiling, the next it looked as if it wanted to bite my head off." Christian looked genuinely perturbed.

"I don't think we're going to find anything here," Andrew said, kicking at a stone. "We'll have to come back later."

"Okay. I need something to drink," Christian said.

"Me too," Andrew replied. "It's so hot today."

The boys left the garden and crossed the street. They were heading toward Virelli's Market when they saw a shop they hadn't seen before. One of the old, vacant storefronts had been transformed into a new toy store. Fresh white paint edged two huge windows filled with toys and games. Between the windows stood a gleaming, bright red door. Above the door hung a large yellow sign that proclaimed:

Oyster Bay Toys

"Look at this!" Andrew said. "I've never seen this place before."

"It must be new," Christian said, pressing his nose against one of the windows. "I wonder what they've got inside."

"Let's look," Andrew said.

The boys opened the bright red door, and a jingly bell rang crisply. They hurriedly stepped into a maze of shelves, packed with toys. Board games, superhero toys, books. From ceiling to floor, it seemed as if every piece of available space were brimming with the best new toys available.

"Check this out!" Christian said in wonderment.

They began to browse the shelves, picking up whatever toys and models, games and puzzles, grabbed their attention. For a few minutes they were lost among the shelves; so it came as quite a surprise when they heard a woman's voice say:

"Hello!"

The boys turned to see an elegant lady standing beside them. Her arms were crossed, and she was staring at them as if they had interrupted her from doing something important. Andrew wasn't sure where she had come from. It seemed as if she had appeared out of thin air.

"Hello," Christian said, trying not to sound alarmed. He suddenly felt guilty, although he was sure he had done nothing wrong.

The elegant woman appeared stern and aloof. She was dressed in black pants and a black, turtleneck sweater. And, despite the heat, she looked as if she were still a little cold. Her short, dark hair wrapped around her smooth, brown face. Her eyebrows were tall arches as she looked at them with sparkling dark eyes.

"We're just looking at the toys," Andrew stammered, putting a box back on a shelf.

"Toys?" said the woman. "Ah, toys...of course. Yes, toys. You were looking at toys. Of course." She seemed distracted, as if she had never seen toys before and the new store were as much of a surprise to her as it was to the boys.

"Is this your store?" Andrew asked.

The woman did not answer. Instead, she asked a question of her own: "And what are your names?"

"I'm Christian, and this is my brother, Andrew."

The elegant woman nodded and said, "You can call me Ms. Waverly."

"It's a great store," Christian said. He was trying very hard to be polite, but it didn't seem to matter to Ms. Waverly. She continued to look at them coolly. Her arms were still folded in front of her. She looked to be on the verge of growing angry with them, although neither boy could tell for what.

"So, are you twins, by any chance?" asked Ms. Waverly, as she tapped a finger against her arm.

Andrew and Christian smiled because they were often mistaken for twins, and they had a standard answer.

"No," Christian said.

"We were born eleven months apart," Andrew completed.

"Oh," said Ms. Waverly. "I see."

There was a moment of silence before Ms. Waverly said casually, "But you live in the town, do you not?"

The boys were confused by the question, just like they had been confused when Mr. Baines had asked it. *Why do these two people want to know if we live in Oyster Bay?* Andrew thought. It seemed a bit odd they would ask the same question.

"Yes," Christian finally said. "We've lived here all our lives. Since the day we were born."

"I see," said Ms. Waverly. "And do you live with your grandfather?"

The boys looked at one another in astonishment. "Yes," Andrew said. "How did you know that?"

Another moment of silence. Ms. Waverly gazed at the toys on the shelves, then gazed back at the boys and smiled.

"Well, you can leave whenever you want to. Don't let me stop you."

Ms. Waverly turned her back on the boys and weaved her way through the maze of shelves, heading back toward the cash register.

She didn't give them a second glance. Andrew could hear her mumbling under her breath before asking herself, "Now, where did I put them...?"

The boys looked in bemusement at each other. They walked toward the bright red door, opening it slowly to prevent the bell from jingling too loudly and disturbing Ms. Waverly. As they were about to step outside, they nearly bumped into another woman coming toward them. She was dressed in bright, colorful clothes and had a big smile on her face as she sipped from a cup of coffee in her hand. "Hello, boys," she chirped. "Having a look around, are you? I just had to pop out and get a coffee. Can I help you with anything?"

Andrew looked blankly at the woman as she brushed past them and entered the store. "Go figure! I step out for five minutes, and a customer comes in!" she said cheerfully.

"So, this is *your* store?" Christian asked, with a puzzled voice.

"Yes. Just opened it yesterday. Today is my first full day of business. What do you think?"

"I think it's fantastic," Andrew said. "But what about the other lady who's here. Ms. Waverly. I thought it was her store."

"I don't know anyone called Ms. Waverly." The owner took a sip of her coffee. "There's no one else here but me."

Andrew pointed toward the cash register...but Ms. Waverly had disappeared.

Andrew and Christian stood on the sidewalk outside Oyster Bay Toys. The sun was still sweltering, even though the afternoon had grown late. The boys were hungry.

"Time to go home and see what Grandpa George has cooked for dinner," Andrew said.

"Right!" Christian answered. "And then we can tell Grandpa George that we want to see Alysse and Jacklyn tonight."

The boys turned down the street and started walking home. But the farther they walked from the toy store and Raynham Hall, the more Christian thought about everything that had happened to them since they had left their house that morning.

"Could today get any weirder?" Christian asked.

"Only—" Andrew said, smiling, "—if we get to see a ghost!"

5

A SPOOKY MEETING

When Andrew and Christian got home, they found that Grandpa George had cooked one of their favorite dinners: chicken cutlets with spaghetti smothered with butter and Parmesan cheese. Both boys were starving; they sat at the kitchen counter and wolfed down the food without saying a word.

Their mom and dad were still frantically typing on their laptops in the family room. It seemed as if they hadn't moved all day. Andrew wondered what was so important that it could hold their attention for so long on such a nice day. His parents didn't seem to talk to anyone anymore, unless it was to talk to someone about work.

Grandpa George cleaned up their plates, carefully placing them in the dishwasher.

"Did you have a fun day?" he asked as he began fixing himself a cup of tea.

"We did," Andrew said.

"Thanks for taking us to Raynham Hall," Christian added. "It was awesome!"

Grandpa George smiled at them both. "I hope that silly old lady didn't scare you too much with her ghost stories," he said. "I think she's a bit eccentric."

"There are no such things as ghosts," Andrew teased his grandfather. "Didn't you know that?"

The old man huffed. "I guess I had that one coming."

"Grandpa?" Andrew asked. "Is it okay if we go to see Alysse and Jacklyn tonight?"

"Now?" said Grandpa George, with a look of disappointment. "I thought we could have a game of Clue."

"We'd love to," Christian said. "But we sort of promised Alysse and Jacklyn we'd hang out with them."

Grandpa George eyed Andrew and Christian suspiciously. Both boys tried their hardest to keep a straight face. If Grandpa George suspected any foul play, he would stop them from going out. After what seemed like an eternity, he nodded his approval. "Okay," he said, "but you know the rules. Home by nine o'clock, sharp."

Andrew smiled and looked at his brother... The ghost hunt was on!

Grandpa George picked up his cup of tea and walked toward the living room. He glanced back and gave the boys another penetrating look then asked, "This hasn't got anything to do with all that mumbo jumbo about ghosts at Raynham Hall, has it, boys?"

Andrew felt a stab of panic in his stomach. He did everything he could to sound composed, but his cheeks turned cherry red as he quickly blurted, "Absolutely not!"

Grandpa George huffed to himself again, sipped his tea, and then picked up a book. Sitting himself down in his favorite chair, he began to read, slowly flipping the pages.

"See you later, alligator!" Christian cried as he and Andrew bounded out of the house. Grandpa George shook his head. "Crazy lunatics," he mumbled under his breath as he took another sip of tea and flipped another page. "I don't know where they get it from."

Night was beginning to draw in as Andrew and Christian ran into town. Stars peeped brightly through the inky sky, and the moon could be seen hovering above St. Dominic's Church like a vivid silver coin. A few cars drove past, their headlights searching the road ahead of them.

The boys were excited. Neither had ever been on a ghost hunt before, and Andrew was thrilled to be setting out on an adventure.

They met Alysse and Jacklyn at the bandstand in front of the post office. Andrew had called them on his cell phone after he and Christian had left the house. Now, the girls were waiting for them, sitting on the wooden rail of the bandstand and swinging their feet.

At thirteen, Alysse was the eldest in the group: she was two grades ahead of everyone else. She towered over the other children and was almost as tall as Grandpa George. Jacklyn was the same age as Andrew, not as tall as her sister but still taller than either of the two boys. The girls looked alike. Both had long blonde hair they usually wore in a ponytail, and each had pale blue eyes.

"So," Jacklyn said, "what's the big rush? Why did you want us to cover for you tonight?"

Andrew and Christian looked at one another, wondering if they should tell Alysse and Jacklyn the truth about the ghost or not.

"Can you keep a secret?" Andrew finally asked.

The four children drew tightly together. "Of course we can," Alysse said. "Jeez, who do you think we are?" She raised her hands in the air. They had often told one another sensitive secrets, and no one had ever snitched.

"We're looking for a ghost," Andrew said firmly.

"We believe it will appear tonight at Raynham Hall," Christian added.

"What?" Jacklyn asked. She rumpled her nose in confusion.

"Are you kidding us?" Alysse stood with her hands on her hips, looking at the boys suspiciously.

"Would we kid you?" Andrew said, peering at the two girls with intent eyes. "Look, there have been two strange sightings around here of what people think is the ghost of a small boy."

"Ethan saw it two weeks ago," Christian said. "Riley saw it last week…and we think we're going to see it tonight."

Christian was emphatic. He really believed that after everything that had happened to them that day, it was inevitable the ghost was going to appear.

"I don't believe in ghosts," said Alysse. "They're not real."

"And I'm not scared of them even if they are real," Jacklyn said, in a determined voice.

"Then you won't mind helping us look for them?" Andrew asked, knowing he could rely on the girls to help.

"Okay," Alysse said, in a disinterested tone, "whatever makes you happy."

The children set off and began walking along Audrey Avenue, past the town hall.

"I got a joke for you." Christian laughed before even saying anything. "Where do ghosts hate to hang out in a house?"

"Where?" Jacklyn asked, her blonde ponytail bouncing as they walked.

"The living room." Christian said. He bent over, giggling hysterically. "Get it?" He was laughing so hard he struggled to get the words out. "The...*living*...room!"

"I've heard better," Alysse said, in a dull voice. She folded her arms in front of her.

"So, when do you think the bogeyman is going to appear?" Jacklyn asked.

"We're just waiting for the sun to set. I have a feeling ghosts only come out after dark," Andrew answered.

"How do you know?" Jacklyn's nose wrinkled with suspicion.

"I don't," Andrew said. "I guess ghosts don't like the sunlight?"

"That's vampires," Alysse replied. "Don't think it applies so much to ghosts."

"I'm sure it does," Andrew said, slipping his cell phone out of his pocket. "Anything spooky is all the same to me."

Andrew looked at his phone. 8:25 P.M. There was hardly any traffic, for a Saturday night. And while the heat of the day had finally died down, the sticky humidity clung to the children like a hot, damp cloth.

"Where is this Raynham Hall place anyway?" Jacklyn said.

"You've lived here all your life, and you don't know where Raynham Hall is?" Christian asked.

"Why would I know where it is?" Jacklyn replied, ponytail bouncing, nose rumpled.

Andrew reassured her: "It's just up here. It's only two minutes away,"

The two boys and girls continued walking toward Raynham Hall. They cut up Maxwell Street and then headed toward West Main Street, past the boutique shop, and toward Virelli's Market.

"So where did Ethan see this ghost"? Jacklyn asked.

"Ethan saw it by his house, which is just over there." Christian pointed across the road.

"And then Riley told me she saw something near Raynham Hall when she was at Virelli's," Andrew said. "It's more than just a coincidence."

They walked the final few feet to Raynham Hall and stopped. During the day, the house had seemed small and unassuming. But now, during the night, the streetlights made the simple white house glow eerily in the dark, and the little carriage light by the front door made the black eagle door knocker seem more impressive. The white picket fence was tinged a faint orange, and the garden that had been so vibrant during the day now seemed dark and foreboding. All the windows were dim. Nobody appeared to be in the house, and the boys hoped the elderly lady had long gone home.

The children walked around the side of the house and peered through some trees to look into the gardens. In the far corner, they saw an arched wooden trellis with a small gate.

"Let's go in," Andrew said. He put his hand on the gate, searching for the latch to open it.

"We can't," Alysse said, looking very concerned. "It's private property. We could get into trouble."

"Do you want to see a ghost or not?" Christian asked, daring the girls forward. "As Grandpa George says—in for a penny, in for a pound."

"Just because your Grandpa George says stuff doesn't mean it's right or makes sense," Alysse said.

"Of course it does," said Christian. "The guy's a genius!"

The children ducked into the dark gloom of the garden. Tall conifers and broad-leaved bushes made the garden seem very secluded, and the children felt they were someplace other than Oyster Bay. In the distance, they heard a car engine roar—and then the car zoomed past them, but they couldn't see anything, and they were sure no one could see them.

Andrew felt they had entered another world....

The sky was nearly completely dark. Purple-blue clouds rolled across the sky, covering the coin-shaped moon, making everything even darker. The children could just about see one another, but beyond their hands, things became murky.

"I don't think we're going to see anything," Jacklyn said. "This is a complete and utter waste of time." Her nose was more wrinkled than ever.

"Give it a chance," Andrew said, impatiently. "We've only just got here."

"But how will we know it's a ghost," said Alysse. Her hands were folded skeptically.

"Shh!" said Andrew. "We don't want to scare it away."

"There's nothing here to scare away," Jacklyn said. "There's nothing here but us!"

"And there won't be anything else if we're not quiet," Andrew said. He was getting frustrated the ghost hadn't appeared already...but there was nothing he could do to change that.

The children stood silently for a few minutes. They could hear a bird singing in the distance. Jacklyn was absently tapping her toe. Andrew kept holding his breath. Alysse was looking at the sky with her arms folded, trying to make out shapes in the passing clouds.

"What time is it?" Christian whispered.

Andrew looked at his cell phone. "Eight-fifty," he said with a sigh.

"We're going to have to go soon," Christian said. "We can't be home late. Grandpa George will ground us."

The children looked at one another in disappointment.

"Just another couple of minutes," Andrew pleaded. "Please?"

Alysse and Jacklyn nodded. There had been plenty of times they had asked Andrew and Christian for a favor, and it was now their turn to help their cousins.

"Did you hear that?" Jacklyn asked, startled.

"What?" Andrew replied.

"Over there. I thought I heard something."

"It was just a squirrel," Alysse said, in a flat voice. "I'm sure there are hundreds of them around here."

Then, suddenly, Christian began to feel the same sensation he had felt earlier inside Raynham Hall. A strange tingling reached from his fingertips through his hands and into his arms. His stomach began to feel warm and tickly, as if he'd just experienced a huge drop on a roller coaster.

Andrew sensed something was wrong, and he looked anxiously at his brother. "Are you okay, Christian?" He put his arm on his brother's shoulder.

"I'm not feeling right," Christian said. "It's like when we were in the house earlier. Something strange is going to happen, I can feel it."

Suddenly, a light shape, quite vivid in the dark, began to appear from the south side of the house. The shape started to shimmer, and curls of pale colored smoke began to slowly form into the figure of a human leg . . . a human arm . . . a small, human body. The smoke swirled more intently, and soon, a young boy stood glimmering like ivory in front of them.

Both Andrew and Christian stood still in amazement. It was impossible for them to say a word. The hair on Andrew's neck stood up. Goose bumps stretched from his head to his feet. Christian could still feel his stomach turning somersaults, and both boys couldn't move. It was as if they had been nailed to the spot.

The young, glowing figure did not look like any boy Andrew and Christian had ever seen. His hair was long and mousy-brown, and it was tied back into a tight ponytail by a piece of black ribbon. He was about as tall as Christian, but his clothes were very strange. He wore short pants and long socks. His loose, light brown shirt was made of coarse cloth and had baggy sleeves. He wore simple black shoes with silver buckles. But the strangest thing about his attire was a black, three-cornered hat that seemed too big for the small boy's head.

The ghost boy stood by the house, almost within an arm's length of Andrew and Christian. He wasn't moving or saying a word. He looked as surprised to be in the garden of Raynham Hall on a Saturday night as the children were to see him there.

Andrew staggered backward. He felt Jacklyn and Alysse standing still beside him.

"Do you see that?" he whispered to the girls.

"See what?" Jacklyn said. She was slowly losing her patience just standing in the garden, and she wanted to go home.

"The ghost boy," said Andrew. "He's right in front of us." He looked at the girls with a wild expression on his face, but it was obvious they couldn't see anything unusual.

"Look," Andrew urged again, "right there!"

"Look at what?" Jacklyn asked. She peered blindly into the black night but couldn't see a thing.

Andrew couldn't believe the girls didn't see the ghost boy. He stepped toward Jacklyn and grabbed her hand in desperation.

"*At that!*" Andrew hissed, and pointed his other hand at the ghost boy.

As soon as Andrew took her hand, Jacklyn felt an icy tingle rush up her arm and into her body, as if she had just been splashed with cold water. Then things began to slow down. Jacklyn looked at the spot where Andrew was pointing. She followed his outstretched finger, and as she did, she could begin to see the gradual shimmer of the ghost boy as he suddenly came into view.

"You have got to be kidding me!" Jacklyn whispered.

"What?" Alysse said. "I don't see anything. What's going on? What's there?"

"Christian, grab Alysse's hand," Andrew whispered. "It's the only way she'll see the ghost boy."

Christian quickly stepped over to Alysse and took her hand in his. As with Jacklyn, Alysse felt the coldness rush up her tingling arm ... saw how the world seemed to slow. And, as she turned her head, she, too, could see the ghost boy, standing like a hologram in the garden.

"What is happening?" she cried in fear. "That can't be real!"

"Shh!" said Andrew. "We don't want to scare him away."

"Don't want to scare him! He's just scared the life out of me!" Alysse shrieked.

The four children stood mesmerized. Andrew held Jacklyn's hand, Christian held onto Alysse. They were standing in a semicircle, staring at the ghost boy with wide, unbelieving eyes.

But the children didn't seem to bother the young ghost boy. In fact, he didn't appear to notice them. He took a few steps to his left, a few steps to his right. Then he put his hand on his chin, as if trying to find his bearings.

Andrew pulled on Jacklyn's hand. Together, they slowly inched toward the boy.

"What are you doing, Andrew?" Christian asked, looking anxiously at his brother.

"Yes, what are we doing?" repeated Jacklyn, in a very concerned voice. She pulled back a little.

"We need to see what he wants," Andrew said. "We need to know why he's here."

"I don't need to know," Alysse said. "I think it's time to go home."

Alysse looked very uncomfortable. Everything she knew about the world had suddenly been thrown upside down. There weren't supposed to be such things as ghosts. She couldn't quite believe what was happening to her.

Then the ghost boy spoke: "Uncle Robert? Uncle Robert? Are you there?"

The voice of the ghost boy was much deeper than his body would have suggested it could be; it was almost the voice of a man. Andrew stood stock-still, as if someone had locked him up.

"I've got to deliver the letter," said the ghost boy. "I've got to get the letter to the general." The boy walked more quickly across the garden, heading toward the house. "Uncle Robert, where are you?" The ghost boy backtracked toward Andrew. "I've got to get the letter to the general!" he repeated anxiously. "If I don't get the letter to the general we will lose the war!"

The ghost boy seemed to be getting more restless; he shone more brightly than ever. He seemed unsure of what he needed to do. He stepped hesitantly left and right—and then stopped next to the children. Turning sharply, the ghost boy stared directly at Christian.

"Who are you?" he asked in a quiet voice.

Christian stood terrified…. Did the ghost boy see him?

"You there—" this time pointing at Christian "—who are you?"

Despite his fear, Christian found his voice. "I'm Christian," he stammered more loudly than he thought possible.

"Christian?" said the ghost boy, glistening like snow in the dark.

"Yes, and this is my brother, Andrew."

The ghost boy turned and stepped toward Andrew.

"So, your name is Andrew?"

Andrew nodded then, summoning all his nerve, he asked, "What's your name?"

"Samuel. My name is Samuel Townsend."

The ghost boy began to look around. Samuel seemed genuinely lost. He looked up at the sky, then over to the trees, then behind him, to the house. Finally, he looked back at the children.

"Where am I?" Samuel sounded sad as he spoke.

"In Oyster Bay," Jacklyn said, suddenly feeling a gush of sympathy for Samuel. She let go of Andrew's hand. Gently touching Samuel's arm, she repeated, "You're in Oyster Bay, New York. We're standing in the garden at Raynham Hall."

"And you are?"

Samuel looked at Jacklyn as if he hadn't seen her before. He gave her a gentle smile. Jacklyn could see straightaway that Samuel Townsend would be a great friend.

"I'm Jacklyn, and this is my sister, Alysse." Jacklyn beckoned Alysse to come forward, but Alysse shook her head and stayed close to Christian.

Samuel Townsend smiled. "What beautiful names. I haven't heard such names before. Where are you from?"

"Oyster Bay. Just like you," Jacklyn said, unable to stop a smile from forming on her face.

Samuel looked around, trying to recognize where he was.

Gaining courage, Andrew asked, "What are you doing here, Samuel?"

"I need to get the letter to the general. Are you for independence—or are you for England?" Samuel asked.

"What?" Andrew said, feeling very confused.

"Are you a loyalist or a patriot?"

Christian shrugged his shoulders. "I'm not sure what you are asking us?"

"I need to get the letter to the general. There's treachery afoot. Villainy of the worst kind...and it must be stopped. Will you help me?"

Samuel looked at Andrew with imploring eyes.

"Help you with what?" Andrew did not know what to think.

"Win the War of Independence!" Samuel looked excited.

"Okay," Andrew stammered, unsure what was happening. "What do you want me to do?"

"I need to get the letter..." Samuel repeated. But before he could finish, he looked as if he had heard something that scared him. His body began to flicker more than ever. "We're not safe!" he warned. "We're not safe!"

Just then, an angry wind began to blow itself around the garden, forcing the trees to sway. The wind hissed through the leaves and *whooshed* noisily across the grass. In the distance, the children heard a door slamming loudly.

"Something is coming," said Samuel. "I have to go!"

He started walking back toward the house, and as he did, he turned grayer, and his image became less distinct. The smoke that had initially shaped him now reappeared, swirling around him and seeming to drain him of all his energy.

"Wait!" Andrew called. "Which general do you need to get the letter to?"

Samuel turned and stared intently at Andrew.

"To General Washington, of course," Samuel said in surprise. "His Excellency, General George Washington."

With his final words, Samuel glowed incandescently bright. And then, as quickly as he had appeared, he disappeared into the darkness.

6

THE GLOOMY MAN

The garden returned to normal. With the faint glow of Samuel gone, everything seemed much darker. The four children stood in silent shock. Only the wind, which was picking up and shaking the leaves, could be heard.

"Did that really happen?" Alysse asked. Her head was in a spin. Now that Samuel had disappeared, it seemed impossible she had just been speaking to a ghost.

"That was just so weird," said Jacklyn, her hands on her hips, her gaze starry-eyed. "I mean, that was absolutely fantastic."

"You're telling me," Andrew said, blinking in disbelief.

"Somebody pinch me," Christian requested, "I need to know I'm not in a dream."

Silence returned as they tried to understand the incomprehensible. The wind was still picking up, and the darkness of the garden became more intense, as if someone were switching off all the lights in a house, one by one.

"So, we can all agree we saw a ghost, right?" Christian turned, looking at his brother and his cousins in turn.

"*Yes*," Andrew, Alysse, and Jacklyn said together, emphatically.

"But only once you held our hands," Alysse said. "Until then, I didn't see or hear anything."

"Me neither. Why was that?" Jacklyn asked.

"I have no idea," Andrew said. His head was spinning, and questions clogged his mind.

The garden was growing darker. Shadows melted into the night. The sky had become blacker than ever. Even the moon seemed to have hidden away in fright. Blackness had steadily crept into every corner of the garden. The orange glow of the streetlights had vanished. But the children didn't notice. They were too busy trying to make sense of what had just happened.

"He seemed lost," Jacklyn said, "and confused."

"And he kept saying he had to take a letter to the general," Alysse said. "He was very insistent about that."

"Yes, General Washington...who died about two hundred years ago!" Christian exclaimed, in complete amazement. "How is that possible?"

The wind gushed across the grass. Christian's shorts began to ruffle like a flag on a pole. He looked around him. The darkness that had been steadily creeping into the garden suddenly became noticeable.

"I feel cold again," Christian said. He stood silently and looked at each of the children with frightened eyes. "Something is going to happen. I can feel it," he warned.

"Is Samuel Townsend coming back?" Andrew's eyes were excited.

"No," said Christian, with a blunt voice. "This feels different. When I felt Samuel, I felt a tingle in my tummy. Now I just feel cold." He gripped Andrew's arm.

The children's mood suddenly changed from excitement to a sensation more like fear. They looked suspiciously around them. The crashing of the wind in the trees became thunderous.

"We should go," Alysse said. "We need to go!" She looked around and suddenly realized how dark the garden had become. She looked for the gate, but she could hardly see anything in the blackness.

"Okay," Andrew said. "Let's go."

They turned to leave, but as they did so, Christian stopped to peer into a corner of the garden. The blackness in that corner was deeper than the darkest black imaginable. It was like a big, never-ending hole of…nothingness. And as Christian stood there, peering, the black began to spread itself and grow. It stole all the light left in the garden, sucking it up like a vacuum cleaner. Plants, flowers, and trees all became impossible to see as the blackness began to swirl in a large circle and slowly began to take shape.

Christian was terrified. He could feel something dreadful was about to happen. "Let's go," he urged. "I don't like the feel of this… This isn't good, Andrew."

The four children ran toward the gate. They groped for the latch like blind mice. They pushed themselves through the entryway, but, after he was through the gate, Andrew stopped and looked back into the garden. Again, he saw the black swirl, taking shape. First, there was a stretched hand…then a thin arm…and then a tall body. The outline of the figure was bigger than Samuel had been, almost double Samuel's size. Andrew stood rooted to the spot as he watched the figure materialize.

"*Run!*" Andrew urged. "I'll catch you up. I need to see this."

He turned his gaze back to the garden. The black shape was getting bigger, filling out, as if air were being breathed into a human-shaped balloon.

The girls looked at Andrew and screamed. "We have to go, Andrew. *Come on!*"

"Just a second. I need to know what's happening," Andrew said, and waved them away.

Andrew couldn't take his eyes from the garden. The dark shape stretched and yawned, and slowly uncoiled itself into the form of a towering man.

"Christian," Andrew shouted in panic, "you *have* to get them *away!*"

Andrew unhooked the lock on the gate, and step by step walked purposefully back into the garden. The shape of the gloomy man had fully formed by now. Now and again, the man would stop to sniff the air and turn his head, as though to see if it had heard something.

Andrew's hands were shaking. Fear was thick in his throat, almost stopping him from breathing. The garden became even darker, and an unsteady calm had descended. The gloomy man touched the ground, then smelled the air inquisitively again, before he slowly turned toward where Andrew was standing. Then, he stopped. His face was still forming. But the gloomy man slowly raised his large hand and pointed a long, knobby finger directly at Andrew.

"Let's *go*," Christian implored from the edge of the garden. *"Please...Andrew!"*

Andrew stood transfixed. The gloomy man's form was becoming clearer to discern. He was tall and thickset. He wore a black cloak that covered him from his shoulders to the bottom of his legs. The hand that was pointing at Andrew was a dirty, coal gray; it peeked out of a long-sleeved shirt. Andrew could see the gloomy man's face finally begin to form. His hair was long and matted, his cheekbones high and arched. His thin mouth, pursed into a grimace, was covered in scabs. But worst of all were the gloomy man's eyes. They were a pure, blazing orange, like polished amber, with two black pupils that fixed themselves upon Andrew.

"I see you," the gloomy man hissed. *"I see you, little boy!"*

"I'm out of here!" Andrew screamed, nearly falling over himself as he began to run for the gate. His arms and legs pumped with all their might to get him as far—and as quickly—away from the garden as possible.

"Let's get out of here, Christian!" he shouted. "Jacklyn...Alysse... *Run!*"

The four children darted down West Main Street. They ran as only fear makes people run, and none of the children stopped until they reached the traffic lights on South Street. Andrew gasped for breath. He felt as if he were going to be sick. Jacklyn bent over, her hands on her knees. Alysse held tightly onto Christian.

"What *was* that?" Alysse asked between gulps of air.

"I have no idea...and I don't want to know," Christian said. He had seen the gloomy man's eyes. Never before had Christian seen so much hate in someone's eyes.

"Is it following us?" Alysse asked. She was looking down toward West Main Street, but she couldn't see anything. Andrew and Christian looked as well; but Oyster Bay had returned to normal. A car was coming up past Raynham Hall, its bright headlights illuminating the road...and the fear on the children's faces. But nothing was out of place.

"I think we're safe," Christian said. "Whatever that was, it hasn't followed us."

The orange streetlights were strangely comforting, a sign of everyday normality. Clouds became visible in the sky again. In the north, the moon had reappeared. It glowed brightly in the night, like a lighthouse.

"I wasn't afraid," Jacklyn said. "It didn't scare me."

But as she said the words, she knew she was insincere. And so did everyone else, although no one said a word.

"So, you could see it?" Andrew asked. "We didn't have to hold your hand?"

"We saw it all right," Alysse said, in a terrified voice.

"*That* was the scariest thing I have felt in all my life," Christian said. "It just *felt* bad. *Mean.* It felt...*angry.*"

"You could feel what it felt?" asked Andrew.

"Yes," Christian replied. "It was horrible. It wanted to hurt us. I could feel its hate."

"And you felt the ghost boy?" Andrew probed.

"His name is Samuel," Jacklyn said. "Samuel Townsend, not 'ghost boy'. "

Christian continued: "Yes, but that felt different. That felt like I was on a roller coaster at Hershey park. I could feel the goodness in Samuel. He wasn't scary at all. Especially when we started speaking to him."

"Are you sure the bad thing isn't following us?" Alysse looked back at Raynham Hall, but nothing was coming. Everything had returned to normal. Two people walked past Virelli's, holding hands and talking to each other. "I'm not going to that place again. I'm glad I've never been there before."

"We should go home," Christian said. "We're in so much trouble. What time is it?"

Andrew looked at his cell phone and was shocked. "It's eight fifty-one," he said, with a puzzled look.

"But it was eight fifty when we went into the garden. And we were in there for ages. So how come it's only eight fifty-one?" Jacklyn asked in disbelief.

"I have no idea," Andrew said.

The children all looked at one another uncertainly. No one said a word.

"What do we do now?" Alysse asked, breaking the silence.

"Keep quiet," Andrew said. "No one should know about this. We have to keep it secret."

"No one will believe us anyway," Christian said.

"Are you going to see if Samuel appears again tomorrow?" Jacklyn asked. "Because that was the coolest thing I've ever seen."

"I don't know," Andrew said. "He seems to be appearing every Saturday, so I'm not sure if he'll come again tomorrow."

"Come on, Jacklyn, let's go," Alysse said. "We'd better get home before Mom and Dad flip out."

"See you later, guys," Jacklyn called as they crossed the street.

Andrew and Christian watched Alysse and Jacklyn leave before walking back up South Street, toward home. Each boy was silent. Neither brother knew what to say to the other. So much had happened...there were too many unexplained events to process. A few minutes past as they walked in lockstep, like brotherly robots.

"What do we do next?" Christian asked. "We can't just keep this secret."

Andrew gave it some thought. He tried to weigh the best decision, as though he were figuring out a critical move in a chess match.

"We have to tell Grandpa George," Andrew finally said.

"I agree," Christian returned. "He's the only one who can help."

7

A SHARED SECRET

"Grandpa!" cried Andrew as the two boys rushed through the front door of the house. They were giddy with excitement—and fear—at what they had just seen, but their minds were buzzing, as if charged with electricity.

"Yes?" Grandpa George said. He sat in the living room, wearing his slippers, his legs crossed. A table light illuminated his face and made his gold-framed glasses glint. In his hands was a hardcover history book, the last few pages waiting to be read. So often they had seen Grandpa George reading this way, the image of him sitting cross-legged, with a book in his hands, etched into their minds like a famous painting.

"We have something to tell you!" rushed Christian.

The boys tried to steady themselves and took big, deep breaths. They wanted to tell Grandpa George everything all at once, but at the same time, each was a little scared to raise the subject of the ghosts.

"Boys, it's late, and I'm just about to start the last chapter of this book. Can this wait until the morning?"

Grandpa George looked tired, but his blue eyes blinked kindly through his glasses.

"No," said Andrew and Christian in chorus.

Grandpa George began to chuckle as he resigned himself to the inevitable. The last chapter would have to wait until tomorrow. He gently put the book down on the table and took a deep breath. "Tell me—and make it quick. It's nearly time to go to bed."

The boys looked at Grandpa George for a long time, then looked at one another before staring at their grandfather again.

"We saw a ghost!" Andrew said, beaming with pride.

"In the gardens at Raynham Hall," Christian explained, taking a step toward his grandfather.

"The ghost was a boy, about our age. He said his name was Samuel. Samuel Townsend," Andrew said.

"He was as real as you and me," Christian insisted. "We *spoke* to him. He told us his name and said he had to get a letter to the general."

"*And* we saw something else," Christian said. "Something that scared the life out of us."

Grandpa George looked at Christian more intently. His jovial mood shifted, and the smile on his lips turned grave. He shuffled to the edge of his chair, as if that would make it easier for him to listen.

"Go on," Grandpa George said, in a quiet voice. "Spill the beans, Christian."

"I don't know what it was," Christian began, "but I know I don't want to see it again."

Grandpa George jutted out his chin and leaned forward. He was sitting on the very edge of the chair, now. It was a miracle he didn't fall off.

"It was the shape of a tall man, and he looked old and gloomy," Andrew said, in a hushed voice. "I wanted to run away but I couldn't. I *had* to see it appear."

"Scared me stupid," said Christian. "It felt horrible. Worse than being sick."

The look in Grandpa George's eyes was serious. At first, he seemed amused by the story of the ghost boy, but now he seemed stern. His caterpillar eyebrows narrowed into an uneasy point.

"You said the ghost boy appeared in the gardens at Raynham Hall and was then followed by a gloomy-looking man?" Grandpa George was very careful with his words, trying not to confuse the details regarding what the boys had told him.

"That's right," Andrew said, beginning to feel a little unsure of himself...and a little uncertain of what Grandpa George was asking.

"And the gloomy-looking man made you feel sick?" Grandpa George looked at Christian, who nodded emphatically.

A moment of silence fell across the room.

"So, you saw a specter," Grandpa George said in a very deliberate voice. "And it was a powerful one, if it appeared so soon after the fissure opening."

The boys looked at each other with stunned eyes. Neither could understand exactly what Grandpa George had just said. Andrew heard words, but none of them appeared to be in the right order, and the ones that were in the right order didn't make sense. He looked at Grandpa George for an explanation.

"What did you say?"

Questions began popping in Andrew's mind like fireworks, each rushing over themselves as though in a panic to be asked.

"You just saw a high-level specter. One that would have probably killed you if you hadn't run away. Or worse, it could have made you like him, someone trapped between time, with no home and only hate in its heart." Grandpa George's voice had turned very solemn.

Andrew sat down in a chair and looked at his grandfather as if he had just told them space aliens had landed in their front yard. He ran one hand through his dark hair, wondering what to ask next.

"You believe us then?" Christian was surprised. "About the ghost?"

"I believe you saw something you shouldn't have seen," said Grandpa George. "Something I thought would never appear again."

"I'm sorry," said Andrew, "what did you say? What's going on?"

Andrew was feeling very disorientated. First, he had been unsure what Grandpa George's reaction would be when they got home and told him about the ghost. He didn't think his grandfather would believe them when they told him about their encounter with Samuel.

But now, not only did Grandpa George believe them, he seemed to know more about what was going on than they did!

"This shouldn't be happening," Grandpa George said. He stood up and started pacing the room. "I thought I'd taken care of this and stopped it once and for all." He took his glasses off and rubbed the bridge of his nose. "Something must have changed. Someone must have done something different."

The living room again fell silent. The boys looked at Grandpa George as if he were a stranger. They couldn't understand the meaning of what he was saying. They watched as he put his glasses back on and stared out of the window.

No one said a word for what seemed like a very long time, and then Christian asked, "What's a specter? What's going on, Grandpa? I'm scared."

"You should be, Christian," Grandpa George said. "The fissure has opened, and a trial is about to begin. And I haven't prepared you, yet."

The old man began to wring his hands with worry. He looked distracted and caught off guard as he paced the room.

Andrew felt even more confused—if that was possible. "Prepared us for what?"

Grandpa George looked at his watch. "It's late. There's nothing we can do now. The fissure is weak; otherwise, I would have felt it. It could be a week or more before anything else happens. It's not certain we've lost. We have some time yet."

"Time for what?"

Andrew's inquisitive eyes were bright and full of unanswered questions. He couldn't believe what was happening. Grandpa George had told them ghosts were make-believe. Now he was telling them things existed they could never have imagined. The boundaries between fact and fiction were beginning to collide in Andrew's mind.

"It's time for bed!" Grandpa George said. The soft, warm smile the boys knew so well had returned to his face, but his eyes were still clouded with uncertainty.

"Are you kidding me?" Christian screamed, throwing up his arms in frustration.

"I'm not kidding. It's late. We have a lot to do tomorrow. Thank goodness, it's a Sunday."

"But Grandpa, you can't make us go to bed like this. We need to know what's going on. We're not going to sleep otherwise." Andrew's small dark eyes pleaded for answers.

Grandpa George sat down slowly in his chair. His head was beginning to hurt. He took off his glasses again and polished them, using the tail end of his shirt. The room was silent. The wind pressed against the windows and then rushed among the trees. The table lamp flickered on and off, and the boys looked around the room, hoping it wouldn't go out and throw them all into darkness.

When Grandpa George eventually spoke, his wary tone scared them both.

"It's tough to explain," he said.

"We will do our best to try and understand," Andrew promised. Both boys sat down on the chairs opposite their grandfather in silent anticipation.

Grandpa George hesitated for a moment, trying to decide the best way to explain things. "Okay," he said at last and took a deep breath. "There are specters, there are fissures. Then there are those who can take the trial, and those who can't."

Both boys stared at their grandfather in bewilderment.

"Those who take the trial are those who can save the present history of the world." Grandpa George spoke methodically, as if he were a professor explaining a complicated equation. "The trial is a test. Succeed, and the world stays as it is. Fail, and the consequences could be catastrophic…for everyone."

Grandpa George took another deep breath. His forehead was wrinkled with uneasiness, but he looked at them steadily and said, "It would seem, from what you have told me, that you have been selected to take the trial."

"Take the trial? Us?" Andrew couldn't stop himself from asking questions. There was so much he didn't understand, and so much he wanted to know.

Grandpa George looked somberly at the boys and nodded. "What you saw tonight is a specter. And a specter only wants to do one thing. Make you fail the trial."

"But what is a specter?" Andrew urged, sensing his grandfather was about to reveal all.

"A specter is someone who has been caught in the fissures of time and is unable to get back to where they originally came from. They were once people, like you or me, who took a trial—but who failed. For hundreds of our years, they could be trapped. Maybe thousands of years. And for each year they can't get home, they become more evil and hateful. They have been warped from the people they once were into horrible deformed creatures, who can only despise their former selves."

Andrew was stunned. His mouth opened and closed, as if trying to chew and digest the words Grandpa George spoke.

"But what's a fissure?" Christian blurted. The sound of the word *fissure* made his tummy tingle, like it had when he stood in the gardens at Raynham Hall.

"It's like a door," Grandpa George said, "but it's a door between different points in time or history. The present, the past, and the future are all joined up by the fissures. They should never have been opened...but they were, many years ago. Every so often, they become loose enough for history as we know it to be changed. And it's up to the trialists to ensure that doesn't happen."

The boys sat looking at their grandfather with unbelieving expressions. They just could not conceive of what he was telling them. The soft light of the room made it possible for them to see that Grandpa George was telling them the truth. He looked tired, but at the same time strangely relieved, as if a huge burden had been taken off his shoulders in sharing the secret.

"And how do you know all of this?" Andrew asked.

Grandpa George was silent for a little while longer and then said, "Because when I was about your age, I saw a ghost boy—just like you did tonight. And before I knew what was happening, I had to take the trial by myself, just like my father had to before me, and his father before him."

"*Are you kidding me!*" Christian shrieked. He bounced out of his chair and looked as if he were about to explode.

Grandpa George laughed, as if all the tension of the last few minutes had suddenly evaporated. The gentleness had returned to his blue eyes, and his familiar smile crept back to his lips. "I'm not. But there's time enough to talk about all this tomorrow. Now, it's time for you to go to bed."

"Really?" Andrew said. "After everything that we've seen tonight you expect us to go to sleep?"

"Yes, *really*," Grandpa George told the boys emphatically. "We have a lot to do tomorrow, and we will have to start early. Your parents are in the family room, and I need to prepare. I don't want to raise their suspicions, so go to bed and get to sleep." He stood up and walked toward the front door. "I'll be back in the morning," he said hurriedly.

"Where are you going?" Andrew looked alarmed.

"To check on a few things," Grandpa George replied. "Make sure all the doors and windows are locked after me. The last thing we want is any ghosts getting in here!"

He slipped on his baseball cap, and, after giving the boys a quick wink, he walked out into the night.

8

THE REUNION

It was very early in the morning when Grandpa George woke the boys. It was still dark outside, but morning's light was slowly inching its way across the horizon. Birds were beginning to sing, their sporadic, bright whistles sounding out here and there. One of the neighbor's sprinklers hissed as it dusted water in the garden.

"What time is it?" Christian asked, rubbing the sleep from his eyes. He was finding it difficult to wake up today.

"Too early for most," Grandpa George whispered, "but not for us. We have to get going. There are things we have to do today. Trust me."

Grandpa George seemed very animated for such an early hour as he tiptoed around the boy's bedroom. He was fully dressed, and his blue eyes beamed brightly through his glasses.

"Of course we trust you," Andrew said in a half yawn. "No one doubts that, but it's so early." He rolled over, trying to get back to sleep, and put his pillow over his head.

"I know," Grandpa George said, "but it's time to get out of bed and get your clothes on. Meet me downstairs. We have some investigating to do. And be quiet, for goodness' sake. I don't want your mum and dad waking up and asking awkward questions."

Grandpa George left the boys alone so they could get dressed. Andrew sat up in bed and scratched his head. "You awake, Christian?"

"No," said Christian, "and I don't want to be." He pulled the comforter over his ears, trying not to hear anything.

"What do you think about all of this?" asked Andrew.

"We should do as he says," Christian mumbled as he reluctantly sat up in bed. "I guess this is important. He wouldn't get us up when it's still dark out on a Sunday morning for no reason."

As the boys dressed, they could hear Grandpa George talking to himself softly as he tiptoed around downstairs. Now and again, they heard a familiar creak of the floorboards and Grandpa George shushing it to be quiet. Within ten minutes the boys were dressed and had slipped downstairs.

Together, they all silently left the house.

The morning's air was fresh, almost crisp. The driveway and street looked semi dark. Birdsong was becoming more prevalent as the sun stretched into the sky above St. Dominic's Church. It was so early in the morning that no one could be seen walking the streets, and no cars could be heard.

"Where are we going?" Andrew asked. He couldn't remember seeing Oyster Bay so early in the morning before. He checked his cell phone. It was just before 5:30 A.M.

"We're going to see what's going on at Raynham Hall, first of all," Grandpa George said.

"Is that where you went last night?" Christian asked.

"No," Grandpa George replied, secretively.

Christian was surprised his question went unanswered. Grandpa George usually gave him an explanation to any question he asked.

"So why are we going to Raynham Hall?" Andrew asked.

"I need to go and feel the garden and the house." He rubbed his fingers together, caressing the air.

"*Feel* the garden and the house?" Christian asked. He still hadn't woken up completely, and was upset he hadn't had his usual pancakes for breakfast. "What do you mean by that?"

They came to a stop outside the fire station on South Street. Grandpa George could see the boys' faces in the soft morning light, eager to learn everything he knew.

"This is the last place on earth I ever thought we'd have this conversation, but we don't have the luxury to discuss this anywhere else. Christian, you said you felt a strange sensation before you saw the specter and the ghost boy, Samuel?" Grandpa George stood perfectly still on the sidewalk while looking at both boys intently.

"I did," Christian said, in a quiet voice. "I could feel a tingling in my tummy when I saw Samuel Townsend and felt all cold when I saw that other thing, the specter."

"So you felt both a tingling sensation and a rush of cold in your tummy?" Grandpa George confirmed. "You felt as if there was evil in the world, and at the same time you felt all warm and comforted, as if there was only good?"

"Yes," Christian said, his eyes wide and startled by what his grandfather was describing.

"Do you know how I know that?" asked Grandpa George, his caterpillar eyebrows raised high on his forehead. "Because I have felt those same feelings more times than I care to remember."

Grandpa George's look was determined. In the half-light, he seemed younger, as if discussing Samuel and the specter invigorated him. "Over time, you can train yourself to feel these things, even if you can't see them," he continued. "And as you get more experienced, you can quickly tell if what you're feeling is good or bad." He put his arm on Christian's shoulder, and the young boy felt comforted by the strength of his grandfather's touch.

"So Samuel is a good ghost then?" Andrew asked. His head was still spinning from the night before, and he had more questions than he could possibly imagine.

"Strictly speaking, they aren't ghosts but projections from other times or other histories," Grandpa George said, emphatically. "For all intents and purposes, the boy you saw last night, Samuel, is alive and well but lives in a different time period. Somehow, he's been able to walk through a fissure into our present...but only for the briefest of moments."

Both Andrew and Christian stared at their grandfather in disbelief. All these years they had only ever considered Grandpa George to be a retired construction worker who did everything he could to look after them. But now their grandfather seemed much more than that. To the boys, he appeared to be a different person, one who had mysterious secrets that had never been told. They weren't sure what their grandfather was going to say next. It was exciting and unnerving at the same time.

Grandpa George paused before continuing: "But the specter is a type of ghost, at least a ghost as we may know the term. It's a lost being, a malevolent phantom, perhaps more of a poltergeist that wants to harm people, than a ghost."

The boys stood opened-mouthed, and Grandpa George could see the stunned look on their faces.

"But maybe not quite a poltergeist." Grandpa George looked perplexed. "Oh, I don't know how to explain it." The old man stood still on the sidewalk and took a deep breath, as much to compose himself as well as to steady the boys' nerves.

"Look, I know this all sounds unreal to you now, but you need to believe me. Things are happening that are beyond our control. And even stranger things will happen before all this is done. You will see things you have been told are only make-believe, but which, in fact, are real."

The boys listened quietly to their grandfather as he continued: "Why do you think we have fairy tales and myths? It's not because that stuff didn't happen. Myths and fairy tales are written because those things *did* happen. Maybe some of the stories have been embellished somewhat, but in one form or another, they happened."

Grandpa George took a breath. He knew he was turning his grandsons' world upside down. There was so much to tell them, but not enough time.

"As we've traveled through history, we believe we've grown more civilized, but the opposite may be true. Now, only a few of us can see the strange and marvelous things in the world. People like you and me. Everyone else continues to believe nothing remarkable can happen. It's as if they've convinced themselves there's no magic in the world anymore. But there is, if you know where to look."

Grandpa George looked around. The sky was getting lighter by the minute. Still, no cars or people had passed, but the chorus of a dozen different birds had grown louder. "Let's get going. We don't have much time. We need to get to Raynham Hall before the day starts and people start bothering us."

They walked past the veterinarian's office and the jeweler's store. They turned the corner onto West Main Street. The boys said nothing. Grandpa George strode quickly in front of them. He seemed impatient to get to Raynham Hall. The boys had never seen him walk so fast. If circumstances were different, they would have been laughing at their grandfather for being so excited, but neither boy spoke. They walked side by side as daylight continued to build.

At last, they stopped at Raynham Hall. The old house stood modestly, like it always did. In the growing light, it was even harder for the boys to believe what had happened the night before.

Everything was quiet. The sky was a pale pink-blue as the sun grew stronger and peaked above the small, surrounding hills. The air was getting warm. Both boys could feel the humidity rising. Summer had begun early this year. Usually, Oyster Bay didn't experience this type of heat until the middle of August. Andrew thought today would be a good beach day as his grandfather strode into the garden at Raynham Hall, but the beach was the furthest thing from Grandpa George's mind.

The boys watched their grandfather as he felt the leaves of some of the plants. He smelled the air. He knelt down and brushed his fingertips lightly across the top of the grass, feeling the light dew wet his hands and the knee of his trousers. He was quiet, intent on examining every aspect of the garden.

"So," Grandpa George eventually said, "did you see Samuel appear over there?" He pointed to the edge of the garden, where the boys had first seen Samuel materialize.

"Yes," both boys answered, with big smiles.

"And the specter. The specter started to form around there." Grandpa George pointed to another part of the garden. "And it must have grown incredibly dark when he appeared."

"Yes!" both boys answered again.

"How did you know that?" asked Christian.

Grandpa George had closed his eyes. His fingers were outstretched just above the grass. "I can feel the boy, Samuel, and the specter that was chasing him. I can feel how the specter was trying to stop Samuel from coming through the fissure and trap him. I can feel him also chasing you, Andrew. You must have been scared. It's the specter's job to stop the trial from happening. That's what they are instinctively supposed to do."

"I wasn't that scared," Andrew stammered. "I just wasn't sure what was going on."

"Specters are cruel, malevolent creatures." Grandpa George opened his eyes and looked at Andrew and Christian. He could see the astonishment in their eyes and wished he could wipe it away, as he had wiped their tears away whenever they had hurt themselves as babies.

The boys watched as Grandpa George got to his feet. He took a little longer than normal, and Christian rushed to help his grandfather stand up. "Thank you, Christian," Grandpa George said in his usual, kind voice. "I'm certainly not as young as I used to be."

The boys smiled, but suddenly Grandpa George became quiet. They watched as he closed his eyes again and then turned toward the road. His hands were outstretched in front of him, as though he were feeling his way through a dark alley. He took two steps forward and then gently turned toward South Street. A moment went by in complete silence. When he opened his eyes, Grandpa George saw the outline of a woman approaching them. He looked excited, as if seeing someone he hadn't seen for many years.

"Ms. Waverly," Grandpa George said in a hushed voice. "I could feel your presence from a mile away. Of all the wonders! I never thought I would ever see you again."

The boys turned. There in front of them was the elegant woman from the toy store they'd met the previous day, but she looked different. Her appearance of haughtiness had gone. Instead, she looked happy. Her black hair shone in the early morning light, and a warm smile lit up her face. It was evident to Andrew that Ms. Waverly was pleased to see Grandpa George.

"So you two know each other then?" Christian asked in an awkward voice.

Ms. Waverly walked into the garden. Her head was held high and steady. Everything about her seemed very graceful.

"I didn't expect to see you here, Anna, but I'm pleasantly surprised all the same."

Grandpa George beamed cheerfully. The look on the old man's face had softened. This was certainly a day of surprises for Andrew and Christian. They had never seen their grandfather look so pleased before. It seemed as if twenty years had suddenly dropped from his shoulders. Grandpa George stood tall and proud.

"Good to see you, too, George," said Ms. Waverly, walking closer to the boys and their grandfather. "It's been some time, hasn't it?" Her voice was as quiet as it had been in the toy store, but now it was warm and welcoming, rather than dismissive and rude.

"You haven't changed a bit, have you?" Grandpa George said in genuine awe. "But now I've become an old man." He looked at himself. "I'm not entirely sure age suits me!"

"You're still the man I know and love," said Ms. Waverly. She reached out and touched him gently on the wrist. As she withdrew her touch, Grandpa George seemed to have a moment of embarrassment. Little buds of red appeared in his cheeks, like rose petals. The boys didn't know if they should squirm or smile as they looked at their grandfather.

"It's good to hear your voice again, Anna," Grandpa George said. His moment of embarrassment quickly passed. "Very good, indeed."

In the silence that followed, Grandpa George and Ms. Waverly looked at each other, as if reacquainting themselves after many years had gone by. No one said a word, but a profound sense of understanding seemed to be transferred like gifts between their grandfather and the elegant woman standing before him.

"So you guys really *do* know one another then?" Andrew eventually asked, breaking the silence. He was feeling a little bit awkward, as if he and Christian were intruding on something very personal.

"Yes," Grandpa George and Ms. Waverly said together.

"We're the best of friends," Ms. Waverly added, looking at the boys. "We've been through quite a lot together."

"You can say that again!" Grandpa George reaffirmed. "We certainly go back a ways. A very long ways, indeed." He couldn't help smiling as he spoke.

But both Andrew and Christian were a little frustrated that neither Grandpa George nor Ms. Waverly was saying much. They wanted to know more. How had they met one another? What adventures had they been on? Why was Ms. Waverly so young and Grandpa George so old?

There was another brief moment of quiet before Ms. Waverly turned to Grandpa George. "So it's started," she said. "The game is afoot!" She smiled sarcastically as she spoke, making light of what she was saying.

"I guess it is," Grandpa George said, nodding his head. He clasped his hands before him. He stood much taller than the boys could remember and was more relaxed than when Ms. Waverly had first appeared. "A trial had to happen at some point."

"And the boys?" Ms. Waverly asked, as if Andrew and Christian weren't standing within six feet of her. "Are they to be involved?"

"Yes, the boys saw the fissure open and spoke to a boy from the past," he confirmed. "They also saw a specter. A powerful one, from what I can tell. It's probably Mr. Mud. He's always been a favorite."

"I see," said Ms. Waverly. "We don't have much time, George. Are they ready?"

"No. Something has changed. I thought we'd stopped all this."

"Yes," Ms. Waverly said, "I'm surprised too. But they seem like strong boys. I'm sure they can be trusted."

"And we are standing right beside you," Christian declared, "but we haven't got a clue what's going on!"

Christian was exasperated. Andrew felt exactly the same way. They were being talked about as if they were invisible.

"And we're not scared of anything, just for the record," Christian added. He set his hands on his hips. Andrew, in a sign of support, rested his arm on his brother's shoulder.

Ms. Waverly turned to the two boys and laughed gently. "I'm sure you're not scared. But you need to be resilient on the trial. We don't call it a trial for nothing. You need to be made of stern stuff."

"Like me?"

A warm, sonorous voice floated into the garden. The voice sounded very familiar to Andrew and Christian, and they turned to see Mr. Baines, standing by the white picket fence. Andrew and Christian recognized him immediately, from the day before. He was wearing a dark black suit, a white shirt, and a blood-red tie. His hair was carefully combed back from his forehead and shone with pomade. In his hand, Mr. Baines held the wolf's head cane. Christian saw it had grown smaller, and that it was paler and less animated than before; but still, he couldn't take his eyes off it.

"Stay back, Baines," said Ms. Waverly more forcefully than the boys would have thought her capable of. "You're not welcome here."

"Be careful, Anna," Mr. Baines said, in a gentle voice. "We don't want to say anything we'll come to regret later. We're all friends here. For now, at least. You have my word on that."

Mr. Baines turned to Grandpa George and twirled the cane in his hand. One twirl—and the wolf's head faced Christian. One twirl—and it was gone. "Good to see you again, George," said Mr. Baines, his voice almost purring. "My, you have got old all of a sudden, haven't you. You look older than me, and I'm ancient. Must be painful."

Grandpa George smiled quietly. "And I see you haven't gained any manners over the years, Baines, if that's what I'm still calling you these days."

"Be careful now, George. Remember what happened last time. Rather unfortunate, wasn't it? We wouldn't want to see that happen again, now would we?" A quick twirl of the cane—and the wolf's head looked at Christian with fierce eyes and a dark snarl. Its teeth were razor sharp and glaring. Another twirl of the cane—and the wolf's fierce expression was gone. Christian felt hypnotized, but, using all his strength, he turned his gaze away from the wolf's head cane and looked at his grandfather. Grandpa George seemed to be the only thing protecting him and Andrew from Mr. Baines.

"Don't you threaten my grandpa!" Andrew shouted.

Mr. Baines started to laugh. His laugh grew louder and louder, filling the street like air in a balloon. He began to wipe tears from his eyes. Even the wolf's head cane looked as if it were laughing. "Oh my goodness," Mr. Baines eventually gasped, "I haven't laughed so much in nearly fifty years!" He slapped his leg with exaggerated bemusement. "My, my, George. You've got a couple of young pups there."

Grandpa George ushered the boys behind him. "Andrew, Christian, that's no way to talk to anyone. Let's be civil, even if others can't be."

As Grandpa George spoke, Ms. Waverly stepped toward Mr. Baines.

"Anna. As charming as ever," cooed Mr. Baines. "You always were the beauty, weren't you? It's been a long time since I last saw you." Mr. Baines's eyes were alight, as though on fire.

"What are you doing here?" Ms. Waverly asked calmly. If she was scared of Mr. Baines, she didn't show it.

"The same thing as you," said Mr. Baines. "It seems as if the trial has started, despite all our wishes." He ran his fingers across the top of his cane, petting the wolf's head. "So I just came down to see what was going on. Same as you. Great minds all think alike, don't they?" Mr. Baines turned his attention back to Grandpa George, but it was obvious to Andrew and Christian he wasn't looking at their grandfather, but was looking *at them*. The feel of Mr. Baines's eyes made Andrew's skin itch, as if ants were crawling up his body.

"Did you have anything to do with the trial starting?" Ms. Waverly asked. She seemed to be trying to grab the attention of Mr. Baines, but he didn't take his eyes from the boys.

"No," said Mr. Baines, vaguely. He didn't look at Grandpa George nor at Ms. Waverly as he spoke. Instead, he took a step along the sidewalk, to get a better sight of Andrew and Christian. The boys stayed behind Grandpa George, but Christian began to feel a cold sensation rising in his stomach. It reminded him of the specter.

Mr. Baines smiled. Then, he twirled his cane again and took his eyes from the boys. He tilted his head and then said, "Sorry, Anna. Did you say something?"

Ms. Waverly did not seem flustered and instead, in a calm voice, she repeated, slowly, "Did you start the trial?"

Mr. Baines made a false laugh. He looked up at the sky. "Maybe," he said. A broad smile crossed his face.

Then, without another word, he started to walk toward the garden.

"Don't come any farther, Baines," said Grandpa George. "Just stay back. You know the rules."

The boys were shocked at how forceful their grandfather had become. They had never seen him like this. He stood like a bodyguard in front of them both, his arms taut as shields.

"You misunderstand me, George. I'm simply going to continue my walk. Such a charming town. Full of history, you know. Full of past tales of bravery, treachery, and hidden secrets. Sounds fantastic, doesn't it?" Mr. Baines looked sharply at both Grandpa George and Ms. Waverly. "I do like a good adventure. Don't you?"

"You're sick, Baines," said Grandpa George. Andrew was shocked how angry his grandfather's voice had become and how determined his eyes looked.

"That's a matter of personal opinion, George. Right now, I don't have the time nor the inclination to change your mind." Mr. Baines twirled his cane once more—and the wolf's head angrily faced Christian. Its eyes and snarling mouth had a venomous look of seething hatred, and Christian couldn't help but feel scared. "But there will be time for that, soon enough. Very soon, indeed." Mr. Baines twirled the cane once more—and the wolf's head was gone.

"See you later, boys," chided Mr. Baines. "Don't believe everything Pop Pop George says about me. We've all got secrets." He looked back at them standing in the garden. "You should ask him about his past. But be careful. He tells lots of lies. Don't say I didn't warn you."

As his words died in the air, Mr. Baines walked out of view of the garden and appeared to vanish in the street.

9

THE HIDEOUT

"**W**hat on earth is going on?" demanded Christian. His mind was racing. Thoughts tumbled over one another in a rush to be understood, but they somehow all got jammed in his head, leaving him dumbfounded. Reality, as he knew it, was slowly unraveling like a ball of wool, and everything he had believed up until now was proving to be either false or not quite the truth.

He looked at Grandpa George and wondered for the first time if he even knew who he was. His grandfather had been the only steady influence in his life. But now his grandfather seemed unknowable, like a doppelgänger. He began to shake his head in disbelief.

"We have to go," Grandpa George said. "We have to prepare. There's lots to do."

Grandpa George looked pale, and Christian thought he could see his grandfather's hands trembling. In the space of half an hour, he'd watched Grandpa George turn from excited and happy to scared and withdrawn. Gone from his grandfather's eyes was the self-composure Christian was so used to. Instead, Grandpa George looked flustered, caught off guard, like someone who hadn't prepared properly for a test, or who had gotten caught telling a lie.

"I understand," said Ms. Waverly. Christian noticed she, too, looked agitated—but only for the briefest of moments. A look of confusion flashed in her eyes, almost too swiftly to be seen by anyone, before she gathered herself and took a deep breath. Ms. Waverly touched Grandpa George's hand, and in the next instant, the spell of Mr. Baines was gone.

"Andrew. Christian. Come on. Let's go," Grandpa George beckoned as he strode toward the gate of the garden.

The boys looked at Ms. Waverly. She smiled at them almost apologetically. "It was a pleasure to meet you both," she said, "at least, more formerly than before." She shook each of their hands very precisely, one by one. The boys smiled timidly back to her as each felt her warm, small hand in theirs.

"Are you going to help us?" asked Christian. Ms. Waverly was slowly growing on him. He had almost forgotten about her rudeness in the toy store. Maybe she'd had a bad day when they had seen her last. Perhaps she hadn't quite known who they were. Either way, that Ms. Waverly was gone. Now every time Christian looked at her, he felt a warm tingling in his tummy that made him recall the taste of sponge cake or hot chocolate.

"I don't know if I can," she answered hesitantly. "It's complicated."

Grandpa George had stopped before the gate. Now he stood still, listening as Ms. Waverly spoke. He didn't turn to look at her—or at the boys. He just stood there, his back turned toward them in silence.

"Baines has grown stronger than I could have imagined." Ms. Waverly seemed shocked at her own admission. "It seems he can bend time of his own free will. Something fundamental has changed." As she spoke, Christian noticed a sadness had clouded her eyes, as if she remembered something that had happened a long time ago. "I don't know if I have the power or strength to fight him anymore. Years ago, maybe, with some help from the others. But now, I'm the only Watcher left. We have to find another way. A way he's not expecting."

"What other way?" asked Christian.

Ms. Waverly took a deep breath as she tried to find an answer. "I'm not sure yet, but we will figure it out, won't we?" She gave a weak smile, as if to comfort him, but Christian didn't believe it. He didn't know how to feel. Whenever there was a problem, he could rely on Grandpa George to fix it. Grandpa George always had the answer to everything, no matter how complicated the problem. But now, the answers seemed to have dried up like a desert...and that made Christian uneasy.

"Don't worry, Christian." She smiled again, this time with more strength, recognizing Christian's apprehension. "We will find a way. We have to." Ms. Waverly reached out and gently stroked Christian's cheek with her fingertip. Christian felt the quick tingle in his stomach again. A warm, rejuvenating feeling.

Still standing before the gate to the street, Grandpa George quietly waved the boys toward the sidewalk. Morning had fully dawned in Oyster Bay. The sun was clearing night away like old dinner plates. In the distance, they could hear the faint roar of an airplane making its way through the clouds.

"I'll be seeing you, Anna," Grandpa George said, turning, at last, to look at Ms. Waverly. Christian could see the sadness in his grandfather's eyes and heard the reluctance in his voice. The old man nodded, as if realizing that after just having found her, he inevitably had to leave Anna Waverly again.

"It was good seeing you again, George."

Ms. Waverly came toward the gate then reached out a hand and touched Grandpa George's shoulder.

Grandpa George looked at the ground before raising his eyes to gaze at Ms. Waverly. "And you, too, Anna," he said. "I just wish...."

"George. It wasn't your fault. You can't keep blaming yourself." Ms. Waverly's grip on Grandpa George's shoulder grew firmer.

"But if I'd just done what you told me..." Grandpa George stammered.

"It's in the past."

"For you, maybe. But it's something I think about each and every day." Grandpa George's blue eyes had grown misty. His voice seemed uneven.

Ms. Waverly sighed, but her hand on Grandpa George's shoulder remained firm.

"Things could have been so different for us," Grandpa George said. "All this time that's been wasted."

"I know, George. I know." Ms. Waverly slowly let go of Grandpa George's shoulder, but her eyes looked steadily into his. It was Grandpa George who finally broke the trance. He nodded again, as if acknowledging something in his own mind, and then he turned to leave.

Christian had never seen his grandfather so affectionate with anybody else but him and Andrew. Who was this woman who had been so important in his grandfather's life? What had happened between them? With every passing minute, Christian's grandfather became even more unknowable. Questions began to bubble up in his mind, but he also knew now wasn't the time to ask them.

Grandpa George marched away from Raynham Hall with his long, familiar strides. The boys took one last look at Ms. Waverly and quickly followed on their grandfather's heels, trying their hardest to keep up. Their tall, proud grandfather had returned, and, as they walked down West Main Street, Christian noticed that he never once looked back toward the garden to see Ms. Waverly for a final time.

He's trying to forget, Christian realized.

"Where are we going?" asked Andrew.

"Somewhere safe," Grandpa George huffed. The farther they walked from Raynham Hall and Ms. Waverly, the more he seemed to become irritated, as if someone had interrupted him while he was doing his morning crossword. "Somewhere Baines can't bother us and doesn't know exists."

They walked past the dilapidated, green storefront of Snouder's drug store, crossed South Street, turned right past Nobman's hardware store, and then continued walking along East Main Street. They continued up the hill and past the library, turning onto Cove Road. Without hesitating, Grandpa George turned up the winding Sandy Hill Road.

Andrew and Christian looked at one another with confused expressions, but neither said a word.

Andrew had never seen his grandfather so agitated before, and he certainly didn't want to say anything to make his grandfather's aggravation any worse. He and Christian weren't sure where they were going, but they had no alternative other than to trust their grandfather.

"Keep to the sides boys," Grandpa George urged in a gruff voice, almost spitting out the words. "Now is not the time to get killed by a lunatic driver."

They walked along the snaking road in single file for nearly half a mile, keeping to the edges, their eyes open for anything—or *anyone*— approaching them. The boys struggled to keep up with their grandfather. Andrew had never seen his grandfather walk so fast, or with so much purpose. A tightness formed in Andrew's throat. He wanted to ask questions, more questions than he knew his grandfather could answer, but try as he may, Andrew couldn't form the words.

"We're nearly there," Grandpa George said as he rounded another corner. "Just another couple of minutes."

The boys rushed along, half-walking, half-trotting. The road wound its way through the woods on the outskirts of town. Large houses, set back from the street, dotted the woods here and there. Each house was different. Some were tall and skinny, others were low and sprawling. The boys occasionally had ridden their bikes down the road, and, at times, they had wondered who lived in the houses. But, most of the time, they simply rode past without really noticing.

Eventually, they walked alongside a tall, neatly trimmed green hedge. Within a few paces, a broad, wrought iron gate faced them. The vertical and horizontal rods of the gate's trellis were interwoven with embellished iron swirls. The trellis and swirls formed a beautiful barrier to keep people out.

Ivy grew around the gateposts. The number "23" was painted white on the mailbox. Grandpa George pulled a small bunch of keys from his pocket; the keys jingled as he fiddled with them, until he found one key in particular. He smiled as he fitted the key into the chamber and quietly unlocked the gate, pulling it open and walking through the gateway, onto the driveway beyond.

"Come on," he said. "We'll be safe here. For now, at least."

"Where are we?" Christian asked, looking around with searching eyes.

Grandpa George pushed the keys back into his pocket. As soon as he had stepped through the gateway, he began to look much happier. A gentle smile formed on his lips as he said, "This way."

The boys walked through the gate then followed their grandfather along the narrow driveway, flanked by trees. The small pebbles on the driveway crunched under their feet as they walked up to the entrance of a beautiful, old house edged by an English country garden. The house was large, almost stately. It was built of brick and was two or three stories tall. An imposing chimney rose along one side of the house, its crowning black from years of smoke. White, sash windows lined the façade. The house was stout and wide—like their grandfather, Andrew thought. Two enormous, black double doors marked the entrance to the house. The doors were decorated with a bold brass knocker that shone brightly in the sun. Two plump flowerpots held bright green shrubs, perfectly manicured into the shape of curled soft ice cream.

"Seriously, where are we, Grandpa?" Andrew asked.

He started to feel disorientated, as if someone had blindfolded his eyes, spun him 'round in circles, and then asked him to pin the tail on a donkey. Within twenty-four hours, everything had changed in his life. What had seemed real to him was now an uncertainty. What had been unbelievable, had now been seen and touched. Within one short day, his life had taken a tilt into the unknown. Ms. Waverly, Samuel, the specter, and Mr. Baines had rushed upon him. *Very* fast. Everything had changed, and Andrew felt out of breath, as though he were running to catch up.

"Should we be here?" Christian looked at his grandfather, who by now was standing proudly in front of him with his usual look of calm. "Are we trespassing?"

Grandpa George began to chuckle. "Of course not, Christian. This is my house. Well, one of them at least." He grew quiet with thought then said, "The most important one of my houses, I guess."

"But you live with us," Andrew said incredulously.

"Yes," replied Grandpa George, "for most of the time. But when you're at school or when I need some peace or quiet, I come here." He began fishing in his pocket for another key.

"Who are you, Grandpa?" Andrew asked. His voice warbled and turned shaky. His anger rose inside him. Their grandfather had deceived them!

Grandpa George saw Andrew's cheeks flush crimson, like fuming clouds. He knelt down in front of both his grandsons. "I'm still your grandfather. Nothing has changed there," said Grandpa George in a very calm and reassuring voice. "My love for you is the same as it's ever been, and I'm still the silly old man you've always known. But now I get to share with you who I really am. Do you know how long I've been waiting to tell you about all of this?" He stood up. "Of course, I didn't want to spring it on you. You had to be ready. The time had to be right."

"But that's the thing," Christian said. "I'm not sure we're ready."

Grandpa George's large, blue eyes grew softer. "Trust me," he said, "for just a little bit longer, at least. Everything's going to work out for the best. You're more prepared than you think you are." He turned to the house. Using a large, ornate iron key, he opened one of the two broad front doors.

"Come in." Grandpa George waved for his sons to enter the house. "I'll put the kettle on."

"I don't want a cup of tea, Grandpa," Christian said, indignantly. He was still feeling a bit irritable.

"Who said it was for you?" asked the old man as he shuffled off into the kitchen.

10

THE WATCHERS OF TIME

Andrew and Christian walked into a large, open hallway. Light streamed through the windows, revealing a black-and-white tiled floor. Some of the tiles were chipped from age, and, in places, the baseboards looked worn. Rooms marched off to the left and right.

Grandpa George left them standing in the hallway, but they heard him pour water into the kettle. Then they heard the *swoosh* of the gas range being lit.

"Sit down, sit down, make yourself at home," Grandpa George said, walking back toward them and pointing toward a small study. The room was filled from ground to ceiling with messy stacks of books. An old leather couch was positioned in the middle of the room, on top of an old rug, with two clothbound armchairs on either side. A fireplace faced the couch. Black charcoal and dust stained the mantel, but a fire had apparently not been lit since the end of winter.

Everything was littered with books. The couch, the chairs, the rug. Andrew picked up some books resting on one of the armchairs. They were old hardbacks with fraying covers, that smelled musty. Christian was looking for somewhere to sit, but was unsure where the best place was. "You should be able to find a spot somewhere," Grandpa George said from the hallway. "Move some books, if they're in your way. There's nothing valuable in this room. Well, I don't think there is," he added, scratching his chin as he shuffled back to the kitchen.

Andrew and Christian did as they were asked. They sat precariously on the edge of the chairs and studied the walls. Hanging between the stacks of books were old paintings of landscapes, yachts, and horses. A few antique plates displaying pictures of English hunting scenes hung above one window. Over the fireplace, two Japanese swords balanced quietly on a narrow wooden shelf.

"Look at those." Andrew nudged Christian. "Do you think they're real?"

"Yes, they are," Grandpa George said. He stood at the entrance to the study, holding a cup of tea. "They were given to me some years ago as a gift from Emperor Hirohito." He blew on his tea to cool it down before taking a quick sip. "Just what I needed." He smiled. "There's not a problem in the world that a good cup of tea can't solve!"

"What's happening, Grandpa? Who were those people at Raynham Hall? What did they want?"

The questions came out of Andrew like water breaking through a dam. He needed answers, and so did Christian. Both boys sat perched in their places, desperate for any information their grandfather might tell them.

Grandpa George walked to an old, small desk in one corner of the room. Like everything else, the desk was covered in books. It was also cluttered with reams of paper, some old pots filled with pens, and other trinkets. He clicked on a desk light and rested his teacup on some old papers, which served as a saucer. He didn't seem in a rush to give Andrew and Christian any answers as he slowly sat on the desk's small leather chair.

"It's going to take some time to tell you everything," Grandpa George began. "Some you will understand, and some you won't. Some you will believe, and some you won't. I wasn't supposed to have this chat with you for at least another year or two, when you would both be a little older."

Grandpa George looked at the boys intently, trying to gauge their reaction. They, in turn, looked back at their grandfather with eyes full of attention.

"What do you want to know about first?" Grandpa George asked, taking another sip of tea.

"Who were those people at Raynham Hall?" asked Christian. "We saw them yesterday in town. We thought they were a bit weird, and now we know we were right. Let's start there."

Grandpa George took a deep breath…and then he took another sip of tea.

"They are the Sentinels. The Gatekeepers. The Watchers of Time. Call them what you will. I call them the Watchers," he said, his eyes becoming narrower as he spoke.

"What on earth is a Watcher?" Andrew said.

Grandpa George let out a small laugh. "Good question," he said. "The Watchers look after time. They look after history. They are the beings who have been tasked with protecting the past to ensure the present or our future doesn't get knocked off course."

Andrew looked at Christian and then looked back at his grandfather. "Are you kidding us?"

"Hang on," said Grandpa George. "Maybe this will help."

He opened a desk drawer and started to rummage around. He pulled out some playing cards, a few marbles, another book, and the remains of what looked like an old sandwich, half-eaten. Then, he pulled out a long piece of string, which he held directly in front of him.

"Time," said Grandpa George, "is like this long piece of string." He walked over to Andrew and Christian and held the string horizontally, just in front of the two boys' eyes. "So, let's imagine the beginning of time is at one end of the string—" he wiggled his left hand "—and the present is at the other end of the string." He wiggled his right hand. "History is everything that happens along the line of string. One thing leads to the other and then to the next. Without the past, you can't have the present."

"Okay," said Christian, with a doubting voice. He felt as if he were in a class at school, but instead of a crazy scientist, his grandfather was giving the lesson.

"Well," said Grandpa George, "the Watchers, when everything is just right, can bend time. They can take one end of the piece of string and join it to the other end." As he spoke, Grandpa George drew the two ends of the piece of string together to form a joined circle. "Or they can take any point along the string and join it to another point." Grandpa George was smiling while he talked. Andrew could see he was having fun.

"Now, when that happens," Grandpa George explained, "the past and the present can join together, and, for a brief period of time, a gateway opens. That's the fissure." He spoke with a proud voice, as if he had just discovered—and named—a new planet.

"So, you're saying that when we saw Samuel, he had come through a gateway in time?" Andrew asked.

"Precisely," Grandpa George said, smiling again. He put down the string.

"But why do the Watchers want to bend time?" Andrew asked. He shuffled in his seat and then pulled a lumpy book from underneath his legs.

"Well, the bad Watchers want to disrupt time for their own advantage," Grandpa George said. "They want power. They hunger for it like flies 'round a sugar bowl. But the good Watchers want to make sure history remains the same and doesn't get distorted for some evil purpose. When these good and bad forces collide, that's the trial. We're tasked with doing a trial to make sure we keep the past from being permanently changed, so our present remains the same."

"Don't tell me," Andrew pleaded. "I guess that Baines wants to change things for the worse? He seems like that type of guy!"

Grandpa George smiled. "Yes, Baines is not the gentleman he appears to be. He is the very embodiment of evil. He wasn't always that way, but now he wants to control everything. He's a very nasty piece of work." Grandpa George hesitated as he gathered his thoughts. "But Ms. Waverly is a good Watcher. One of the best."

"So, what do you do on a trial?" Andrew was excited. Thoughts of adventure cluttered his mind.

Grandpa George smiled. "It depends. But, generally, you have to ensure a critical event in the past happens as it should, or you have to stop some new event from happening that could change the present. It could be as simple as making sure two people meet at the right time, or as difficult as averting a plague, or an earthquake, or a war."

"And what happens if something goes wrong during the trial?" Christian asked.

"Then things, as we know them today, could be very different tomorrow," said Grandpa George. "We'll know the difference, but everyone else will just wake up in the morning and think it's normal, even if things are a hundred times worse."

"So how do they, these Watchers, bend time?" Christian asked. "How come they can make a fissure and no one else can?" His face was perplexed, as it often was when he was trying to solve a math problem or figure out a complicated concept.

"No one knows for sure," Grandpa George replied, shrugging his shoulders. "I'm not sure they understand how they do it. The Watchers have many ancient powers I don't even know about."

Andrew was trying his hardest to take everything in. But trying to understand what his grandfather was telling them was like trying to eat a huge plate of food in one bite.

"Okay," said Grandpa George, "let me tell you what I know. To bend time, the Watchers need the conditions to be right. Normally, they can't just do it when they want to. Things have to be aligned the right way. And they can only bend time in particular locations, like Raynham Hall." The old man sipped his tea. "Problem is, Ms. Waverly and I thought we had fixed it so that no more trials could be taken. But, somehow, Baines has been able to bend time and start a trial once again."

"How would that be possible?" Andrew asked.

"I'm not sure. As Ms. Waverly said, something has changed. But I don't know what." Grandpa George finished his tea and put the cup back down on his desk.

"So, how many Watchers are there?" Christian asked.

"Many, many years ago there were lots of Watchers, but now there are only two that I know of. Baines and Anna—or Ms. Waverly, to you two." Grandpa George raised one caterpillar eyebrow higher than the other, looking at the boys like he always did when he wanted them to behave.

"You like Ms. Waverly, don't you, Grandpa?" Andrew said. The question came out before he could stop it. He immediately felt embarrassed as he heard his words leave his mouth.

Grandpa George smiled to himself, and Andrew and Christian could see the memories marching through their grandfather's bright blue eyes. "Ms. Waverly is a good Watcher. She wants to ensure history stays the way it's supposed to, and she'll do everything she can to keep it that way. It's Baines who wants to change everything."

"Why?" Christian asked. "We've done nothing to hurt him. Why does he want to hurt everyone else so badly?"

"I don't know for sure. No one can tell why bad people want to do bad things. Perhaps he just wants to see what happens. He's got an evil heart."

"How many fissures are there?" Andrew asked.

"I'm not sure, to be honest," Grandpa George said. "Probably too many to count, and they seem to be everywhere. Some people think these places are special, like Stonehenge or the pyramids. Some are places that people say are haunted, like Raynham Hall. And then there are some places that we don't even know about."

"All this is so hard to believe," Andrew said, shaking his head. "I mean specters, fissures, Watchers."

Grandpa George looked at Andrew with keen eyes. "You still find it hard to believe, even though you saw it? I'm still not sure what made you go down there in the first place, by yourselves."

Andrew took a quick look at Christian. He was undecided whether he should tell Grandpa George they weren't at Raynham Hall by themselves.

Christian nodded. "We should tell him, Andrew."

"Tell me what?" Grandpa George asked.

"We weren't the only ones who saw Samuel and the specter," Andrew said, timidly. "Jacklyn and Alysse were there, too."

"Excuse me?" Grandpa George stood bolt upright, surprised. "Did they see everything?"

"Yes," said Christian, unsure why his grandfather seemed so animated. "But not before we held their hands."

"Exactly," Andrew confirmed. "We could see everything. But they couldn't see a thing. And then we grabbed Jacklyn and Alysee's hands, and they could see and talk to Samuel."

Grandpa George sat back down in his chair with a heavy thump. He looked very troubled, as if a new complication had been added to the puzzle. He rubbed the hair on the side of his head, trying to tease out a solution to the problem, but, after what seemed like a very long time to Andrew, he still hadn't said anything.

"Is something wrong?" Christian was almost afraid to talk, in case he further upset his grandfather.

"Yes," said Grandpa George. "This changes everything." He stood up and started pacing around the room. "Very unusual this. Very unusual, indeed." He began rubbing his head again. "If you speak with someone from the past, you have to take the trial." He stopped pacing. "Not everyone talks with someone from the past. Most people don't see anything, because they're too busy doing other things."

Andrew wasn't quite sure who his grandfather was talking to. He seemed to be talking to himself, mostly. He watched as Grandpa George paced in circles, unraveling his thoughts into sentences.

"Some people, especially children, may see something accidentally, but there's no harm in that," Grandpa George said. "But if you talk with someone from the past, then that's different. That's very different. That's interaction. That's an invitation to the trial." He stopped pacing and suddenly grew quiet and calm. "There's no other thing for it. We have to tell them about the trial." Grandpa George sat down at his desk and put his head into his hands.

"Perhaps we all need a cup of tea?" Christian asked. He put a big smile on his face.

After what seemed like a very long pause, Grandpa George spoke again. "You have to bring the girls here," he said. "They have to take part in the trial. There's no alternative but for them to be involved."

Christian innocuously asked, "How?"

"I don't know," Grandpa George shouted sharply, slamming his hand onto the desk. His face all of a sudden looked very red and bulbous. His eyes were fierce and pinched together, just as they had been in the garden at Raynham Hall, when he was arguing with Mr. Baines. "You need to start thinking these things through for yourself!" he snapped. "You can't rely on me all the time. Contact them by one of those text things on your cell phone, or think of something else to do with all your fancy technology. Tell them to meet. Tell them what you know, and then come back here."

Andrew sat bolt upright, as if shocked by electricity. "Okay," he said. He'd never seen his grandfather look so angry. No matter what they did, Grandpa George never seemed annoyed.

Christian also looked at his grandfather. He felt a nervousness he had never before felt in the presence of Grandpa George. He watched as Andrew slowly pulled the cell phone from his pocket and sent a text to Alysse.

Meet us in town. Now. Urgent.

Grandpa George stood from his chair and left the study. Andrew and Christian heard his feet stamping the floor as he walked back toward the kitchen. "I need more tea," he said, his voice whining down the hall. The boys pictured their grandfather rubbing his temples wearily as he walked.

"What's wrong with Grandpa?" Andrew asked. "I've never seen him like that. He never loses his cool."

"I think he's been taken by surprise, I mean with Baines and the girls seeing Samuel," Christian said. "It's a lot to take in, even for Grandpa."

"But it's not our fault," Andrew protested. His face was contorted in shame. "We didn't do anything wrong." He felt hurt, as if someone had kicked him in the shin.

"But sometimes you lash out at the people you love most." Grandpa George had silently walked back to the study and was standing in the hallway. "I'm sorry I snapped at you, Christian. I didn't mean to."

"It's okay," Christian said. He looked silently at the floor, so as not to show his grandfather his embarrassed face.

"And I'm sorry, Andrew, if I hurt your feelings." Grandpa George looked genuinely remorseful.

Neither boy said a word, scared of upsetting Grandpa George any further.

"You have to understand," Grandpa George explained. "You have to do this trial. You have to think on your feet and solve problems by yourself. I can't be there for you." He looked helplessly at them.

Andrew's phone chirped. It was a text from Alysse.

See you there. What's up?

Andrew quickly responded, his fingers dashing effortlessly across the screen.

Will tell you later.

Grandpa George walked into the study, and started looking at the bookcases. Apparently, he was looking for a specific volume. Every so often, he would pull out a book, take a quick look, and then put it back. He did this a few times, mumbling to himself, before finally finding the book he had been looking for. He pulled it off the shelf, and Christian peered as best as he could to take a look without being noticed. The volume was an old book about the American War of Independence.

"What do you think is going to happen?" Christian asked. "With the trial and the fissure and…everything?"

Grandpa George looked up from examining the book's cover. He had calmed down from his earlier outburst. Even so, his cheeks were still flushed. He looked tired all of a sudden. *Maybe getting up so early this morning is beginning to have an effect on him,* Christian thought. Both he and Andrew would often giggle to themselves when Grandpa George took afternoon naps, a book or two resting on his snoring chest.

"I'm not sure, Christian. But go and meet the girls. Bring them here, and by the time you get back, I may have more of an answer for you." Grandpa George smiled kindly at both Andrew and Christian. "Give me five," he said, holding up one of his large hands, and both his grandsons obliged.

Then, Grandpa George tickled them both until they were gagging with laughter, and for the briefest of moments, the fear of the trial was forgotten.

11

A PROBLEM SHARED

ndrew and Christian waited for the girls at the bandstand outside the town hall. It was midafternoon. Everything was quiet for a Sunday. A few people were out on the streets, going about their business. Nothing extraordinary, especially compared to what the boys now knew about the Watchers of Time.

As Andrew waited, he saw two black crows looking down at him from a telephone pole. "Caw," cried one of them. It hopped up and down on the pole and bobbed its head, as if dancing. The other crow then looked at Andrew. Its black eyes stared at him blankly before it tilted its head. "Caw. Caw," it screeched. The first one then picked up the song: "Caw, caw, caw, caw." It seemed to be laughing at Andrew again, like the crows in the park the day before. The crows became bolder, taking turns to caw at Andrew. *Go away you silly birds*, Andrew thought. But he said nothing to Christian. He watched as the crows jumped from the pole to the trees nearby before cawing a few more times and then flying away.

It seemed like a long time before the girls eventually turned up. They ran down the street and came hurriedly up to the bandstand.

"Couldn't get away." Jacklyn panted. Her face was all apologetic, and she held her hands up, to excuse herself and Alysse.

"Dad wanted us to help him in the garden," Alysse said. "I've never weeded so much in all my life."

"It's okay," Andrew said, with a smile.

"We've got a problem," Christian noted seriously. "There's some gnarly stuff we've got to tell you."

Christian told them everything about the Watchers, the specters, and the fissure. The girls listened intently, their eyes widening with every revelation.

"You have got to be kidding me!" Jacklyn exclaimed. "That's the biggest load of crazy nonsense I've ever heard."

"But you saw Samuel," Christian said, emphatically.

"*And* you saw the specter," Andrew concurred. "We didn't make that stuff up!"

"I know," Jacklyn said reluctantly. "But is this really true?" Her face was incredulous.

The girls had hardly slept the night before. They had stayed up well past midnight, talking about what they had seen, and then each had nightmares about the specter chasing them in their sleep. Even so, what the boys had told them seemed like make-believe, or fairy-tales parents told their children to make sure they behaved themselves. Despite everything they had seen and experienced, it all still seemed impossible.

"It *is* real," Andrew said. "I don't want it to be real, but I guess we've been pulled into something none of us wants to be involved with."

"What do we do now?" Alysse asked.

"Let's go and see Grandpa George," Andrew said. "He said he has more to tell us."

"As if he hasn't told us enough already!" Jacklyn exclaimed. "Any more of this and my head will blow up!"

"Knock, knock," said Christian.

"Who's there?" Alysse said, in a mocking tone.

"Boo."

"Boo who?" Andrew said, anticipating the answer.

"There's nothing to cry about. We only have to save the world from complete and utter destruction!" Christian's voice was sarcastic, and the four children looked at one another, not knowing whether to laugh or cry.

It was late afternoon by the time the children got to the house. Swallows dipped and swooped across the long grass yard at the back of the house. The birds chattered noisily in flight. Alysse stood with her hands on her hips. She had never known this part of Oyster Bay existed.

"This place is unreal," Jacklyn said in awe.

Alysse looked around the garden. "How long has he lived here?"

"We have no idea," Andrew said.

"There are lots of things we don't know about Grandpa George anymore," Christian said. "It's like he's a secret agent or something!"

The children ambled around the gardens. A huge lawn unfolded before them. A brick patio with a table and chairs looked out over the gardens, and a large, oversized umbrella protected the chairs from the sun. Trees and shrubs grew in an ordered structure. Wildflowers and herbs grew amid curvy borders, and a large white birdhouse with a copper-colored roof stood among some tall bushes.

"Let's go in," Andrew eventually said. "We'd better see what Grandpa George has been up to."

"We're back!" Christian cried, as they came through the front door. The air of the house was refreshing after the heat of the afternoon.

Grandpa George came out of his study. He was holding a book in one hand, and he pushed his glasses up on his nose with the other hand. He looked exhausted, but at the same time, his bright blue eyes were relieved to see the children. He smiled at Alysse and Jacklyn.

"Come, come." He ushered them into the house and led them back toward the study. "Come take a seat. Make yourself at home." The old man placed the book back down on his desk. In the background, classical music played very softly, almost inaudible.

Andrew and Christian had entered the study and sat down comfortably on the couch. But Alysse and Jacklyn stepped gingerly into the room. While they had known Grandpa George since they first could remember, both now seemed a little wary of him, as if he were a stranger they had never seen before. Jacklyn kept an eye on Grandpa George as she moved a pile of books off the leather couch, placed them on the floor, and sat down next to the boys. Alysse perched on one of the chairs, next to her sister. She smiled at Grandpa George, but the air was tense with uncertainty. Both girls, usually so lively around the old man, sat frozen and didn't fidget.

"Have the boys told you about what's going on?"

When he spoke, Grandpa George's voice was very soft and calm.

"Yes," said the girls, together.

"I'm sorry you are involved in all of this. I really am. But when you talked to Samuel, there really was no going back."

"Back where?" Jacklyn asked.

Grandpa George suddenly looked sad. "Back to how things were before yesterday, I'm afraid.

"Generally, it's just one person—maybe two—who take the trial," Grandpa George continued. "But there's never been four people before. And I don't know if it's a right or wrong thing." He scratched the side of his head. "I guess everything happens for a reason."

"But I don't see why it has to be us?" Alysse hardly moved as she spoke.

Grandpa George nodded. "There's a reason. I don't know what. But it seems as if you've all been selected for this trial." The old man looked at the children. He could see they were worried...scared, even. They were all so very young, so much younger than him.

The children sat still.

"So, what's this trial we're supposed to do?" Jacklyn asked.

"I'm not sure yet. There are some clues to what it could be about, and I do have a theory." Grandpa George patted the side of his nose with a finger. "The fissure opened at Raynham Hall. You met Samuel Townsend, who's family was prominent in colonial America. If we add the clue about General George Washington to the mix, then it seems the trial may have something to do with the War of Independence."

The four children stared at one another, aghast.

"And you think we are supposed to do something in the War of Independence to make sure history doesn't go crazy?" Alysse still did not move as she spoke.

"Precisely," Grandpa George said. "Think of it like this. You know that game where you stack dominoes in such a way that if you push the first one, it tumbles all the rest?"

The children all nodded.

"Well, imagine if one domino was taken away. The rest of the dominoes wouldn't fall the same way. It's the same with history. You make the dominoes fall correctly, or you don't."

"One thing is still bothering me," Alysse said. She was finally beginning to relax. Instead of sitting bolt upright, unmoving, she leaned into the conversation with alert eyes.

"And what would that be?" asked Grandpa George.

"How do specters become specters?"

"Well, sometimes people do trials and fail, and unfortunately they can't get back to their own time. Sometimes, people from the past come through fissures and get caught in the wrong history."

"Can specters hurt us?" Jacklyn asked. "Really hurt us?" She looked a little scared.

"Specters can trap you in time, or they can kill you. One bite is all it takes." Grandpa George didn't mean to scare them, but he knew the importance of ensuring they knew the truth.

"They *bite* you?" Alysse was horrified.

"Yes," said Grandpa George. "A single bite will either take your life or turn you into one of them. Have you ever heard of a succubus? Why do you think we have the legend of vampires? It's not because that stuff is made up. It's because of the specters."

The room grew quiet. No one fidgeted. No one spoke.

"So, you're saying there are such things as monsters?" Alysse said.

Grandpa George nodded. "And they have names."

"What do you mean?" Christian asked.

Grandpa George considered for a moment and then began to speak very quietly. "There are quite a number of specters I have come across. All are evil, but some are worse than others. The nastiest is called Mr. Mud. He's an exceptionally powerful specter, and I think it could have been him who you saw at Raynham Hall."

The four children were held in thrall by Grandpa George's revelations. All their lives they had been told there were no such things as monsters, and now here was Grandpa George, naming them.

"And then there's Grendel. I call him that, after the monster in an old poem, 'Beowulf'."" Grandpa George said. "Goodness knows what his real name is."

"What's 'Beowulf'?" asked Jacklyn.

"A story for another day." Grandpa George smiled briefly.

"And the others?" asked Alysse.

"Well, after Mr. Mud and Grendel, there are many others, and they all bite. There's Rebus, Dybbuk, John G. Samuel, and finally, but not least, Lady Matilda." Grandpa George let out a big sigh. "She's the most spiteful of them all. She looks pretty on the outside, but her very being is foul. All of them are monsters from the past."

The day was growing late. Somewhere in the house, the deep, resonant sound of a grandfather clock chimed six times.

Grandpa George stood up. He stretched his back, took off his glasses, and then rubbed his nose. Putting his glasses back on, he smiled at the children. They all saw the Grandpa George of old. Andrew thought he seemed much happier, as if telling them everything he knew about the Watchers, the specters, and the fissures had taken a huge weight off his shoulders. He watched as his grandfather went to sip some tea from an empty cup. A look of disappointment made his blue eyes open wide, and he huffed to himself, as only Grandpa George could. Then, he chuckled before asking, "Who wants a cookie?"

"I never thought you'd ask," Christian said, smiling. "I could eat a horse."

"So what now?" asked Andrew.

He looked at Grandpa George, then at Christian, and then at the girls. They had brought a plate of cookies into the study and had just resumed their discussion. Christian was just finishing his sixth cookie—and he was trying to reach for a seventh without anyone noticing.

"You said the boy, Samuel, who came through the fissure was carrying a letter for General Washington, correct?" Grandpa George looked at the children inquisitively, one caterpillar eyebrow raised. He held a fresh cup of tea in his hand and seemed very content.

"Yes," Jacklyn said. "He said it was a very important letter."

Alysse reiterated Jacklyn's claim: "Samuel was adamant the letter had to be delivered to the General. He said it was a life-or-death matter."

Grandpa George turned quiet for a time. He mulled over his thoughts as he sipped his tea. Then, he walked over to the books he had placed on his desk and brought them over to the couch to talk to the four children.

"I now think it's definitely about the War of Independence, also known as the Revolutionary War," Grandpa George said. "I think Baines wants to change the course of history, to stop the United States of America from winning the war and becoming an independent country."

Like Christian, Alysse, and Jacklyn, Andrew had learned all about the Founding Fathers, the Declaration of Independence, and the Revolutionary War at school. It seemed impossible that someone would want to stop the birth of America from happening. He took one of the books and started to flip slowly through the pages. Between paragraphs of text, he saw pictures of maps and famous military men, hands on swords or sitting proudly on horses.

"Did you know that a huge battle in the War of Independence was fought here on Long Island, in seventeen seventy-six?" Grandpa George was smiling again. "The British, commanded by General Howe, surrounded George Washington's army and forced his troops out of Brooklyn. Washington was able to evacuate his army over the East River, to Manhattan, by using hundreds of boats to ferry away the soldiers. He got lucky, because a mysterious fog suddenly appeared and masked his escape. Without that fog, the War of Independence could have been over before it even started."

"The War of Independence happened on Long Island?" Jacklyn asked. "I didn't know that." She sounded excited.

Grandpa George nodded. "A lot happened around here. You'd be surprised. The War started in seventeen seventy-five, but it didn't end until seventeen eighty-three. George Washington didn't become president until seventeen eighty-nine. It was a long time, from start to finish." Grandpa George broke away from the conversation for a moment and scrambled to find a particular book. Once found, he opened it to show the four children a painting of General Washington, in full military uniform, staring out at them, astride a white horse.

Andrew studied the picture carefully. He saw a man who looked very calm and sure of himself. The blue uniform with white trim made him look stately and imposing. The person who was George Washington, though, was still a mystery to Andrew. All he knew was that he was the first president.

Andrew touched the picture in the book, as if trying to get a better sense of Washington himself through the illustration on the page....

"We know that Raynham Hall was also the center of Washington's secret spy ring." Grandpa George went hunting for another book. He found a second volume and brought it back for the children to look at. This book described Washington's spy network during the war.

"That's right," Andrew said as the pieces began to click into place. He remembered the trip to Raynham Hall with Grandpa George the day they saw Samuel. "The old lady who showed us around the house told us about that. She said the spy ringmaster had a unique code name."

"Culper Junior," said Christian confidently. "That was the code name for Robert Townsend. Agent seven twenty-three."

"That's correct." Grandpa George nodded. "And the Culper Spy Ring played a large part in defeating the British during the War of Independence. Without the spy ring, Washington might not have won the war."

Grandpa George was buzzing around the books now, like a bee around flowers. His blue eyes were invigorated. He picked up another book and opened it to a drawing of Raynham Hall from 1780.

"So, you're saying we're supposed to make sure the War of Independence is won by the colonists?" Jacklyn asked, with an incredulous smile on her face. "I mean, I've only just turned eleven!"

Andrew and Christian began to laugh, but Alysse looked seriously at Grandpa George. "You think that's what this is all about?"

"Yes," Grandpa George said sincerely. "The evidence seems to point that way."

Jacklyn sat back in her chair and let out a huge sigh, almost like a balloon losing all its air. "This is freaky," she admitted. "This is beyond freaky."

"Why would Baines want America to lose the War of Independence?" Alysse asked.

"It's tricky," Grandpa George said. "But, perhaps, if the British had won, then a monarchy would have been created in America. Perhaps the United States as we know it wouldn't have been formed. Maybe there would have been a lot of smaller countries in what is now America that were owned by the British, the French, and others. If America didn't exist as it does today, who knows what things would have happened in the world, and how Baines would gain power as a result."

Alysse was confused. All she had ever known was her home being the way it was. Her school, her friends, her family. She couldn't begin to imagine what her life would be like if all of these things were different.

"If America had a king, then perhaps our concept of having a president who only serves two terms wouldn't have been put into place," Grandpa George surmised. "It was Washington himself who initiated the two-term presidency. And without that idea, perhaps America would have succumbed to a dictator."

"What's a dictator?" Jacklyn asked.

"Someone who has absolute power," Christian said. "They can do what they want, and they don't care about the consequences."

"And someone who is all-powerful could do magnificent things or terrible things," Andrew said. "I guess they do a lot of terrible things, especially if that person is Baines." He looked at Grandpa George for an answer. Grandpa George smiled and nodded in agreement.

A moment of silence passed before Grandpa George said, "Well, it's impossible to say for sure how history would change if America didn't win the war. Best not to speculate too much. We need to focus on making certain we know as much as we can about the war, so that you can pass the trial."

"What else do we need to know?" Christian asked.

"Too much to learn," said Grandpa George. "But for now, I need to do some reading and understand as much as I can, so that I can tell you the things to look out for. But it's getting late. It's been a long day. Perhaps you should all go home, and we pick this up tomorrow."

Andrew could see that his grandfather looked exhausted. "What about you?"

"I'm going to stay here awhile and do what I can for tonight. I'll be home a little later." He smiled at Andrew. "The trial is important. Let's all get ready for it."

12

THE TRIAL BEGINS

The next day at school seemed the longest the boys had ever known. Andrew found it difficult to focus. All he could think about was the trial, and what was about to happen. Christian kept thinking about the wolf's head cane and wondered if it could bite, like a specter.

When the school day eventually came to an end, the boys walked home along their well-trodden route. School bags hung heavily on their shoulders. The heat was oppressive, and sweat slowly trickled down their faces and backs.

As they walked up South Street, they saw Grandpa George half-walking, half-running toward them. He had a look of distress on his face, almost a look of panic, as he shuffled down the road as best his old frame would carry him.

"Boys!" he called when he knew he was in earshot. The words barely escaped his lips, he was so out of breath. "Boys, something is happening!"

Andrew and Christian dropped their backpacks on the ground and ran toward their grandfather. Andrew could feel a knot of panic build in his chest and throat. He had never considered anything bad happening to his grandfather, but he suddenly felt a strong sense of fear.

"What's wrong?" Christian asked.

He grabbed ahold of his grandfather before he could collapse in a heap on the ground. Christian felt the weight of Grandpa George pushing down on him, and he was surprised at just how heavy his grandfather was.

"It's beginning," said Grandpa George. He was gasping for breath, like a fish out of water. "I can feel it. The fissure is starting to form. It's Baines. He's trying to catch us off guard. He's become more powerful than I thought, if he can now bend time when he feels like it."

Grandpa George leaned over and rested his hands on his knees. Christian was glad his grandfather was able to hold his own weight. The old man was still panting loudly, taking huge gulps of air. It had been a few years since he had run any significant distance. Andrew suddenly realized just how old their grandfather was becoming, and how vulnerable he seemed.

"Are you okay, Grandpa?"

"Yes," Grandpa George said. He tried to stand upright but then decided against it and rested his hands on his knees again. "I'm going to be fine. Just a little out of breath, that's all." Beads of sweat gleamed on Grandpa George's head. His skin looked red and sunburnt. His glasses had slipped a little down the bridge of his nose. But within a minute or two, he began to regain himself. His breathing became more regular. He pushed his glasses to the top of his nose and once again stood upright. The old but brilliant blue eyes began to shine.

"We have to move," he said at last. "We only have a short time to do the final preparation. We need Alysse and Jacklyn. Can you ask them over to my house?"

"We can ask," Andrew said, "but I'm not sure if they can come. I guess that will depend on what Uncle Pete and Aunty Jay are doing."

"They have to be here," Grandpa George insisted. "We will fail the trial without them."

Andrew nodded. He fished out his phone and started to text.

It's going down 2night. Meet us at Grandpa's at 6. B there!

"Come," said Grandpa George. "Let's go to Raynham Hall. We need to check what's actually happening."

"How will we know for sure?" Christian asked.

Grandpa George gave Christian a little knowing wink. "Because we're going to be able to feel it, young man," he said.

"What about Mom and Dad?" Andrew said.

"I told them I'm taking you for hot dogs and a movie. I've got you covered." And with a mischievous smile, he ruffled the hair on each boy's head and strode toward Raynham Hall. The boys ran back to retrieve their backpacks, then quickly followed him.

They stood outside the garden of Raynham Hall. It was late afternoon. No one appeared to be in the old, white house, not even the elderly lady. Even West Main Street was quiet. No one walked up and down the sidewalk. There were no cars or trucks, either. It was as if everyone knew something strange was about to happen and had decided to avoid the area at all costs.

"Can you feel anything, Christian?" Grandpa George asked.

"Not really," Christian said.

He was looking around, trying to see what he was supposed to be feeling. He looked at the trees, the buildings, the parked cars dotting the street. He could see the sun still high in a very blue sky with few clouds. It seemed like a typical Monday afternoon. Nothing different or exceptional was happening.

"Close your eyes," said Grandpa George, "and try to ignore everything else that's going on. Just feel with your tummy."

Christian felt a bit self-conscious as he stood on the sidewalk with his eyes closed, but he did what Grandpa George asked. He concentrated as much as he could and tried not to let anything disturb him. But no matter how hard he tried, he could still hear the distant sounds of the town. Birds singing…car engines accelerating and decelerating...even the noise of the traffic light signal singing *beep-boop, beep-boop.* Everything seemed to be conspiring to distract him.

"Any better?" Andrew asked.

"Not really. I can't feel a thing, but I can hear a lot of stuff. I can't focus."

"Come," Grandpa George said. "All you need is a little bit of practice. Let's go into the garden. Perhaps you need to touch something closer to the fissure to help you along a bit."

Their grandfather opened the gate and calmly walked into the garden, as though he owned it. "Come on, Christian," Grandpa George instructed. He bent down toward the ground, taking a knee. "Come here and touch the grass."

Christian put down his backpack and gingerly walked into the garden. He knelt down and stroked his hands along the top of the lush, early-summer grass.

All of a sudden, his stomach began to tingle.

"I can feel it," he said. "The fissure. It's not as strong as when Samuel appeared, but I can definitely feel something." He was smiling, delighted with himself that he had actually managed to sense something. He looked at Andrew, who was looking back at him. "It tickles!"

"Good," said Grandpa George. He had closed his eyes, and there was a very peaceful look on his face. "I can feel it, too."

"It seems to be getting stronger," Christian said. He let his fingers gently caress the ground. "It's still not ready yet. But I know something's going to happen tonight."

"How do you know that?" Andrew asked. He was standing beside his brother and grandfather, watching them in awe.

"I'm not sure," Christian replied, looking up. "I can just feel it. It's difficult to explain, but it's definitely getting stronger. It's like it's speaking to me without words."

"What you're feeling are time ripples," Grandpa George explained. "Before the fissure opens completely, it slowly wakes up, and only those who are Feelers can sense the ripples getting stronger. As the time draws near to when it's fully open, the ripples begin to feel stronger and stronger... It's almost time, boys. Another couple of hours or so, I guess."

"It's amazing," said Christian. "I can feel it all through my body. I've never felt anything like it before." He was grinning. "It's unbelievable."

"So, what do we do now?" Andrew said.

"We wait until the fissure is fully opened," Grandpa George answered, looking at both boys with calm eyes. "That's all we can do for now. In the meantime, we'll go and have something to eat."

Andrew felt a buzz in his pocket. He pulled out the phone. There was a message from Alysse.

We'll be there.

"I guess the girls will be joining us, after all," Andrew said with a smile. He showed the phone to Grandpa George and Christian.

"Jolly good," Grandpa George said in his strong English accent. He smiled in relief.

"Grandpa!" Christian looked concerned. He was still stroking the summer grasses. "I can feel something else."

"What is it?"

"It's something terrible. It's nothing to do with Samuel or the fissure. It's something completely different. It feels like... It feels like..." Christian closed his eyes and tried to concentrate more than ever.

"Take your time, Christian. Relax." Grandpa George coached his grandson in a quiet voice. "Calm your mind. Let the feeling come to you, and don't try to rush it."

Christian took a deep breath and cleared his mind. He was completely still, his hand now resting an inch or two above the ground. "Baines," he said, at last. "I can feel Baines, and he is getting closer."

Grandpa George closed his eyes and spread the fingers on his hands. He took a deep breath and waited. "You're right, Christian," he said, at last. "I can feel Baines, too. We should go. I'm not ready for him yet. And there's still something I have to do."

They returned to Grandpa George's house. The boys sat on the patio. As the afternoon ticked away, they began to feel a bit worried. Andrew kept looking at his cell phone, checking the time: 5:55...6:00...6:05....6: 10 . . . But still no Alysse and Jacklyn!

Where could they be? Had something happened? Had Uncle Pete or Aunty Jay stopped them somehow? What would happen if they couldn't be part of the trial? Would they fail before they started?

The sky began to become overcast and gray. "Looks like we could have a storm a bit later," Grandpa George said as he served the boys their hot dogs. He paused for a moment to look at the brooding clouds beginning to form like smudged charcoal. "They didn't forecast that today! They said it would be clear skies, hot and humid." Grandpa George tutted to himself.

"I bet that storm has something to do with Baines," Christian said.

"He can control the weather now?" Andrew looked intently at his grandfather.

"I wouldn't be surprised what that evil man can do." Grandpa George huffed contemptuously. "I don't know where he gets his power from."

"Where are the girls?" asked Christian.

"I don't know," Andrew said, checking his phone. *No messages.* It troubled him that they hadn't already turned up, but he knew he had to be patient.

"It's getting late," Christian said. "They better be here soon, or we may have to start the trial without them."

"But if what Grandpa George says is correct, we'll fail it without them." Again the niggle of impatience dug at Andrew.

Just then, a noise came from the driveway. The sound of metal scraping against stone could be heard as the big, black gate opened and then closed. The boys looked up and saw Alysse and Jacklyn walking toward them. Their dog, Macy, strained at the leash.

"What are you doing with Macy?" Christian asked.

"It was the only way we could get out," Jacklyn said. "Dad said we had to walk Macy."

"What are we going to do with her when we're doing the trial?" asked Andrew.

Grandpa George stepped from the house onto the patio. "I will look after her," he said. "Girls, good to see you at last. I didn't know if you were going to make it. And it's lovely to see you too, Macy!"

It was getting late. Everyone had eaten. Macy sat under the patio table, curled up, snoozing on Jacklyn's feet. The sky was becoming unnaturally dark for a summer's evening, and it seemed cooler than normal, so much so that Alysse asked Grandpa George if he had a sweater or blanket to put around her shoulders.

"How's everyone feeling?" Grandpa George asked. "Scared?"

No one spoke. The four children all looked at one another with questioning eyes, before Jacklyn said, "I'm okay."

Grandpa George smiled. It became quiet again, as each of the children wondered what was going to happen next. Andrew checked the time. Seven o'clock. He was surprised it was so early, because the dark sky made it feel so much later.

"I have something." Grandpa George put a worn, brown, leather satchel on the table. "We never talked about the talismans, did we?" He looked at the children with a raised caterpillar eyebrow.

"No," Christian said. "What are they?"

"Well, they are things that were made by the Watchers in ancient times. And some of them have special powers." Grandpa George rummaged inside the satchel and pulled out a gold-shaped star about the size of his palm.

"What *is* that?" Andrew asked. He desperately wanted to reach out and touch it but sat on his hands instead.

"It's a unique weapon," Grandpa George said. "One that has been used throughout the years to protect humans from specters. Ordinary weapons can't hurt a specter. But this throwing star can wound a specter, and if it strikes its heart, it will kill the specter outright."

Grandpa George handed the gold throwing star to Jacklyn. "This is for you, my brave little Jacklyn. Use it well, and only when you need to."

Jacklyn was stunned. She took the throwing star and turned it over and over in her hands, studying every part of it. Then she looked back at Grandpa George. "Thank you."

Grandpa George nodded. "You're welcome."

The old man began to rummage in the satchel again. "I only have one other talisman, although there are many others out there. But perhaps this one is the most important of them all." He pulled out a small wooden box and opened it. Inside was what looked like a small copper-colored coin, no bigger than a quarter. It had no markings on it. It was smooth to the touch, and the edges were thick and blunt. He picked the small coin out of the box and held it up.

"This is the key to the fissure," Grandpa George said. "When you saw Samuel, it was only because the fissure let him stay in our present temporarily. To truly go back in time, to take the trial, you need this. I call it the copper-colored key."

He passed the key to Andrew.

"For many years, Andrew, I thought it would be just you and me having this conversation," Grandpa George said. "I always assumed you would be the boy to take my place. But I guess the fissure needs more help to make sure things stay the way they should be." He nodded to Christian, Alysse, and Jacklyn. "Perhaps you will all have a say in how the trial will end. But you can't take the trial without the key."

"It's beautiful," said Andrew. "I've never seen anything like it...."

Grandpa George nodded in agreement. "It's what Baines has always coveted. If he had the key his power would be absolute. You must keep it safe. Don't lose it. Without the key, you can never come home."

Andrew swiftly put the copper-colored key deep into his pocket and kept his hand on it to keep it safe. It felt warm, as though it were alive.

"Can you feel anything, Christian?" Grandpa George asked.

Christian closed his eyes and stretched his fingers like he had seen Grandpa George do in the garden at Raynham Hall. He tried to remove everything from his mind and breathe deeply. Slowly, everything around him began to disappear and crumble into nothing. The lights...the sounds...the feel of the weather on his skin... Everything disappeared, except the tingling in his stomach. Only, this time it was more powerful. It pulsed like one hand rhythmically slapping the surface of a table. He began to feel drawn out of his chair, wanting to be pulled through the fissure...

"It's started," said Christian, with wide eyes.

"It certainly has," Grandpa George said. "It's time. Come on. Let's walk down to the garden."

"And I can feel Baines," Christian added quietly.

"So can I," said Grandpa George. "So can I."

13

THE FATEFUL MEETING

The walk from Grandpa George's house to Raynham Hall seemed to take a long time. The children walked up front. Grandpa George ambled behind them. Macy was enjoying the walk. She stopped and sniffed the grasses and shrubs whenever she could. On more than one occasion, Jacklyn gave her a gentle pull to get her walking again.

"Do you think it's going to start raining?" Christian asked. "Those clouds look ominous."

Alysse looked up to the sky. "Probably," she said. She wore an old sweatshirt that belonged to Grandpa George across her shoulders. She held the sweatshirt tightly against herself, to thwart the cold.

"Great," Christian said. "So, we're going to have to save the world and get soaked at the same time!"

"It would seem that way." Grandpa George nodded. "Nothing is ever easy in this world, my boy."

They continued to walk in silence. Eventually, they came to South Street, where they turned onto West Main Street. As they did so, Christian let out a loud moan.

"What's wrong?" Andrew asked.

"It just felt like someone punched me in the stomach." Christian gasped for breath as he coiled over like a folding table.

"Christian!" Andrew grabbed his brother.

"I'll be okay," Christian said. "Just had the wind knocked from me."

"It's Baines," said Grandpa George. "He's trying to stop you from taking the trial. If that happens, he'll win. We must be on our guard from here on. He's going to be watching for us."

A crack of loud thunder shuddered across the sky. Macy slunk down on her haunches. The clouds rolled in angry swirls, like black spinning tops. Everything was now completely dark. Oyster Bay had been thrust into a premature midnight. Cars turned their headlights on. People walking along the streets pointed up at the sky in alarm and amazement, wondering what was happening.

Grandpa George helped Christian to his feet. "We must get to Raynham Hall." He looked anxiously around him. "I have to get you all through the fissure."

"Come on, Macy," Jacklyn called. "It's going to be okay." But Macy was scared, and Jacklyn struggled to get her back on her paws. In a swift movement, Jacklyn bent down and whisked Macy up, into her arms. "Don't worry, Macy," she said reassuringly. "I've got you." Macy licked Jacklyn's face gratefully.

Despite the darkness, they could see someone standing in the middle of the road in front of them. They couldn't quite tell who it was. The shape was blurred, out of focus. But it looked like a man.

"Who's that?" Alysse asked.

"Baines," Christian said. "I can feel him."

"You don't need to feel him to know it's that jerk," Andrew said.

"Hush now, Andrew," his grandfather said. "Calling people names isn't going to help anyone." Grandpa George hurried the children forward while keeping his eyes firmly on Mr. Baines.

Just then, a bright streak of lightning cracked the sky. It raced to the ground, bouncing along the far end of the road until it exploded against a tree behind Mr. Baines. Everyone crouched down, unsure of what was happening, and Macy let out a loud yelp. But Mr. Baines didn't flinch. The tree that had been hit began to slowly fall into the street behind Mr. Baines. The sound of bark and wood tearing was earsplitting, and, as the tree crashed onto the road, it made a tremendous din.

Unsteadily, the four children and Grandpa George got to their feet. Macy was quietly whimpering; she had jumped out of Jacklyn's arms to hide behind her legs. The distance between them and Mr. Baines had narrowed. He stood in front of them, in a simple black suit, shirt, and tie. His shoes were polished mirror-bright. He held the wolf's head cane in his hand and twirled it from time to time.

"George!" Mr. Baines called like a teacher scolding a naughty child. "Give up, George. You can't win this. Give up now and save us all a lot of trouble."

"Baines!" shouted Grandpa George. "You have to observe the rules of the trial. You can't stop it from happening."

Baines began to laugh quietly to himself. "The rules of the trial?" he mocked. "What rules? *I* make the rules now, George, not you or anyone else. Can't you see that yet?" Mr. Baines raised his arms. "Look what I did!" he shouted proudly. "I created this storm, I caused the lightning, I opened the fissure. I can do anything I want."

"Baines, you don't have to do this," Grandpa George shouted.

"Oh, but I do!"

Mr. Baines started walking toward them. His cane clicked on the road, in perfect time with his steps. The fallen tree was on fire; flames stretched and danced into the sky. The fire was the only light around them all. All of the lights of the shops and the houses were dark. No streetlights were lit. Andrew wondered if the storm had knocked out the power. No people, no cars, no signs of life were visible.

Christian felt nauseous again. His stomach was doing somersaults. All the warmth from the fissure had been washed away. He could see the wolf's head cane. The wolf's face appeared to be getting bigger in Mr. Baines's hand. Its teeth were glaring in the night sky, the sharp points more prominent than ever before. Its eyes were narrow and focused, as though it were hunting prey. Christian felt overwhelmed and was unable to turn away, or even just close his eyes. He knew it was Mr. Baines that was making him feel sick, but there seemed to be nothing he could do to stop it.

"*Let's go!*" Andrew shouted.

With every step, Mr. Baines further closed the gap between the children and himself. Soon, it would be impossible for them to get into the garden at Raynham Hall and pass through the fissure.

Andrew realized it was time to act. He grabbed his brother by the arm and shoved Jacklyn and Alysse forward with his body. "*Move!*" he commanded. "We have to get to the garden. We have to get to Samuel and get through the fissure."

Rain began to fall. Gently at first, but then more steadily. It bounced off the blacktop like wet ping-pong balls. Soon, the children's clothes were soaked, and their hair was matted. But the rain woke them up. They found their feet and started to rush toward the gate of Raynham Hall. As they drew closer, Christian began to feel the rhythmic beat of the fissure again. Its smooth warmth slowly replaced the nausea brought on by Mr. Baines. He suddenly felt stronger, as if the fissure were giving him some of its power. Christian looked up to see Mr. Baines striding vigorously toward them in his smart, black suit. The wolf's head cane didn't appear so scary anymore.

"Baines!" Grandpa George shouted again. "You can't stop this."

Mr. Baines halted and turned his head angrily toward Grandpa George. "Shut up, you stupid old man. Your time has come and gone." Mr. Baines shot the old man an aggressive look. His refined composure had gone, revealing the hatred Mr. Baines felt for Grandpa George.

But instead of standing still, Grandpa George started jogging toward Mr. Baines. Slowly at first, but summoning all the strength he had, he began to run. Mr. Baines watched Grandpa George as the old man gingerly shuffled toward him.

"I don't want to do this, George. Don't force me to do it."

Mr. Baines smiled as he spoke, but the look of hatred on his face grew darker, and his eyes had turned completely black. Mr. Baines held the wolf's head cane in front of him, raising the snarling face so that it gazed directly at Grandpa George.

The children reached the gate. In the half-light, Andrew reached toward the latch and immediately opened the gate. He ushered them all up the brick path and into the garden as quickly as he could, rounding them up as though herding sheep into a pen. Even Macy did as Andrew asked: Jacklyn set her to the ground, and she trotted quickly into the garden. Her leash trailed quietly behind her.

"Christian!" Andrew said sharply. "Has the fissure opened? Can you see Samuel?"

Christian spread his fingers into the air before him. "A few minutes more, Andrew. Just a few minutes more."

Andrew turned toward the street. Between the trees, in the half-light, he saw Grandpa George come to a stop about ten paces away from Mr. Baines. Both men seemed to be staring at each other intently.

"Stay here," Andrew commanded. "I have to help Grandpa George."

Christian looked nervously at his brother but did as he was asked. Andrew rushed out of the garden the way he had come in. The rain was falling heavily, pelting all the children, as well as Grandpa George; but Mr. Baines looked desert dry. Andrew's mind was racing, and his heart felt on fire. As he reached West Main Street, he heard Mr. Baines laughing, as though he had just told a joke.

"So you think four silly children and a stupid dog will help you win the trial, George?"

"I beat you before, Baines," said Grandpa George. "And I wasn't much older."

"Ah," Mr. Baines goaded, "but I'm more powerful now, George. I can pretty much do as I want. I took the power of the other Watchers, and I've made it my own. I'm going to make time do my bidding. And you think you can stop me?"

Suddenly, Grandpa George fell to his knees and clutched his head. He let out a low, quiet scream of intense pain. Every muscle of

Grandpa George's body stiffened. It looked as though he had been stunned with a hard blow.

Mr. Baines started to laugh. But the very next moment, he gasped loudly, as though he were choking. Then he, too, clutched his head. Abruptly, he lifted off the ground, as if some unseen power were forcing him into the air.

"Maybe he can't stop you," said Ms. Waverly, appearing from out of the darkest edges of the street, "but I can."

Swiftly, Ms. Waverly raised her hands as though she were pushing against an unmovable wall. The next instant, Mr. Baines—still a foot above the ground—*whooshed* backward then suddenly dropped onto the road, in a heap.

Gasping, Ms. Waverly turned toward Grandpa George, to make sure he was unharmed. He was still on his knees, but the pain in his head had gone. "I'm okay," he said to her as he looked up. "I'm okay."

Andrew had come to a halt before his grandfather. He gazed at Ms. Waverly, his eyes growing in wonderment. She suddenly looked tired, and a little older. He realized that pushing Mr. Baines over had taken all the energy Ms. Waverly had.

"Get back to the garden," she said. A glint of determination still emboldened her eyes. "You don't have much time. I can't hold Baines forever. Take the key and get through the fissure. I will meet you there."

Andrew nodded. Next to him, Grandpa George struggled back to his feet. Andrew shot one final look at him before running back to the garden gate.

"Christian," Andrew shouted, "is it time?"

Christian urged Andrew back into the garden. The pulsing sense of the fissure was now one continuous wave. It raced across his arms, his legs, and his body and head, like a warm breath.

"*It's time, Andrew!*" he shouted.

In the garden, the children saw a gentle light shining in front of them. Like a flower opening, the fissure began to form. It shimmered and grew bigger and bigger, until it was the size of a door. From the shimmering light came a hand...then a wrist...a foot...and a neck. Gently, the shape of Samuel Townsend came into view. The young boy stepped out of the light and walked into the garden. He grew pale before them.

"Samuel!" Jacklyn shouted. "We have to go with you!"

Samuel looked at Jacklyn and smiled. "Where are we going?"

"Back to where you come from," she said. "And we have to go *now!*"

"We're going to help you take the letter to the general," Christian shouted.

Andrew felt the copper-colored key in his pocket. It had grown hot against his skin—almost burning. He looked back, toward West Main Street. Mr. Baines had got back to his feet and was slowly walking toward Ms. Waverly and Grandpa George.

"That wasn't very nice of you, Anna," Mr. Baines said, standing right next to Grandpa George. He dusted off his trousers with his hand. "Do you have any idea how much this suit is worth?"

"You can't stop this, Baines!" Ms. Waverly warned. "If the fissure is open, then we each get the chance to take the trial. You can try to change history for the worse. I will try to make sure it stays the same. You know the rules."

"When I kill you, Anna, there will be no one to stop me," Mr. Baines replied, in a cold voice. From the garden, Christian sensed a sudden new presence in his stomach. It wasn't the warmth of the fissure, this time, or the nauseating hatred of Mr. Baines. It was the same cold feeling he had felt when he had sensed the specter. A freezing touch began to fill his body. The air around him turned intensely cold. The hairs on his arms and legs stood up, as though called to attention by a military officer.

"Andrew!" called Christian. "I can feel a specter. *We have to get through the fissure!*"

Alysse looked at Jacklyn in pure fear. "We have to go home!" she cried. "We shouldn't be here.... *Let's go.*"

"We have to do this," Jacklyn said. She picked up Macy's leash and held it in one hand while holding her sister's hand in the other.

"We'll get through this. We have to. I'll look after you." Jacklyn had never felt so scared in her life, but somehow that realization made her feel stronger. "Look at me, Alysse," she urged. *"We've got this."*

All at once, a thin hand appeared through the fissure, then extended out into the darkness. The hand was a murky gray, like old rags. An arm then slowly slithered from the fissure, like a snake. The tall, dark form that Andrew had watched take shape the day before began to form again.

"Come this way!" Samuel cried as he ran to the corner of the garden. "We'll be safe."

The children followed Samuel as Jacklyn urged Macy along, and the specter slowly came to life.

"You think you can stop me," said Mr. Baines, laughing. "Don't you know I have friends in low places who are only too happy to help me?"

Grandpa George was about to respond to Mr. Baines...but a look of fear suddenly crossed his eyes.

All at once, he felt the specter.

He turned to Ms. Waverly. "You have to help them, Anna," he said. "You have to watch over them. Leave Baines to me."

"So noble of you, George," Mr. Baines goaded. "So admirable. We could still make a gentleman out of you yet, George, if you want it."

"Go to hell, Baines."

"You would like to see me there, wouldn't you?"

Mr. Baines flipped his cane upward and held it with both hands in front of him. The ivory wolf's head pommel was glowing a blood red. As Mr. Baines held the cane, he gently stroked the wolf's head. Slowly, it began to change shape, until the pommel reformed itself into the tapered handle of a sword. Pulling the wooden cane away like a sheath, Mr. Baines revealed a long, deadly blade. It flickered against the fire of the tree burning behind him.

"Run, Anna. Save the children!" Grandpa George shouted.

"Yes...run, Anna," mocked Mr. Baines. "Run for your lives!"

Mr. Baines was laughing as he turned his attention back to Grandpa George. In one swift movement, he raised the sword up and then plunged it into Grandpa George.

Grandpa George gasped. He looked down at the sword, thrust through his chest. A look of surprise flickered across his blue eyes. Flailing, Grandpa George tried to grab the sword, but he couldn't get a firm grip. Mr. Baines stood staring at Grandpa George with his emotionless black eyes.

Grandpa George let out another sigh then slumped to his knees.

"Run, Anna," Mr. Baines mocked again. "Run as fast as you can. There's nothing you can do for him now."

⌇

Christian felt the sword almost as if it had struck him directly. He screamed in pain. Alysse and Jacklyn held him as he fell to the ground.

"What's happened?" Jacklyn screamed.

"It's Grandpa George," said Christian. "He's been hurt."

Andrew ran to the fence and looked into the street. His heart nearly stopped as he saw Grandpa George kneeling on the ground, with Mr. Baines's sword pushed through his chest. Anger rushed over Andrew, and a thick, hot bile filled his mouth. "*No!*" he screamed. "What have you done?" He began to shake the fence with his hands. "What have you done?"

"What needed to be done," said Mr. Baines, coming up to the gate and turning to look at Andrew. An empty smile formed on his face. "And now I'm going to change time, and you can't stop me."

Andrew stared in fear at Mr. Baines. But then he felt a presence behind him. He turned and watched as the specter stepped through the open gate and walked into the road. Its steps were stiff and deliberate, as though it had been caged up for a long, long while. Its black cloak rippled in the wind and the rain. As it walked, it pulled back the cloak's hood to reveal a long, drawn face. Loose, saggy skin hung from its cheeks and neck; but its eyes looked young and keen.

"Good to see you again, Mr. Mud," Mr. Baines said.

Mr. Mud nodded but didn't say a word.

Mr. Baines looked at Mr. Mud and smiled again. "You know what to do. Finish the job."

Mr. Mud remained perfectly silent. Then, he walked up to Grandpa George as he knelt in the road, gasping, trying to take the sword out of his chest. As Mr. Mud looked at the old man, he licked his chapped, gray lips. Grandpa George's head was lolling weakly in front of him. Blood had seeped into his shirt and he had set one hand on the road, propping himself up as best as he could.

He turned toward Andrew, and in the strongest voice he could muster, shouted, *Make this right. . .!*"

Mr. Baines laughed and then hissed between his clenched teeth. "Georgie, Porgie, pudding, and pie, kissed his boys and let them die. And when the ghosts came out to play, Georgie Porgie died away."

Andrew watched as the specter drew still closer to Grandpa George. Carefully, Mr. Mud put his hand on Grandpa George's shoulder. Grandpa George let out an agonizing cry as he tried to swat Mr. Mud away. *"No!"* shouted Andrew again. *"Don't do this. Please...don't do this!"*

From the garden, Jacklyn quickly approached Andrew. She shouted at him, "Move!" From her pocket, she fished out the gold throwing star. It glinted in the night, as though it were happy to have been drawn. With all her might, she threw the star as best as she could at Mr. Mud. The throwing star buzzed and cut through the air like scissors through paper. It seemed to weave through the night by itself, cutting left and right, looking for its target. Rushing upward and then spinning in a circle, it carved through the night...and sliced into the back of Mr. Mud.

Mr. Mud let out a piercing scream that lasted for almost a minute. The specter's arms thrashed from side to side as he tried to pull the throwing star from out of his own back. But he couldn't reach it. Grandpa George, released by the specter's hold, fell on his side. Mr.

Baines glanced at Grandpa George, and then at Mr. Mud. He was more furious than ever before.

"Get through the fissure!" Ms. Waverly suddenly stood in the garden. "You haven't killed it. Only a direct hit to the heart can do that. It will come at us again, but next time will be worse."

Amid the chaos, Ms. Waverly had found her way to the gate and was now pushing the children to where the bright light of the fissure had first appeared.

"I know you," said Samuel, looking at Ms. Waverly. "Aren't you from…."

"Not now," barked Ms. Waverly. "Andrew, Jacklyn, Alysse—*move!*"

Jacklyn turned and did as Ms. Waverly commanded. But Andrew stood still, like a statuette. He leaned on the gate and looked at his grandfather who lay gasping in the road. He couldn't take his eyes from Grandpa George.

Andrew felt Ms. Waverly grab his arm. "There's nothing we can do. We have to go *now*, or we will all die." She pulled his arm harder. "We *have* to go before Baines stops us." Her voice had become calm. Andrew turned and looked at her as though she were a stranger. He was trying his hardest not to cry, but tears were flowing uncontrollably. "I'm going to kill Baines!" Andrew shouted. "I'm going to kill them all!"

They walked quickly to the corner of the garden. Alysse and Jacklyn were holding onto Macy. Samuel stood next to Christian. They could hear the screams of Mr. Mud, but they were weaker now, less intense. Christian hoped the specter would die. With tears streaking his cheeks, Andrew pulled the copper-colored key from his pocket. "It's time to go," he said. "Let's do this."

The children held hands. Ms. Waverly walked behind them. The light of the fissure began to burn more brightly than ever before. "Follow me," said Samuel as he marched toward the cold, shimmering light of the fissure. As they neared the entrance, Andrew looked back. He saw Mr. Baines, standing at the edge of the garden. He had grown calm again. All the anger he had shown toward Grandpa

George and Ms. Waverly was now gone. In his hand, he held the wolf's head cane. All signs of the sword had vanished. The wolf's head pommel had returned and was smiling, as though it had just eaten its favorite meal. Their eyes met. Andrew looked with loathing at Mr. Baines. Mr. Baines's eyes were neutral, blank and uncaring.

"I will see you soon," Mr. Baines said, leaning on the cane nonchalantly. "No matter where you are or what you do, I will be there," he warned. "And next time, there will be no one to save you."

"I'm going to find you and kill you for what you've done!" Andrew screamed. He felt Ms. Waverly's hand on his arm again.

"Let's go, Andrew."

Andrew turned back toward the garden, and with the rest of the children and Ms. Waverly beside him, he stepped into the fissure.

14

INTO THE PAST

It was morning.

Christian felt something wet flicking against his nose and cheeks, like a wet tissue or rag. He was trying to wake up, but he felt so tired he didn't want to open his eyes. The wet flicking continued, darting around him like an annoying fly. He started to swat it away but the harder he swatted, the more intense the wet flicking became. He opened his eyes but was dazed for a few seconds. Sunlight stung his sleepy eyes. He tried to see where he was. Slowly gathering his bearings, he realized the wet flicking was Macy licking him—and as soon as Macy saw that Christian was awake, she began licking him more vigorously.

"Good morning, Macy," Christian said, groggily. His head hurt. A throbbing sensation pulsed across his temples like prickly spikes. He got to his feet, and, rubbing his eyes, realized he didn't know where he was.

He was in what looked like a barn. Bundles of hay were stacked in towering piles along the near wall. Pitchforks and shovels were lined up against the far wall. Riding gear and tack hung from black, iron hooks, and empty pails were stacked upon one another. Through cracks in the barn door, Christian could see the sun streaming through like thin, flat poles of light. On the floor, not too far away from him, he could see Andrew, Alysse, and Jacklyn, deep asleep.

Macy was very excited to see Christian awake. She bounded and pushed her head against his leg, willing him to play with her. Christian petted Macy's head. "Good girl," he said in a croaky voice. Macy welcomed the attention as Christian scratched her ears. "Do you know where we are, Macy?"

Christian gingerly took a few steps. Bits of straw covered his shorts and T-shirt. He could feel straw even in his hair. Macy started jumping in excitement, thinking she was going for a walk. "Take it easy, Macy," Christian said, in a quiet voice.

He walked over to one of the larger cracks in the barn door and looked through it.

It was early. The sun was just beginning to seep into the sky, turning it a reddish gray. Below the sky, Christian could see nothing but fields. Some looked as if they were planted. Others seemed left to grow wild, the long grass gently swaying. A rugged dirt path led off toward the right side of the barn, but he couldn't quite see where the dirt path went. The path looked muddy, as if it had just recently rained. Christian took a deep breath. The air smelt strong of animal poop—a thick, foul smell that made him wince. In the near distance, he could hear what sounded like hens clucking and scratching in the dirt. And then he heard a deafening sound as a cow mooed.

Christian staggered back from the door, a little shaken by the noise of the cow. He'd never heard one low so closely to him before, and it had taken him by surprise. Christian looked around the barn again and felt very unsettled. He had no idea where he was, and he couldn't remember how he had got there. He sat down on one of the hay bales and scratched his head while Macy gently nudged his legs before sitting beside him.

Christian tried his best to think. He could remember walking into the fissure and seeing some bright lights and feeling as if he were falling. He could remember seeing Alysse, Jacklyn, and Andrew holding hands. He thought he could remember seeing Ms. Waverly, but she seemed distant. His mind then went foggy. He couldn't remember anything else, or how and why he was now in a country barn.

He willed himself to remember more. In his mind he retraced his steps, trying to think of the events that had led up to now. He remembered walking to Raynham Hall with Andrew. He could remember seeing Mr. Baines with his wolf's head cane, and the storm he conjured out of nowhere. He could remember racing into the garden and seeing the gloomy-looking specter, as it lumbered like a nightmare into the street.

Suddenly, Christian's mind was full of the image of Grandpa George on his knees in the road. Baines had stood over Grandpa George, gloating, like someone who had won a prize. Christian felt a sudden sorrow cover him like a damp rain. His stomach felt empty, and as he closed his eyes, he felt a slicing pain in his chest.

Christian again looked at Andrew, Alysse, and Jacklyn. They were still asleep. He had to do something. He had to find out what was going on. He walked up to his brother and gently shook his arm. "Andrew." He prodded his brother again: "Andrew, wake up."

Andrew began to come around. He flickered his eyes and looked at Christian as if he were a stranger.

"I need ten more minutes," Andrew mumbled. He rolled over and tried to go back to sleep.

"Andrew," Christian implored, "you need to wake up."

Andrew slowly came around and sat up. Christian watched as Andrew suddenly realized he wasn't home.

"Where are we?" he asked, rubbing his eyes, making sure he wasn't dreaming.

"I have absolutely no idea," Christian replied. "Seems we're in a barn, by a farm, somewhere in the countryside."

"My head hurts," Andrew said, rubbing his temples. Macy sauntered over and began to lick Andrew's knee. "Where are the girls?"

"Sleeping. Just over there," Christian replied.

Andrew gradually stood up. He felt woozy, and unsure of his feet. He looked around, trying to understand where he was. He saw the inside of the barn, the tools, the hay.

"How did we get here?" Andrew asked.

Christian shrugged his shoulders. "The fissure?"

Andrew remembered the fissure. It was like walking into a dream. He remembered a lot of bright lights, and the copper-colored key, hot in his hand. And then he remembered Grandpa George. A wave of sadness hit him like a slap.

"Grandpa George...?" Andrew asked, holding back hot, angry tears.

"I don't know what happened," Christian said, in a dull voice. He stared silently at his feet.

Andrew shook his head. He remembered the look of agony on his grandfather's face as Mr. Baines laughed. Andrew clenched his teeth in rage, and he felt his fists scrunch rigidly into ironlike balls.

"Come and have a look. You're not going to believe where we are."

Christian gestured for his brother to come to the door, but before they got there, the cow mooed loudly again.

"There are no cows in Oyster Bay!" Andrew said, eyes wide in surprise.

Christian peered through the cracks in the door again. The day was growing brighter, but even though he strained to see more of whatever was outside, the wooden slats of the door blocked his view.

"What's that smell?" Andrew asked.

"Poop," Christian said, flatly. "Either cow poop or chicken poop. But it's poop."

"Smells disgusting," Andrew said, waving his hand near his nose.

Christian peeked outside again. He spotted something moving that blotted out the light. He looked harder, trying to make out what it was, but he couldn't see clearly. Then, he saw a blurred shape slowly walking along the dirt path. It was moving toward them.

"Someone's coming," he hissed.

"Who?"

"Don't know, but he's coming right for us."

Andrew and Christian stepped back from the door. Andrew looked around and grabbed one of the pitchforks leaning against the barn wall. He moved closer to the door, so that he could attack whoever—or *what*ever—entered. Christian shifted to the other side of the door, and Macy cowered behind him.

"If it's a specter, stab it in the heart," Christian whispered.

"Got it," Andrew replied. His hands tightened on the handle of the pitchfork. His eyes were steady on the door.

From outside, Andrew and Christian heard a bolt being unlocked, and then the soft creak of the hinges as the door slowly opened. Andrew steadied himself. A look of grim determination was etched on his face as he held the pitchfork at chest height. He wasn't going to allow a specter to hurt anyone else he loved.

The door quickly swung open. Brilliant sunlight flooded the barn in an instant.

The boys felt momentarily blinded as shards of bright light stung their eyes like broken glass. Andrew waved the pitchfork around, frantically blinking, trying to see. Christian held his hands up to his eyes as Macy slunk behind him, into the shadows.

"Are you going to kill me with that thing, or is that your way of saying good morning?"

When the world eventually came back into focus, the boys saw Ms. Waverly standing in the barn.

Andrew breathed a sigh of relief and dropped the pitchfork. Christian smiled as Ms. Waverly stepped into the barn, closing the door behind her. Even Macy came out from behind Christian. She walked up to Ms. Waverly to lick at her hand. Ms. Waverly smiled. "Good morning, Macy. I never thought I'd ever see the day when a beautiful dog like you would do a trial," she said, gently petting Macy.

Ms. Waverly looked very different. She wasn't wearing her usual black slacks and turtleneck sweater. Instead, she wore a plain cream dress with puffy sleeves. A simple apron was tied around her waist. She wore ordinary black shoes and a small bonnet on her head. She carried a large basket in the crook of one arm and a cloth sack in the other. Christian couldn't help but think she was dressed like the elderly lady who had told them about the ghosts at Raynham Hall.

"What's going on?" Andrew asked.

"And where are we?" Christian wanted to know.

Ms. Waverly put down the sack and the large basket on a hay bale then smiled as she flattened her apron.

"We're in Oyster Bay," she said eventually. "It's the year seventeen eighty, and the trial has now officially begun."

The boys looked at one another in shock and disbelief.

"Are you kidding me? We're really here?" Christian asked.

"What did you think was going to happen when you stepped through the fissure?" Ms. Waverly put her hands on her hips, and a broad smile spread on her lips "You've looked outside. What did you see? Does it seem like the twenty-first century out there?"

"I've only seen what I could through the cracks," Christian said. "I couldn't see much. The door was locked."

"That's because I locked it when we got here. I wanted to make sure you could rest in peace." Ms. Waverly went back to the door and took a peek through the gaps. "We'll be safe here, for a little while, at least."

"What do we do next?" Andrew was trying to process what had happened. "How do we start the trial?"

"We should wake the girls." Ms. Waverly looked over at Alysse and Jacklyn. "There is a lot I have to tell you, and I don't want to have to repeat myself."

Alysse and Jacklyn were just as surprised as Andrew and Christian to be waking up in a dust-filled barn. They, too, had sore heads, as if they had slept too deeply, or not slept quite enough. Macy was excited to see the girls awake; she wouldn't leave Jacklyn's side. Jacklyn, in turn, held Macy very close, as if clinging onto a piece of the present.

"I can't believe we're in the past," said Alysse.

"Indeed, we are. Today is August third, seventeen eighty," said Ms. Waverly, in a very precise manner. She opened a small, silver-colored pocket watch, "And it's about six thirty in the morning. Although watches in this period can be a little unreliable."

Looking at the confused expressions on the children's faces, Ms. Waverly continued—with a *very* patient expression. "I know this is difficult for you to comprehend, but the sooner you do, the faster we can get things done, and I can get you home to your own time period." Her voice was calm but firm as she continued: "We are definitely in the past. But this is only the past to you. You must remember that for everyone else you meet, this is their present day. This is their normal time. We're the odd ones out here."

The barn grew quiet. Macy chewed on some hay and then scratched at her ear. All the children looked at Ms. Waverly as they slowly came to terms with what had happened. Andrew felt, for the first time in his life, very lonely. Everything he knew was gone. His house, his school, his parents, Grandpa George. The only things he had from his old life were Christian, Alysse, Jacklyn, and Macy.

"Did you see what happened to Grandpa George?" asked Christian. He was trying his hardest not to cry, but his eyes were brimming with tears.

Ms. Waverly looked kindly at Christian. "I'm sorry my boy. I saw what Baines did to your grandfather. But I don't know if he's okay or not. I came through the fissure with you. Your grandfather is a wonderful man. And he's strong. We just have to hope he will be all right."

"Baines didn't have to hurt him." Andrew could feel the rage building in him as he thought about what happened. "Grandpa George never hurt anyone."

Ms. Waverly turned her attention to Andrew. She saw the pain in his eyes and the rage inside him, like boiling water about to bubble over. She gave him a hug, covering him tightly in her arms. Andrew was taken by surprise. He could feel Ms. Waverly's warmth and smell the clean scent of her dress and apron. Andrew wanted nothing more than to run away, but Ms. Waverly held him close. He tried to wriggle free, but Ms. Waverly would not let go. Andrew relaxed. The protective guard he had put up before the others dropped away, and he began to cry quietly.

Ms. Waverly said, "I understand. I love your grandfather very much, as well."

The children all stood quietly for a moment, not wanting to interrupt Ms. Waverly and Andrew.

Eventually, Ms. Waverly let Andrew go, and he went to sit by himself on a hay bale.

"I don't want to be here," Alysse said, breaking the silence. "I want to go home. I don't want to be in seventeen eighty, or any other year. I want to be with my mom and dad."

Alysse turned to Jacklyn, looking for support. "I don't care about this trial. It has nothing to do with me. I never wanted to do it, and you all forced me to be here." Her face had turned scarlet, and the veins on her neck bulged.

"We had no option," Christian said. "You saw what happened at Raynham Hall. We have to do this."

"No!" Alysse said, defiantly. "*You* have to do this. I don't want no part of it. I just want to go home." She looked at Ms. Waverly. "Take me home now," Alysse ordered.

"We can't do it without you, Alysse." Andrew's voice was barely audible in the barn. He was still sitting on the hay bale, looking at his feet. "We have to do this for Grandpa George. The last thing he told me was to make this right. I need you to help me do that."

Alysse stood quietly. Tears of frustration welled up in her eyes and began to streak her cheeks. "I just want to go home," she mumbled, more to herself than anyone else. "I want to be at home."

"You must all be hungry," Ms. Waverly said, at last. She pulled a cloth from the top of the basket she had been carrying and pulled out some bread and cheese. Placing the food on the checkered sheet, she said, "Here, let's all eat some breakfast."

The children looked at one another—and then began to eat. To Christian, nothing could beat pancakes for breakfast, but the bread and cheese were the best he had ever tasted. The food was fresh and full of flavor, as if it had just been made.

"Wow," said Jacklyn. "This cheese is fantastic. Is it organic?"

Ms. Waverly smiled and then began to chuckle to herself. "In this century, everything is organic."

"Oops! I guess so," Jacklyn said, sheepishly. "I never really thought about it."

"That's not the only thing that's different around here," Ms. Waverly said. "We'll need to be careful."

15

MS. WAVERLY

Within a few minutes, the four children had eaten all the cheese and bread; then, they sat in a semicircle around Ms. Waverly. The day continued to brighten. Bits of hay floated in shards of sunlight that streamed through the cracks of the barn. Now and again, the cow outside would unleash a long, deep *moo*, sending Jacklyn into fits of laughter.

"So," Andrew said. "The trial. How do we get started?"

"I'm not sure," Ms. Waverly said, truthfully. "We're in the middle of the War of Independence. We're in Oyster Bay, in a barn by Raynham Hall. And I guess there's something here we have to do as part of the trial, but I have no idea what."

"We saw the boy, Samuel Townsend," Alysse said. "He wanted us to deliver a letter. Do you think that could have something to do with it?" After eating breakfast, Alysse had become more like herself.

"That's one possibility," Ms. Waverly said. "If someone stopped letters to General Washington, that would adversely affect the war. Whether or not that's the actual trial is uncertain. No one knows for sure. But Christian and I will feel when the fissure is ready to open, and that generally means the trial has been completed, or is about to end."

"Well," said Andrew, "as Grandpa George always says, the sooner we start, the sooner we finish. Should we go and find Samuel Townsend?"

"That would be a logical next step," Ms. Waverly agreed. "But we need to sort some things out first."

"Such as?" Jacklyn asked.

"Your clothes," Ms. Waverly said. She stood up and walked over to the hay bale where she had left the cloth sack. "Printed T-shirts were not the fashion in the seventeen eighties. Here," she said, "put these on." She threw some clothes across to Andrew and Christian and then to Alysse and Jacklyn. "You need to blend in. We can't draw attention to ourselves. We can't let anyone know we're from the future. The last thing we want is a time paradox."

"A whatadox?" Christian laughed.

Ms. Waverly sighed. "A time paradox is when someone from the past learns something they're not supposed to know about the future. If that happens it could change our present. It's a rule of the trial, and I don't even think Baines can break that one."

The mere mention of Mr. Baines made Andrew feel prickly with anger again. All he could think about was how he was going to make Mr. Baines pay for what he had done to Grandpa George.

"Something else you should remember. During the War of Independence, Oyster Bay was a British stronghold. There are over three hundred British troops stationed in the fort just up the hill from Raynham Hall. Strictly speaking, they are the enemy, but it's much more complicated than that, because most people who live in Oyster Bay are loyal to the British crown. They think independence is not in their best interest. So they don't like people who are in favor of the War. The British troops won't bother you unless you do something to raise their suspicion. So keep away from them. Keep quiet and don't say anything to anyone unless you can trust them."

"How will we know who the British are?" Jacklyn asked.

"You won't be able to miss them. They wear either bright red or green uniforms, and they all talk like your Grandpa George!"

"And who can we trust?" Andrew pointedly asked.

Ms. Waverly turned somber. "You trust no one outside this barn. Everyone else needs to earn our trust."

"This dress doesn't look good," Alysse complained. She held the dress up against her body. The neckline was as high as the hemline was low, and the sleeves puffed out at the wrists.

"Don't worry, it's fashionable for the time," Ms. Waverly said. "And it's all I could find, so it will have to do."

"And what about you?" Andrew asked. "How do you fit into all of this? You said before you may not be able to help."

"It's complicated for me," Ms. Waverly affirmed. "As a black woman in this time period, most people expect me to be a slave."

The children stared at Ms. Waverly with open mouths. It had never crossed their minds that Ms. Waverly would be considered a slave.

"It's okay," Ms. Waverly said. "Some time periods can be challenging for me. Some countries and some historical periods don't treat black people with dignity. Most of the wealthy families around Oyster Bay have slaves. Unfortunately, it's normal to them. It's not your fault." She smiled at the children. "So, we have to do what we can."

"And what can you do?" Christian was furious that Ms. Waverly could be hated or disliked by anyone. Since meeting her in the garden that Sunday morning with Grandpa George, Christian had quickly come to trust Ms. Waverly. And now, every time he saw or spoke with her, he felt the same way he did after eating cotton candy.

"Well, I am a documented free woman and not a slave. That certainly helps." Ms. Waverly pulled out a small leather wallet and unfolded a neat and formal handwritten letter. "Do you know what this is?" she asked politely.

"No," said Christian.

He could see that the small, square piece of paper was old, because it was the color of stained coffee. The handwriting was an elaborate script that ran across the page in perfectly straight lines. He thought it looked beautiful, like a piece of art.

"This is a manumission document. Very few of these are issued, but a manumission gives freedom to slaves. It makes people like me legally free." She carefully folded the document back into the wallet.

"Now, that doesn't mean bad things can't happen, but it allows me to come and go with some small amount of freedom."

From outside, the children heard the cow moo again. Nearby, some chickens seemed frantic as the morning wore on.

"We need to get moving," Ms. Waverly said. "Baines will be trying to figure out where we are. He would have entered the fissure after us, but he won't know for certain how to find us, just like we don't know where he is. The only thing that's certain is he would have come here at the same point in time we did. Our paths will cross soon enough." She started cleaning up the breakfast and putting the leftovers in her basket. "And that specter, Mr. Mud, will be hunting us by now. Its only goal will be to stop us and make us into one of them."

Jacklyn stood firmly in place. "I thought I took care of the specter," she said. "I hit it. I heard it screaming."

"You only hurt Mr. Mud," Ms. Waverly explained. "Only a direct hit to the heart could kill him. All we've done is make him angry."

"And both Mr. Mud and Baines are here?" Andrew asked.

"Somewhere around here, yes," Ms. Waverly said. "Baines has been here before. He knows people in this time period, just like I do. He will talk to who he knows and do everything he can to learn the whereabouts of four peculiar children." Then, Ms. Waverly looked at Macy. "And—" she said "—a beautiful-looking dog!"

Alysse and Jacklyn smiled as each sister ruffled Macy's ears. "Perhaps you will be the hero of this adventure," Alysse said. "Baines wouldn't see that coming."

"Don't underestimate him," Ms. Waverly warned gently. "He has more power now than any Watcher would ever think possible."

"How did you become a Watcher?" Jacklyn asked. "Where do you come from?"

Ms. Waverly looked startled. Then, she started to laugh. "You know, Jacklyn, I haven't thought about that in a long time."

"How long?" Christian asked.

Ms. Waverly thought for a moment before responding. "In over two hundred years or more."

"Are you kidding me?" Christian yelped.

Ms. Waverly laughed again. "No, I'm not kidding you." She sat down on a hay bale. Taking the small bonnet from her head, she ran her fingers gently through her hair.

"I wasn't born this way," she said eventually. "None of us were. Some of us were born many years ago, some in the present, some many years from now. Time doesn't really matter that much when you're a Watcher."

"So, you didn't want to be a Watcher?" Christian sat down next to Ms. Waverly, the taste of cotton candy distinct in his mouth.

"No," Ms. Waverly said. "I was like you. I was an ordinary person. I was born in Ethiopia around the twelfth century, by Western calendars. I was an average child, until one day, when I was about nine or ten, I was pulled through a fissure near my village."

"How?" Andrew asked. "I thought only those who had the key could walk through the fissures and stay in that time period." His small brown eyes began filling up with questions again. He wanted to learn more.

"Not if you are born a certain way," Ms. Waverly said. "And I guess I was born differently, although I'm not exactly sure how."

"So what happened?" asked Alysse.

"The fissure spoke to me," Ms. Waverly said. "I didn't know it was a fissure back then, but I felt drawn to it, as if it was calling to me. I saw it open, and it asked me to walk through. I did what it told me to do. I was too young to know any different. I don't know how long I stayed in the fissure, but it talked to me," she said again. "It told me I had a great responsibility. It told me I was to look after time and make sure history unfolded in the correct order."

"And then what happened?" Alysse asked.

"I ended up in Michigan in nineteen eighty-four and didn't know what on earth to do."

"What?" Andrew exclaimed. "Why Michigan?"

"I have no idea." Ms. Waverly laughed. "I can remember it being cold. I had never felt the cold like that before. It must have been around January or February. It was dark. I think it was late. I just appeared and ended up standing outside a pharmacy in a shopping mall. I knew no one. I didn't know the language."

Silence.

Ms. Waverly looked lost in memory. She stared into the distance as she remembered what had happened to her all those years ago.

"A woman found me. She took me in. She gave me food and somewhere to stay. She taught me how to speak the language. She gave me clothes. She fed me. It took me some time to admit it to myself, but she became the closest thing I had to a mother. I couldn't believe how lucky I was."

"And what happened then?" Alysse was perched on the edge of a straw bale across from where Ms. Waverly and Christian were sitting. She was listening intently to everything Ms. Waverly had to say.

"I grew up. I went to high school. Then college. I started a job. I dated. Life was pretty normal. I never forgot about my real mom and dad or my home, but every day the loss was easier to bear. I stopped thinking about the fissure and what it had told me. It never really entered my mind. But things didn't stay normal for long. One summer's night, I felt something I hadn't felt for many years. It was a tickly feeling in my stomach, like I had felt when I was a little girl. Then it dawned on me. It was the fissure, calling me again. I found it, and I saw it open. There was nothing I could do to stop it, and when I walked through, things were never the same."

Ms. Waverly turned quiet.

"What do you mean?" Andrew asked.

Ms. Waverly paused before answering, as if wondering how much to tell the children. Then, making up her mind, she said: "I don't age. I may live in one time period for three days or three months. Then in another period for a hundred years or more. Now and again, the fissure speaks to me. It shows me things. It gives me the power to do things I couldn't ordinarily do."

"How many trials have you done?" Jacklyn asked. She reached down and petted Macy, who had lain down by her feet.

"More than I can remember. The fissure allows me to bend time. I can't do it when I want, but when the fissure is ready. And I only ever do it to rectify time and fix something that has been altered. For many years, there were no trials. The Watchers lived in harmony. And then things began to change."

"Baines?" Alysse inferred.

"Yes, Baines," Ms. Waverly said. "He appeared some time ago. It's difficult to remember exactly when. But I can remember the first day I met him, and I knew something was wrong. I just wish I knew then what I know now."

"What do you mean?" Andrew asked.

Ms. Waverly picked at a piece of straw. "What I didn't know about was the secret war that was being waged. Some of the Watchers fought Baines. Others joined his cause. Over time, they all disappeared. Some of those who died were my friends."

Ms. Waverly paused. Andrew could tell she hadn't thought about these things in a long time, and for each memory she recalled, an element of sadness was associated with it.

"And then I met your grandfather. He appeared as a young boy one day, not much older than Andrew, and took the trial. I've never seen a young boy be so confident, so assured." She smiled. "And then he took the second trial, when he was much older. That wasn't supposed to happen, and things went wrong."

"*Another* trial?" Christian looked perplexed.

"Didn't he tell you?" Ms. Waverly looked at the children with questioning eyes.

Andrew and Christian shook their heads.

Ms. Waverly looked surprised. "Well . . . your grandfather was supposed to pass the copper colored key to your father when he was about your age. But before he could do so, the fissure called to your grandfather. It selected him and not your father to do the trial. That had never happened before. The key is passed from father to son. That's the way it's always been. Until then."

"What *did* happen?" asked Andrew. He was determined to learn more about his grandfather as a young man. Grandpa George had never really talked about his past, other than to say he was from England and was in construction.

"We spent a lot of time together during that second trial. You could say we got lost in time," Ms. Waverly said.

"For how long?"

"I'm not entirely sure. Forty-five years, I think, more or less. You don't age when you are in a time period different from the one you were born in."

"Is that why Grandpa George never told us how old he was?" Christian asked.

"Maybe," Ms. Waverly said.

Andrew thought about this for a few moments. "When you add it all up, he's probably around one hundred and twenty years old."

"Maybe older," said Ms. Waverly. "You sort of lose track of age. And besides, it's difficult to get all the candles on the birthday cake."

The barn was filling with morning light. Andrew could hear the walls creak gently as a light breeze pushed against the beams and rattled the siding. The straw smelled warm and comforting, and even the cow mooing in the background made them feel more at peace. Ms. Waverly began gathering her things and putting them together in the basket. The children changed into the clothes Ms. Waverly had brought them.

"I look weird," Jacklyn said, looking down at the dress she was wearing. It was long and reached down to her shoes. The skirt and sleeves were puffy. And she wore a simple bonnet that covered her hair, which she had curled up into a bun.

"Nothing new there then," said Christian, with a smile.

"You don't look so fantastic yourself." Alysse sniggered. "Those britches are the bomb!"

"Just remember," Ms. Waverly said, "we don't look weird for the time. This is their normal. Try not to attract any unnecessary attention.

Keep your eyes and ears open for any clues about the trial. It may not be obvious what it is, so pay attention."

A glint in the far corner of the barn caught Jacklyn's attention. She wasn't quite sure what it was, so she walked over to take a look. As she got nearer, she could see the shape of the glinting object slowly form. A gold prong. Then, another four gold prongs. Suddenly, Jacklyn saw it was the gold throwing star.

"Look at this!" She held up the throwing star for everyone to see. "I thought I'd lost this last night."

Andrew looked at Ms. Waverly. "I guess we're ready," he said. "Let's go and find Samuel Townsend."

16

AN HONEST PATRIOT

They left the barn in silence, walking in single file and looking around carefully as Ms. Waverly led the way, with Andrew close by her shoulder. Christian, Alysse, and Jacklyn followed with Macy.

It had turned into a warm morning. Just outside the barn, the children could see fields of tall grass, undulating like water in the gentle breeze. To the right of them, they spotted a dirt path leading to a small, white saltbox house that stood alone amid the fields.

"Is that what I think it is?" Christian asked softly. "Is that Raynham Hall?"

Ms. Waverly nodded. "It is."

The 1780 version of Raynham Hall looked both remarkably similar to and incredibly different from the building they remembered. The garden was larger, and there was no white picket fence enclosing it. The surrounding space was open farmland. The two big trees that hid Raynham Hall from view in the present day weren't there. Instead, smaller trees and bushes were clumped in small crops. There was no West Main Street, as the four children knew it. Instead, there was a dirt road that led toward where the main part of town would have been. But all the buildings they recognized were gone. There were no traffic lights, no paved sidewalks, no other houses overcrowding

Raynham Hall and very few other buildings within eyesight. Only a few barns and outhouses could be seen.

Andrew stopped and stared. How could something so familiar to him seem so foreign and strange?

Everything was quiet. Andrew couldn't believe how quiet it was without the rush of cars and the sounds of everyday people. The franticness of modern day life was gone. Instead, the town seemed still and calm, like a picture in one of Grandpa George's history books. He could clearly hear the breeze as it rose and fell, brushing against the leaves in the trees. Around him, birds were singing. Their songs seemed amplified, as if freed from not having to compete with the sounds of present-day Oyster Bay. The air was fresher, purer, and the scent of the ocean water from the bay was pungent, as if Andrew were holding a piece of seaweed in his hand.

Andrew tried to get his bearings. There were other small houses, but they were spaced sporadically along the road, and nothing seemed familiar. Each house looked similar to Raynham Hall. Small box houses with large timber frames and pale-colored siding.

"This is freaky," said Jacklyn.

"This is beyond freaky," Alysse returned. "And this dress is *so* itchy." She scratched her legs and arms.

"Don't forget," Ms. Waverly said, "Samuel doesn't know that you're from the future. The fissure pulled him into your present only temporarily. He probably thinks you're from his time period. Play along. Don't make him suspicious."

They made their way along the dirt road beside Raynham Hall.

"He'll be out soon enough," Ms. Waverly said. "And remember. Be careful of the British soldiers, and don't go talking to too many people." She looked at the four children kindly. "Now, I have to go."

"Go where?"

A sudden sense of panic rushed over Andrew. What would they do without Ms. Waverly to help them? He didn't want to be left alone in 1780.

"I am going to see if I can find out what's going on with Baines. And besides, it's best I'm not seen too much—and certainly not with a group of children and a dog from the future." She looked at them seriously. "Be careful. Trust no one. I'll be back soon enough. I'll find you."

And with that, she left and walked westward along the dirt road, until she was soon out of view.

‍♐

"Now what?" Jacklyn said.

"I guess we speak to Samuel," Christian suggested.

"And how do we do that?" Alysse asked.

"Well, we walk up to him and say hello," Christian said, pointing. "Because he's right there!"

They all turned and saw Samuel by the side of the house. He was dressed as before, in a simple baggy shirt and what looked like shorts. He had a pail in his hand and was walking toward a water pump. He looked strangely normal, not like the ghostly spirit they remembered. The pale light that had made him shimmer when they had seen him in the gardens at Raynham Hall had gone. Instead, they saw an ordinary boy, tall, very slim, with blond-colored hair. They watched as he began to pump water. The squeak of the pump was loud as the cold water rushed into the pail Samuel held beneath the waterspout.

Andrew walked closer to the house, with Christian, Alysse, and Jacklyn beside him. He wasn't quite sure what to say, or how Samuel would react. Would he remember them? Could he be trusted? Would he help them? More and more questions filled Andrew's mind as his heart began to pound anxiously.

"Samuel…?" Andrew called in a nearly silent voice. "Samuel…?"

Samuel turned and looked at Andrew.

"Is that you, Andrew?" A huge smile of recognition spread across Samuel's face. "And is that you, Christian? I thought you all had gone after last night. I didn't know where you went."

"Things got a little crazy, didn't they?" Christian said. "We must have lost each other in the chaos."

"What about that gloomy-looking man that was chasing us? He was horrible." Samuel looked fearful as he spoke about Mr. Mud.

"We don't know where he is," Andrew confessed. "But I don't think we've seen the last of him."

Samuel shuddered. "I can't remember everything that happened. It was as if I was in a dream."

"I know how you feel," Christian said.

"Hi, Samuel." Jacklyn raised her hand in greeting.

Samuel blushed a little. "Good to see you again, Miss Jacklyn."

He put down the pail and walked over to them.

"Samuel, we need to talk to you about something."

"What?"

"The letter," said Andrew. "The one you need to deliver to the general?"

Samuel looked around, as if he were scared of being seen or overheard. He beckoned the four children closer before speaking. "Do not mention that here," he warned, in a quiet voice. "The enemy is all around us." Samuel looked toward Raynham Hall. "The British have taken over my uncle's house. It's not safe to talk about such matters here."

Andrew looked at Samuel anxiously. The last thing he wanted was to cause trouble, but he needed answers. Samuel gestured them toward the side of the house, and the children huddled in a ring, with Macy in the middle.

"Is your uncle a man called Robert Townsend?" Alysse asked.

"Yes," said Samuel. "He's my uncle. But he's not here. We are expecting him from New York any day now. He was away for business matters."

"And the letter you told us about?" Jacklyn asked. "Did it get to the general?" She spoke in a hushed voice, barely audible.

"There are always letters to be sent," said Samuel. "I'm sure my uncle will have one to send after his return from New York."

"And will you have to get that to the general also?" Jacklyn probed.

"I will need to get it to the courier."

"Who's that?"

"An honest patriot who can be trusted with my life. His name is Austin Roe. He picks up the letters from a known location and makes sure they get to where they need to be."

"General Washington?" Christian asked.

"Ssh," said Samuel, turning pale. "Be careful when you speak his name in these parts. People are still loyal to King George the Third despite the cruelty imposed upon us by the British troops." Samuel looked intently at his friends. "His Excellency George Washington is a noble and honorable man," he continued. "And we will do what we can to help him and our country win the war."

"Can we speak to your uncle when he gets back?" Andrew asked. His heart was beating a hundred times a minute, as though he had just been running. Every fiber of his body felt prickly and energetic. He had never felt such excitement in his life.

"I will see what I can do," Samuel promised. "But he doesn't trust strangers."

"But we're your friends. Hopefully that counts for something." Jacklyn gave Samuel a warm smile...and Samuel blushed again.

They heard the door of Raynham Hall open, and then a woman's voice shouted, "Samuel? Samuel? Where's the water?"

"I'm coming," Samuel shouted back. "I'll be there in a moment."

"Who's that?" Alysse asked.

"That's my Aunt Sally. It's time for breakfast; I need to get the water to her. Meet me down by the bay around noon." Samuel pointed in the general direction of where present-day Theodore Roosevelt Memorial Park would be. "Perhaps my uncle will be home by then." He picked up the pail, full of sloshing water. "You need to go. I will speak to you later. I promise to come find you."

Samuel rushed back to the front of the house, and was gone.

"Now what?" Jacklyn had her hands on her hips. "Everyone wants to leave us today!"

"Well, I guess we've got a couple of hours to kill, so why don't we have a look around?" Andrew said.

"Where?"

"The town of Oyster Bay. Come on, let's go."

Andrew led the way. They walked toward where the town would eventually be; but, in 1780, there was no semblance of Oyster Bay as they knew it. Instead, there were a few houses randomly dotting the landscape. Fields dominated the horizon. Some were used to grow crops. Others were full of cows and sheep, feeding from long troughs. They saw chicken coops and paddocks for horses. They walked toward the area they would have known as South Street, but now it was only a wide dirt road that led out of the village and wound its way up the hill, toward the town of East Norwich.

And then, from the direction of the town center, they saw two soldiers walking toward them. They wore light-colored breeches, white shirts, and vests, with black shoes and long, red coats. Tall muskets stood upright in their arms. The two soldiers appeared to be talking to one another, laughing now and again.

"Are we seeing what I think we're seeing?" asked Christian.

"Redcoats?" Jacklyn asked.

"I guess you could be right," Christian said. "The British are coming! The British are coming!"

"That's not even funny," Andrew said.

The children turned and walked away as quickly as they could, down toward the sea. They crossed a small stream and followed a dirt road in the general direction of East Main Street. They passed some houses and saw people who nodded at them when they walked by. The townsfolk were dressed in the same manner as Ms. Waverly and Samuel. Simple clothes, dull colors. From some of the houses, they could see smoke rising from chimneys; the smell of burning wood was overpowering.

Cooking fires, thought Christian.

The children turned down a path close to what would become Ships Point Lane. In the bay, they could see a half dozen or more sailboats. The boats all had tall masts, with furled sails hanging like bunting below the crossbeam. They saw rowboats and whalers moored with straw-colored rope. Men were working on the ships, cleaning, fixing, loading and unloading. Voices rose as the workers yelled to one another. Other tradesmen were working in what looked like small warehouses that lined the wharf, just opposite the moored ships.

"This must be the main harbor," Andrew said.

"Seems busy," Christian noted. "I guess this is where people work?"

"Or in the fields," said Alysse.

"Let's go back toward the barn." Andrew was growing nervous. "I don't want people asking what we're doing here."

They slowly made their way back toward Raynham Hall. A small trail meandered toward the beach, and they followed it. They heard crickets chirping, birds singing, and the occasional pig squealing in the distance. As they drew closer to the water, they could smell the sea and hear the waves lapping on the beach.

"I wish we knew what to do," Jacklyn said. "At least then, we could just get it done and go home."

"Let's just wait here," Andrew returned. "Samuel said he'd come find us."

The day passed. The children sat on the stony beach and watched the ships slowly move through the water like huge, stately swans. Seagulls cried and circled the ships. Some seagulls walked along the beach, scratching at the water or the sand with their long, yellow beaks. Christian looked toward Center Island and wondered if it was called by that same name here, in 1780.

"I need something to take my mind off things," Andrew said. "I bet I can skip stones better than anyone else here."

"You're on!" Jacklyn said, only now growing excited. She loved competitions and would do anything she could not to lose. "Come on, who's going first?"

Pockets of clouds dotted the summer sky. The sound of the water lapping the pebble beach was soothing. The four children stood at the far edge of the beach, skimming shells and flat stones into the water. Macy raced in and out of the waves, barking as she tried to catch rocks in her mouth.

"Five skips," Jacklyn proudly announced. "You're not going to beat that."

"You wait and see," said Andrew.

A black crow sat on a large stone by the beach, watching them. It was looking at Andrew, who was too busy to notice. The crow made one huge "caw" and then flew off and quickly disappeared.

In the distance, Alysse could see people standing on their moored sailboats, still cleaning them and doing general repairs. Now and again, a boat would sail by, silently cutting through the water on a gentle afternoon breeze.

"Do you honestly believe this is happening?" Alysse asked aloud.

"What do you mean?" Christian asked. He was getting ready to launch a particularly well-shaped skimming stone.

"All this?" Alysse replied.

"It's hard *not* to believe," said Christian. He drew back from throwing the stone. "We're here, aren't we?"

"I know. But somehow I wonder if we're just dreaming this."

"We can't all be in the same dream," said Andrew. "At least, I don't think so."

"I just wish it was a dream," Alysse said. "I wish I could forget all of this and go back to normal. I'm not cut out for adventure." She sounded incredibly sad, as if something had been taken away from her...something that would never be returned.

Everyone stopped and looked at Alysse. She was staring at the ground, trying not to look at anyone, in case she started crying. It had been a very dramatic day, and everyone was feeling unsure about what was going to happen next.

"I guess I'm just scared," Alysse confessed.

"So am I," Christian said. He hunched over and got himself into a throwing position again. With a flat stone in his hand—and with a deft movement—he gently let the stone leave his arched throwing arm.

One, two, three, four, five, he counted to himself. "Almost," he said.

"But not good enough," Jacklyn noted.

Andrew stood next to Alysse. He put his hand on her arm, as if to comfort her. Alysse smiled weakly. "It's going to be okay," Andrew said. "We're going to stick together no matter what happens, and we'll be there for each other."

"We sure are," said Christian. "We've always been there for each other, since the day we were born."

17

"**I**'m getting hungry," Jacklyn said, as all the children waited on the beach for Samuel.

"So am I," Andrew said.

"I guess we can't just go grab a pizza?" Jacklyn asked, in vain hope.

"Doubt that's possible in seventeen eighty," Andrew returned. "Let's just wait for Samuel. Hopefully, he can help us."

The time seemed to pass by slower than on a tedious day at school. The children sat under the shade of some trees and waited for Samuel to show up. The sun was becoming intensely hot. The clothes the children wore seemed to make the sun feel even hotter. No one felt like moving, and they listlessly watched the water as it ebbed backward and forward.

Then, in the distance, they heard someone calling.

"Andrew?" the voice called. And then, "Christian?"

They saw Samuel coming toward them. He was smiling and carrying something in his arms. As he came closer, they saw the object he carried was a basket, like the basket Ms. Waverly had brought to the barn. Christian hoped it was full of food; his mouth watered at the thought.

"Good to see you, Samuel," Andrew said.

"I brought you something to eat," Samuel said.

"Thank goodness," said Alysse. "I'm starving."

Samuel put the basket on the ground and shared cornbread, some pickles, and salted meats. He also had some apples.

"Is your uncle home yet?" Andrew could just about get the words out between bites of cornbread.

Samuel grinned. "Arrived home about an hour ago," he said. "His boat got in around noon."

"Boat?" asked Christian.

"Yes," Samuel said. "How else would he get to New York? Ride by horse? Takes too long. And nowadays, with the war, it's best not to be out on open roads."

He looked happy to see them eat and encouraged them to finish everything.

"I know we are friends," he said shortly, "but I don't even know where you are from." He looked at Andrew first, and then Christian. "I know you helped me with that gloomy man in the garden, but who are you? I need to know where are you from?"

"A long way from here," Andrew said. "Farther than you can imagine. But we're here for the same reason as you. The War. General Washington has to win the war. And we have to do what we can to help. Otherwise we'll never get home."

"And how are you going to do that?" Samuel asked, biting into an apple.

"The letters you send to General Washington. They are from your uncle Robert. Do you know what they are about?"

Samuel looked at the ground. "He writes to the general and tells him about what is happening in New York. I don't get to read the letters. I just deliver them to Austin. My uncle spends most of his time in New York City. He's not at home as much as I would like. His letters tell Washington what the British are doing and what we can do to win the war."

Andrew smiled. "Exactly. We need to make sure those letters get to the general."

"Because we think someone is going to try and stop the letters," Christian warned.

"Who?" Samuel asked. He suddenly seemed alarmed and looked around to be sure no one could overhear them.

"A man called Baines," Jacklyn said. "And that scary man from the garden, Mr. Mud."

"And we're here to stop them," Andrew said.

"It's a dangerous business," Samuel replied. "We could all be executed for spying."

Alysse grew alarmed. "Executed?"

"Like Nathan Hale," Samuel explained. "The British hung him for being a spy."

"When did that happen?" Alysse looked more terrified than ever.

"When the war started. Everyone was shocked by the news, and we all know that if the British catch us, we will suffer the same fate."

Everyone was quiet as they thought about the consequences. A crow in a tree above them began to caw. Andrew looked up, and the crow met his gaze. "Caw," said the crow. "Caw, caw, caw." Andrew held his gaze. He stared intently at the crow until the crow cawed once more before flying away.

"I'm beginning to hate crows," Andrew said, sullenly.

"You told me you wanted to meet my uncle?" Samuel asked.

"That's right," Andrew said. "We need to ask him some questions."

"Well, that's him there," said Samuel.

They all looked up to see a man walking toward them. He wasn't very tall. He wore what looked like a frock coat, breeches, and buckled shoes. On his head lay a pale, gray wig under a three-cornered hat. He looked very unassuming, but, as he got closer, he started looking around, as if concerned he was being watched.

"That's my Uncle Robert. I told him I had some friends who wanted to speak to him," Samuel said. "He thought it best to meet you out here in the open, where no one could overhear us."

The children stood by Samuel. Andrew stepped slightly forward and felt a twang of panic as he wondered what might happen next. He watched as Robert Townsend drew closer. He saw a stern expression on the man's face.

"Who are you?" Robert barked when he reached the children.

"My name is Andrew Redmond." Andrew was scared. He wasn't quite sure if Robert Townsend would be a friend or an enemy.

"How do you know me?" Robert hissed as he took a step toward Andrew.

"My grandfather told me about you," Andrew stammered.

"Who is he? What's his family name? Tell me and tell me quickly."

Andrew could feel his throat go dry with fear. He wasn't sure what to say next, worrying that it might make Robert Townsend even angrier with them.

"My grandfather told me about you. He told me you went by the name Culper Junior, and that your code name is seven twenty-three."

Robert Townsend stumbled backward, as if someone had hit him in the stomach. A look of desperate confusion spread across his face. He looked at Samuel and then back at Andrew and the other children. Christian moved forward, "We don't mean to scare you," he said. "But we know that someone is trying to stop you from delivering your letters to General Washington, and we know who it is. We want to help."

Robert Townsend struggled to speak, as if he were fighting for words. "We could all be killed for this," he eventually said, through clenched teeth. "It's not a game for small children," he whispered.

He looked around. No one else was near. Nothing but the sound of the trees, the soft, flowing grass, and the lapping of the waves against the pebble beach. "How did your grandfather know who I am? Tallmadge? Brewster? Who told him?"

Andrew saw that Robert was desperate for answers, and he could see the fear in Robert's eyes. "We know you want to help General Washington," he answered. He felt some of the strength returning to his legs after his initial fear of meeting Robert Townsend.

"You know His Excellency? How would a bunch of children know General Washington?"

"We know you need our help," Andrew said, sincerely. "And believe me, we need to help you so we can go home."

"Uncle." Samuel spoke softly. "They saved me from the shadowy man we've seen around these parts. The one I told you about."

Robert looked at his nephew with suspicion, trying to determine if he was being told a lie. Then, he looked back at the children.

"You know of the shadowy man my nephew is talking about?"

"Yes," said Jacklyn. "We call him Mr. Mud. I thought I'd killed him, but somehow he's still alive. He's one nasty specter."

At last, Robert Townsend allowed himself to smile. Then, the smile turned to a warm laugh. The fear and anger in his face gave way to a calm handsomeness. Robert Townsend suddenly wasn't the same intimidating man.

"He is an evil phantom, I'll give you that, young lady. The most wicked man I have ever seen around these parts. We thought he was a British spy, sent to hunt us out." Robert studied the children carefully, as if weighing them up before addressing Samuel. "And you saw this young woman hurt the gloomy man?"

"Made him scream like a stuck pig," said Samuel, with a broad smile.

"But there's more than just one of these specters," Andrew added, hurriedly. "They work for this man called Baines, and they're all out to stop us."

Jacklyn looked Robert firmly in the eye. In the pocket of her dress, she could feel the throwing star. The hard, firm warmth of the star gave her an inner strength.

Robert looked back at Jacklyn. "I don't know where you be from, but I know courage when I see it."

"I'm not scared of anything," Jacklyn asserted.

"And how are you supposed to help me, young master Andrew?" Robert now spoke very softly.

"We need to make sure the information you have gets to the general. If it doesn't, the war will fail and we won't be able to go home."

"But we've been doing that," said Robert. "Maybe it takes too long to get the letters to him in Connecticut, but His Excellency has been getting reports from the Culper Ring for these past two years."

"We know," Christian said. "But we think that Baines knows all about you. And if he does, he's going to do everything he can to betray you. And us."

"Who is this Baines man you keep talking about?" Robert asked.

The children all looked at one another, unsure of what to say.

"Let's just say Baines is the bad guy, and he wants the British to win. If the British win, he will become incredibly powerful," Christian finally said.

"And he controls the specters," Alysse added.

"*And* they know of the Culper Spy Ring," Andrew observed. "Baines knows a lot stuff."

The color seeped from Robert Townsend's face like red wine spilling from a glass. He pulled his hat and wig from his head to reveal dark, stubby hair underneath. "We are done," he said at last. "Everything we've accomplished will be for nothing."

"Not yet," said Andrew. "Baines will try and stop the letters. But we're here to make sure they get delivered."

"And how will you do that?" Robert said.

Andrew took his time trying to find the right answer, but nothing came to mind. "In all honesty, I don't know," he said. "We've got to figure that one out."

Robert Townsend smiled. And then he began to laugh again. "This war has seen some very strange things indeed. And there's nothing more unusual than you four children and—" he added, stretching his hand toward Macy "—that silly dog."

Macy looked at Robert and then started to lick his outstretched hand. Robert petted Macy's head and scratched her ears. He seemed more at ease, and Andrew could tell he believed they were on his side and weren't out to betray him. Robert put on his wig and straightened it carefully, then replaced his three-cornered hat. He stood tall and tugged at his coat to straighten it around his shoulders and waist.

The waves lapped against the pebble beach. A seagull screamed. The sailboats slowly eased their way through the sea on a gentle breeze. Men shouted to each other as they piloted the ships. It looked as if Robert were thinking about something, weighing the right and wrong in his mind, before saying, "It's hot out here. Come with me. You can stay in the grist mill by the pond for now. I have some apple cider for you, and we can get you some food. We can talk later. I may have something I need you to do."

Robert then looked at his nephew intently. "If anyone asks, these are your cousins. They are visiting from Setauket. Do you understand me, Samuel?" The young boy nodded and winked at Andrew. "Stay here until I'm gone and then go home," Robert continued. "We will all meet later, at the mill."

That evening, the four children sat in the grist mill by the pond on the edge of Oyster Bay. The old mill was a small, square, run-down building. Stubby windows peeked out over the pond and the stream that powered the mill wheel. The mill looked as if it hadn't been used for some time, and it didn't look like a very comfortable place to stay. But it was quiet and secluded. *The perfect hiding place,* thought Andrew. Trees surrounded it on all sides, and the bordering dirt road led one way to the town of Bayville and the other way up a steep hill to Mill Neck.

The children had eaten. As the light from outside dimmed, Samuel lit a small, whale oil lamp, providing a close halo of yellow light. The children sat where they could: on the floor, on hay bales, and on a small wooden bench that looked as if it might break at any moment. Macy lay on the ground, her eyes closed; Jacklyn hoped she was dreaming of chasing rabbits. The air was still hot in the mill, and the children felt sleepy, even though the hour was still early for them. Samuel was eating an apple. They had spent the afternoon and early evening talking about the local history and prominent families, like the Townsends, the Lloyds, the Youngs, and the Underhills.

"Not everyone wants American independence," said Samuel as he took another bite of the apple. "That's why we have to be careful.

There are still some who are loyal to King George the Third and the British. We are spying on the British, but the people loyal to the crown are spying on us. We just hope we find out more about them than they learn from us!"

"And they hang spies?" Andrew asked.

"Yes," said Samuel. "Or worse. They torture them for information."

"So, how do you know who supports who?" Christian said.

"You don't," Samuel replied. "Sometimes it's not immediately obvious. You have to be careful. Even some families are divided, with fathers supporting one cause and sons helping the other. It's a terrible time. We just hope His Excellency wins the war and all this can be over."

"Seems very complicated," Jacklyn said, "not knowing who's who."

"Or being able to trust anyone," Alysse said.

"It's the way of the world for now," Samuel conceded. "Let's hope it's all over soon."

"We have to trust one another," Andrew said. "And we trust you, Samuel."

The door to the mill opened. Robert Townsend walked in. He wore the same clothes from earlier in the day, and his hat was perfectly perched on his head.

Robert closed the door carefully behind him. His face was stern, and then he took a deep breath.

"I need your help," he muttered, quietly. "I need you to get this letter to Austin Roe. It has to get to Setauket tonight. Samuel knows where to meet him and drop the letter." From the pocket of his frock coat, Robert pulled out a small, square piece of paper. The letter was sealed with a piece of red wax. "It will be noticed if I leave the house tonight, but it won't be noticed if four children, who shouldn't be here, leave the town."

"What is the letter about?" Christian asked.

Robert looked around, as though to make sure no spies had lately snuck into the mill and were hiding among the rafters and the hay bales.

"While I was in New York last, it was told to me the British will be sailing to Rhode Island in considerable force over the next few weeks." Robert was very hushed. The children edged closer to him to listen. "His Excellency is relying on the French fleet, stationed at Rhode Island, for support in his push to win the war. If the British surprise and defeat the French, our cause is lost. We can't let that happen."

"And this letter will warn General Washington, so he can do something about it?" Alysse asked.

Robert nodded. The children sat silently.

"We'll get the letter to Austin Roe," Andrew said, standing up. "Leave it to us. We will make sure it happens."

Robert held the letter for what seemed like a very long time before he reluctantly gave it to Andrew. A look of understanding passed between them. Both Andrew and Robert knew the importance of the letter and the significance of what would happen if the letter failed to get delivered. For Robert, it would mean losing the war. For Andrew, it would mean he, his brothers, and his cousins would never get back to their Oyster Bay.

Andrew carefully put the letter into the pocket of his breeches.

"I am trusting you with every fiber of my being," said Robert Townsend. He looked at the children like a man who had lost everything and needed salvation. "Quite possibly, the fate of the War of Independence rests on your success."

"We understand," Christian said, with a solemn voice.

"You have to get to the meeting point and be back before curfew," Robert continued. "The British will be patrolling the town, and if you get caught, I don't know what will happen to you next. Samuel knows the way. He will guide you as best he can."

"We will be back in time," said Andrew.

"Where's the meeting point?" Christian asked.

"It's to the east," Samuel said. "On the road to Huntington. I know where it is. It's a few miles from here."

"Austin knows to meet there tonight," Robert said. "I told him I would be there when I was in New York a few days ago, but I have to stay back at the house. I can't raise any suspicion. There's a new British officer in town called Major John Andre. I will have to entertain him tonight."

A crooked smile formed on Robert's mouth. Everyone could see entertaining Major Andre was the last thing he wanted to do.

"You have to leave now," Robert said. "It's getting late, and you don't want to keep Austin waiting. He's a grumpy, old man. One of the grumpiest men I've ever met. Heart as good as gold—but grumpy all the same."

The children looked at one another. "We're ready to go," Jacklyn said. "Come on, Macy."

18

THE HUNTINGTON ROAD

They left the old mill quietly, like four young church mice. "We will walk across the fields and through the orchards," said Samuel. "It will keep us off the roads, for now."

The other children followed Samuel, and Macy followed the children, sniffing the grass as she trotted behind them. They walked parallel to the bay, toward the area where Cove Road would eventually be.

Christian ambled close to his brother and whispered, "Do you think this could be the trial?"

"I'm not sure," Andrew replied. "It could be. Can you feel the fissure?"

"I feel nothing," Christian said. "Everything feels quiet."

"Let's get the letter to Austin Roe, and we'll see what happens after that. Maybe the fissure will open then, and we can all go home."

They walked along the edges of the fields. Christian grabbed a piece of long grass and put it in his mouth. The sun was quickly sinking. Dusk had begun to settle like a gray mist. Jacklyn heard the high-pitched buzz of a mosquito, and she slapped her leg. "Got it!" she said to herself.

"We have to take the road from here," Samuel said as they emerged from the edge of a field. They were in the general area of where the library would be on East Main Street.

"What road is this?" Christian asked.

"We call it Broadway or Main Street," Samuel said. "We have to take this all the way to the Huntington Road. It's a good three miles from here. It should take an hour or so to get there."

Andrew looked behind him. He saw lights being lit in the distant town, against the backdrop of the oncoming night. Outside one of the houses, he vaguely made out five or six British soldiers standing in a semicircle. In the middle of the group, he saw a well-dressed, elderly man holding a long cane, laughing. A shudder ran up Andrew's spine as he watched the elderly gentleman walk toward Raynham Hall.

"Over there," Andrew whispered to Christian. "Is that Baines?"

Christian squinted into the distance. "Could be. Hard to tell for sure in this light."

"Let's go," said Samuel. "We have a long way to travel."

The children blended into the evening shadows and walked as fast as their legs would allow. Trees edged the side of the road, which was nothing more than compacted dirt. Every so often, a plop of horse manure stood in a pile like a pyramid, attracting flies.

"That smell," said Alysse. "I don't think I'll ever get used to that smell!"

"Is anyone following us?" Samuel asked.

Christian looked back down the road. "I can't see anyone."

They heard the crickets and the occasional scramble of a squirrel in a tree. Macy began panting. The road was winding down toward the water, and the smell of seaweed became intense again. No one could be seen. Evening was growing darker, and the crescent moon provided them little light to see by.

"I guess a flashlight is out of the question?" Alysse asked Jacklyn.

"Let's just hope we have some candles," Jacklyn replied.

They walked mostly in silence for the next hour. The road weaved and twisted like a coiled rope. The wind blew in short, weak bursts, and, despite the gentle rustling of leaves in the trees now and again, the countryside was silent.

"We're not that far away now," said Samuel. "It's just up beyond that hill. Perhaps a quarter mile more."

As they walked, Jacklyn heard a strange noise behind them. It sounded like a muffled thudding on the earth. The sound was getting louder, and Jacklyn thought she could feel the road vibrating.

"What's that noise?" she warned.

Everyone froze in place to listen.

Jacklyn thought the thudding was definitely getting louder, but she couldn't think what it could be.

"Let's get off the road," Samuel advised. "Into the trees. Quick. And...hide."

The children scrambled through the brush and hunched as best as they could amid the thick nest of trees. Jacklyn made Macy lie down. "Stay quiet," she ordered, and Macy obliged, putting her head on her paws. The children stayed very still and breathed as quietly as possible. The thudding became thunderously loud.

"It's a rider," Samuel said. "Perhaps a Redcoat."

No one spoke as the sound of the snorting horse grew closer.

The rider galloped by on a brown–black stallion. He wore a black, three-cornered hat and a long, dark cloak that reached all the way down his back; the cloak flowed behind him like the wind. The rider was whipping the horse onward, and the poor creature struggled for breath as it ran. Within a few seconds, the rider passed by the children in their hiding place. They watched as he galloped out of sight. Then, they breathed a sigh of relief as the sound of the clopping hoofs grew distant. Jacklyn held tightly onto Samuel's arm. Nobody moved.

"Has he gone?" Alysse asked.

"For now," Samuel said. "But let's just stay here a few minutes to make sure."

Christian turned to his brother. "Did you see his face, Andrew?" .

"No. It was too fast."

"Do you think it was a specter?"

Andrew shook his head. "I'm not sure, but let's do as Samuel says. Let's stay here a little while and make sure he's gone."

"That wasn't a British rider," Samuel said. "He wasn't in uniform. Perhaps he was a highwayman."

"What's that?" Alysse asked.

"A thief," Samuel replied, "who robs travelers."

The children huddled behind the trees. The road became silent again. Around them, the crickets were strumming steadily. Nothing else could be heard.

Andrew didn't know how much time passed. It seemed like forever, but he was sure it was only a few minutes.

"Should we get going?" Alysse suggested.

As she spoke, the children faintly heard the slow and quiet steps of a horse coming up the road. As the horse came closer, it whinnied. The children heard the rider pull on the reins, and they heard the creak of leather as the horseman shifted his weight in the saddle. Before Jacklyn could scream, Samuel put his hand over her mouth and looked at her, his eyes urging her to be quiet. Andrew and Christian ducked as low as they could, behind the trees, while trying desperately to see the rider through the thick, dark undergrowth.

They could hear the horse breathing and biting on the bit. As Christian peered out from among the trees, he could see a white sweat covering the horse's neck like soap foam. He saw the worn, black boot of the rider in the stirrup, and he could hear the reins being twisted by the rider's hands.

"What is it?" said the voice of the rider. "What do you hear?" he hissed.

All the children crouched as close to the forest floor as possible. Even Macy hunched into a small ball, sensing the danger. The wind picked up and swayed the branches of the trees.

"I smell something." The rider sniffed the air. His voice was crackly, as if his throat were covered in sandpaper. The horse paced in a circle then snorted and stamped a front hoof on the ground.

Jacklyn gripped the throwing star in her pocket and could feel the cold metal pressed against her hand. The boys were huddled, completely still, and fearing to move. Alysse risked a quick peek above the leaves of a bush in front of him, but she still could not see the face of the rider. The hood of the rider's cloak cast his face in shadow.

"I don't see anything. Must be a raccoon," the rider said eventually, almost choking on every word. "C'mon."

He kicked the horse through the stirrup then pushed it into a gallop. The horse neighed loudly in protest even as it rushed away, throwing dark clumps of dirt into the night air as it went.

"That was a specter," Christian said, in a hushed voice. "I could feel it. It felt evil."

"How did the specter know we were here?" Alysse whispered.

"Could it smell us?" Samuel said.

Christian looked at Andrew. "I think it could sense us, like we can sense them sometimes."

"Must have been a specter," Andrew agreed. "There's no other explanation for it."

"That was a different one, though," Christian said. "That's two we've seen. Mr. Mud and…Mr. Sandy Voice."

"There's likely to be more," Andrew said. "Perhaps a lot more."

"Yes." Samuel agreed. "My father says phantom spies are all around us these days."

They sat still. Everyone feared to move, in case the rider should come back.

"We need to move," Samuel finally urged. "Austin will be expecting us, and he won't wait around forever."

The children gathered themselves together and gingerly stepped from their hiding places. Macy sniffed the air and ground where the rider had been. "Let us know if you smell him coming, Macy," Jacklyn said. "We're counting on you." Macy licked Jacklyn's hand, and Andrew believed Macy knew exactly what she had to do.

Nightfall was nearly complete. Only a few wisps of daylight touched the sky, and bit by bit, they began to disappear, as if being covered by inky blue curtains.

The children trod carefully down the road. It was hard to see in the dark. Macy sniffed the way forward, her tail wagging as she walked. Now and again she would pause and stand at attention. Whenever that happened, the children would stop and crouch down. But the rider didn't reappear, and the road remained clear.

"Over there," Samuel whispered eventually. He pointed to the Huntington Road ahead of them. "That's the drop-off point. Austin should be around here shortly. There's a spot along the side of the road. We should wait there."

They rushed to the Huntington Road. Samuel got out a small, gray-colored neckerchief and gently tied it to a tree branch that could be seen from the road. "This tells him we are here. Otherwise, he'll ride on a bit and then come back. The last thing he wants is to be seen waiting here. It will look suspicious. If he doesn't come tonight, we'll leave the letter where he can find it."

The children made their way off the road and into the cover of the trees not far from where Samuel had tied the neckerchief. They could see through a slight opening among the thickets and branches. "We'll wait here," said Samuel.

"For how long?" Andrew asked.

"For as long as it takes," Samuel said.

Andrew was concerned. He didn't know if it would be minutes or hours before Austin Roe would arrive. What he wouldn't do to be able to use his cell phone right now, Andrew thought. How easy would it be to send a text and ask, "Where are you?" But his cell phone had disappeared the night they came through the fissure.

They waited. No one spoke. Now and again, Macy would sniff the air and then settle down again to sleep. They heard the buzzing of mosquitoes and swatted them away. Andrew could feel the folded letter in his pocket. He hoped Austin Roe would turn up soon. If this was the trial, and if they delivered the letter, they could all go home and begin to live their lives again. No one wanted to be here. Andrew knew that everyone, not just Alysse, was sad they weren't with their families.

Then, they heard the sound of horse's hoofs. The horse wasn't walking or galloping but trotting rhythmically. The children stayed silent. Macy was sniffing but didn't seem alarmed. The sound of the horse became louder...and then stopped. Jacklyn could hear the horse breathing and the sound of its hoofs clipping the ground as it became restless again.

Only after what seemed like a very long time did they hear a voice. "Robert?"

"It's Austin," Samuel said, relieved.

The children made their way back onto the road. Austin sat astride a horse that looked impossibly large. Christian marveled at the horse that was staring at him, its nostrils flaring as it chomped the bit. The horse circled the children, and Austin Roe stared at them all in turn with a look of complete surprise.

"Get that dog away, little missy," he bellowed. "It's scaring my horse."

"Sorry!" Jacklyn stepped back toward the tree line. She pulled Macy as close to her as she could, so as not to alarm the horse. All the time, she kept her eyes on Austin. He was dressed in dark, muddied clothes. He wore knee-high leather boots and thick leather gloves. Austin had dark, keen eyes; a black, messy beard covered his face. If she didn't know he was here to help them, she would have thought he was the enemy.

"Who are your friends, Samuel, and where's yer uncle?" Austin seemed angry. It was obvious to Christian he was expecting to see Robert Townsend and not four children and a dog he didn't know.

"He had to stay at the house," Samuel explained, breathlessly. "He had to meet a British officer for dinner and didn't want to cause any suspicion. These are my friends. They are here for the cause."

Austin eyed the children with a deep distrust. The horse was bucking a little and stepping side to side in a skittish way. It didn't like standing still, and, by the look on Austin Roe's face, he didn't want to be where he was right now, either. He looked around, as if almost expecting someone else to turn up at any moment and discover them.

Andrew felt his heart was about to burst through his chest, but he summoned up all the courage he could. "We have a letter for you," he said. "You have to get it to General Washington."

"Where is it?" Austin said flatly, pulling hard on the reins to control his horse.

Andrew pulled the letter from his pocket and held it up toward Austin. Just then, Macy started barking, sending Austin's horse into an agitated panic. Macy was straining as she looked up the dirt road in the direction of Huntington. She could sense something bad was coming. Her face was panicky as she barked, her lips pulled back in a mixture of fear and anger.

Austin Roe struggled to keep his horse from bucking. "Shut that dog up!" he shouted. "It'll get us all hung."

Christian looked at Jacklyn, then at Alysse, and then at his brother. "The specter," he warned. "It's the specter. I can feel it again. That's why Macy's barking."

Jacklyn was doing everything she could to keep Macy quiet. She crouched down to hold Macy in her arms and was talking gently to her.

"What do we do?" said Samuel.

"Alysse. Jacklyn. Go down the road we just came up. Hide in the trees," Andrew instructed. "You go as well, Samuel. Look after the girls." Then he looked at Christian. "Stay here with me."

Christian nodded. Andrew walked toward Austin Roe. He saw the horse's eyes wild with fright. Austin writhed with all his strength to keep the horse under control. "Give me the letter, boy!" Austin Roe commanded.

Andrew pushed the letter to Austin, who tried his best to grab it, but the horse wouldn't keep still. The sound of the oncoming rider was beating louder and louder, and the earth was vibrating like a bass drum. Andrew rounded the horse so as not to get trampled, but he couldn't get the letter into Austin's hand. With an almighty effort, Austin dug his heels into the horse's flanks and leaned down to where Andrew was standing. Andrew stretched as high as he could, and Austin Roe grabbed the letter.

"You have to warn Washington," Andrew shouted. "The British know about the French navy at Rhode Island and will try to stop them from helping us."

Austin Roe stared directly at Andrew. A look of acknowledgment passed across his eyes. Austin knew the message. He was certain of what he had to do.

The sound of the other rider was almost upon them. With one final look at Andrew, Austin Roe tucked the letter into his coat, and then he allowed the coiled horse to be unleashed. He shouted as hard as he could, "Yah!" and dug his stirrups into the horse's flanks. "Yah!" he shouted again. "Go my beauty, or in hell we'll burn!"

The horse sprung forward. Andrew dived out of the way and landed in a pile of dirt. Christian ran into the undergrowth as Austin Roe, with unbelievable speed, charged up the road to Huntington.

19

MR. SANDY VOICE

In the dark, Andrew and Christian could see the specter galloping toward Austin Roe. They saw Austin draw a sword. The specter charged to the left of Austin as they raced at each other, like in a joust. For a moment, Andrew and Christian thought they would collide head on, but Austin Roe jerked to the side and then lashed out with his sword. The specter raised his arm and parried the blow. At that moment, Austin pushed his horse as hard as he could. The specter pulled back on the reins, his horse screaming in pain as it tried to come to a sudden stop. The specter seemed to be using all his strength to control his horse. Andrew stood up and walked into the middle of the road. Christian rushed from the undergrowth and soon stood next to his brother.

"Looking for us?" shouted Andrew.

The specter stopped and turned to the boys. In the distance, they saw Austin Roe galloping up the road, *yahing* his horse onward. Within moments, he was gone.

A glint of moonlight filled the road. Christian could see the face of the specter. He had a livid look in his eyes, as if he'd just lost a wager. His eyes were snake-orange. Under the glow of the moon, his skin appeared cracked and ashen gray. He snorted contemptuously as he pulled his horse around, then guided the horse up the road until he was looking directly down at Andrew and Christian. Then, the specter let out an exaggerated sigh. "So," he said, "here we are at last." The raspy voice of the specter filled the air and echoed along the road.

Andrew was terrified. He felt the blood racing through his body and pulsing in his temples. His hands were shaking. His stomach felt as if he were about to vomit. Christian stood behind Andrew. Now and again, as Andrew backed away from the specter, he could feel Christian like a shadow beside him. *At least I'm with my brother,* Andrew thought.

The specter slowly edged his horse forward. The horse stepped reluctantly, shaking its head, as if it didn't want to do what the specter was commanding.

"Do you feel it?" the specter jeered.

The boys looked at him silently.

"The fissure? Is it about to open, boys?" The specter began to chuckle like a croaky toad. "You think you've won? Did you believe it would be that easy?" The specter started to laugh. "One little thing, and it's all done? Perhaps I wanted you here. Perhaps that was my plan all along?"

The horse snorted and stamped its front foot hard into the ground. It was trying to pull away from Andrew and Christian, but the specter held it firmly in place by the reins.

Samuel came out from the undergrowth. He stood on the other side of the specter, across from Andrew and Christian. In the loudest voice he could muster, Samuel shouted: "Go away, you evil rogue!"

"What do we have here? A little runt! Go home, boy, before I cut out your heart and eat it."

"It's us you want!" Andrew shouted. "Leave him alone!"

The specter started to laugh again. His eyes gleamed a mustard–amber in the darkness. "You're right. It's you I want."

The specter pulled out a large knife from under his cloak. The long, thin blade glistened like soft water in the moonlight. "Without you, there is no trial. And then there's nothing that can stop us."

The specter seemed about to dismount his horse in order to engage Andrew and Christian in hand-to-hand battle. But the next moment, from out of nowhere, Macy ran onto the dirt road. She barked so loudly and so fiercely that she took everyone by surprise. The specter's horse shied, raising up on its hind legs, almost falling backward. The specter was stunned: his arms flailed wildly as he quickly fell onto the ground with a loud, dull thud. The horse, spooked, bolted toward Andrew and Christian. For a split-second it seemed as if they might be plowed down, but Samuel, sprinting toward them, pushed them both out of the way. Christian fell hard to the ground, the breath knocked from him. The horse thrashed in panic and then galloped down the road, to Oyster Bay.

The specter lay motionless on the dirt road for what seemed like a long time before he finally began to twitch and shudder. The boys, getting to their feet, watched in horror as the specter let out an angry howl that raced into the air and along the road like a fierce gush of wind. Soon the howl gave way to a guttural laugh as the specter rolled around on the ground, slapping his leather-gloved hand in the dirt.

"That dog," the specter spat. "I'm going to get me a dog like that, and I'm going to eat it for breakfast."

He hunched himself on the ground, and then slowly but surely, got to his feet.

Standing, the specter seemed much taller than the boys thought possible. He had broad shoulders and thick, strong legs that made him look even more formidable. He pulled back the hood of his cloak to reveal a thin face and straggly black hair. In his hand he still held the long knife, only now it seemed to be shining a faint hue of daylight-blue.

Alysse and Jacklyn both ran from the undergrowth to grab Macy. She had stopped barking as the specter had picked himself up from the ground. Now Macy was growling again, doing her best to protect the children.

"Time to end this now," said the specter. His voice had turned serious.

The specter darted toward Andrew with a speed that was impossible to believe. He was upon them instantaneously. Andrew and Christian both staggered backward and fell to the ground. The two boys were helpless, unable to get back to their feet. The specter stood above them and slowly raised the long-bladed knife into the air.

There was nothing anyone could do. Everything seemed to be happening so quickly.

Alysse screamed.

"Too easy," the specter hissed, and grinned dreadfully.

He held the knife above his own head with both hands. His tall, dark frame was the only thing the boys could see. Andrew stared, terrified, as he saw the knife rise above him. Christian hugged himself, fearing the worst. The specter went to plunge the knife downward with all his might.

Suddenly, the knife flew out of the specter's hand and spun helplessly into the air, like a leaf blown by a gust of wind. The specter gawked at his empty hands with bewildered eyes then looked around in confusion before scrambling to retrieve the knife from where it had fallen in the dirt.

From down the Huntington Road, Ms. Waverly walked quietly into view. Her hands were stretched in front of her. The wind rose through the trees, and the leaves rustled in protest as she approached the children. The children saw that she was furious, her eyes wide and angry.

The specter stared at Ms. Waverly with complete hatred. His amber cat's eyes squinted into furious slits as Ms. Waverly drew closer. Christian, with some effort, got to his feet and pulled Andrew up. Alysse and Jacklyn quickly walked behind the boys. Samuel watched as Ms. Waverly marched fearlessly toward the specter.

"Watcher!" the specter cried.

He ran back to where his knife had fallen by the side of the road and scooped it up with a single hand. The blade seemed to shine with more intensity as he turned to confront Ms. Waverly.

"Ms. Waverly!" shouted Andrew. "We have to run!"

"Not now!"

Ms. Waverly's voice sounded different. It was deep and fierce as if it were coming from someone else. Andrew could see her eyes were blazing with rage and he edged away from her in fear.

Ms. Waverly stood still. The wind began to blow harder. The dress that she wore fluttered silently in the darkness. The specter was no more than twenty paces in front of her. His lips formed an ugly smile as he stared venomously at Ms. Waverly. He patted the knife against his thigh and took two or three steps toward her.

A gust of wind rose up. Ms. Waverly pulled a long, sharp object from the waist of her dress; then, she seamlessly launched the blade at the specter. The specter went to parry, but the wind pulled at his cloak. The garment wrapped around his arm and prevented him from raising his hand. He tried to turn away, but the blade struck him in the stomach. He screamed loudly as he doubled over and knelt on the ground.

The next moment, the specter began to laugh. Andrew couldn't believe it. The children slowly backed away, unsure of what might happen next.

Almost as quickly as it came, the wind now died. The trees became still again. Ms. Waverly doubled over, out of breath. Still laughing, the specter stood bolt upright. "You got me good," it chuckled. "Got me really good." But as he pulled the blade from his stomach and wiped the black blood away on his trousers, he said, "But not good enough, Watcher."

Ms. Waverly's eyes grew wide. "Now, Jacklyn!" she screamed.

Jacklyn realized her hand was on the throwing star. It seemed to have found its way there by itself. She looked up to see the specter and then closed her eyes. Imagining she was skimming stones at the beach, she released the throwing star. It *whooshed* through the air, circling overhead, and then, in an arching loop, spun toward the specter. It hit with a thump, sticking directly into the left side of the specter's chest.

The specter stood still, confused. His hands reached up to the star, which was lodged in his heart, trying to grasp it away. His face went slack. His eyes flashed wide open, and then dimmed. With a long, slow sigh, the specter dropped to his knees and then toppled over, onto the ground. Within a few seconds, the shape of the specter disintegrated into dust…and then vanished amid the dirt on the road.

Ms. Waverly fell to the ground. She was still breathing heavily, exhausted. Andrew looked at Jacklyn, who stood a few feet away from him on the road. She was smiling in amazement.

For a few moments, no one knew what to say. Eventually, Macy walked over to Ms. Waverly and started to lick her face. Ms. Waverly began to laugh. "I love you too, Macy,"

"What just happened?" asked Samuel.

"We just beat the bad guy," said Christian.

"*Jacklyn* beat the bad guy," Ms. Waverly noted, with a weak voice.

"Only after you softened him up." Jacklyn laughed.

Then they all began to laugh. The fear that had frozen the children just a few moments before melted like ice cream on a hot day. Now, they all looked exhausted but were happy to have escaped the specter.

"We have to get back," Samuel said. "It will be curfew now. We will need to be careful."

Ms. Waverly slowly stood up. She brushed off her petticoat and, after taking a deep breath, walked over to the children. "Do as Samuel says. You have to get back. Baines will know soon enough what happened here. He'll feel it—and, believe me, he'll be furious." She talked sternly but as someone who wanted to ensure the children understood just how dangerous the situation was.

Christian and Andrew nodded.

"Where did the specter go?" Alysse asked. "He just vanished."

"I have no idea," Ms. Waverly said. "And right about now, I don't care. We were lucky. That wasn't one of the powerful ones. Baines was testing us. He knew this wasn't the trial."

"Let's go," Samuel said. "It's not safe here. Austin will get the message to Caleb Brewster, and within a few days, it will be with General Washington. We did what we had to do, but now it's time to go."

"Go," said Ms. Waverly. "I can't come with you. I have to rest. And then I have to see someone. But go now."

"Thank you," said Alysse.

Ms. Waverly looked up, surprised. "For what?"

"For saving our lives." Alysse nodded.

And then the children turned and walked down the road, toward Oyster Bay. Ms. Waverly watched as they slowly dimmed into the dark night.

"We have to get back to my uncle's house without being seen," Samuel said. "The British guards will be out. If they find us, there will be trouble."

The children walked as fast as they could. At times they jogged, until they were out of breath, and then they walked again. The pale moon helped light their way. Alysse was amazed at how bright and beautiful the stars were. She had never seen the stars shine so brightly before. They covered the sky like pale jewels lain on a black blanket. No sounds could be heard apart from the crickets. Macy wagged her tail happily, and the children drew comfort from how relaxed she was.

The walk back seemed so much quicker than the walk there. Within the hour, Andrew could tell they were nearing Oyster Bay.

"We have to be quiet," Samuel warned. "The last thing we want now is to be trapped by the Queen's Rangers. Stay close to me."

They got off the road and edged along the fields, toward Raynham Hall. They saw the watch fires and the British troops standing guard, their rifles strung across their backs. And they heard the voices of the soldiers as they laughed and joked.

They soon came to the road that led to the mill, and they stopped to catch their breath. Everyone was exhausted, except for

Macy, who looked as if she could run another ten miles. Andrew and Christian smiled to one another. They had made it. Despite everything, they had done what Robert Townsend had asked them to do.

Christian looked toward the town to see if they had been followed. From the entrance to Raynham Hall, barely visible, he saw two men emerge. One was a British soldier, the other was an ordinary man dressed unusually well. They paused to talk to one another. The children couldn't hear what they were saying, but could see the men spoke with the comfortable familiarity of close friends. Then, they shook hands and parted.

"Does that look like Baines?" Jacklyn asked, pointing to the well-dressed man as he strode away, walking with his cane in hand.

Andrew stared as hard as he could. "Perhaps. It's dark, and it's a long way off, but I think it is."

"Who was that guy with him?" asked Christian.

"If you mean the British officer," Samuel said, "then he was the man who was with my uncle tonight. Major John Andre."

They all looked at one another with amazement. Could Baines have had dinner with Robert Townsend, Andrew wondered?

"What was it that Grandpa George used to say?" Christian said. "Curiouser and curiouser."

Andrew nodded. "Samuel, we need to talk to your uncle."

"I thought you might say that," Samuel said. "He's not a very social man, and I fear tonight he might be tired or in a bad mood."

Alysse began to yawn.

"You're not the only one who's exhausted," Jacklyn said. "Seems as if we're all tired."

"Bring him to the mill, if you can," Andrew said. "We can talk to him there."

It was around midnight when Robert Townsend appeared at the mill. The children were barely awake. It had been such a long day; they all felt the heavy weight of exhaustion pressing down on them. Macy was sleeping. Now and again, her legs twitched, as if she were running. Jacklyn wondered if she was fighting a specter in a dream. A small oil lamp shone brightly as Robert looked at the children sitting on the ground.

"You got the letter to Austin, I hear," Robert eventually said.

"Yes," Andrew said, standing up.

"But not without incident?"

"We killed a specter," Jacklyn said, defiantly.

Robert's eyes opened wide in surprise. "One of those bad people?"

"Exactly," Jacklyn said, proudly.

"No attention was drawn to our cause?" Robert asked.

"We are safe, Uncle," Samuel said. "That evil man is gone, no one saw anything."

Robert stared fiercely at his nephew. "I hope that to be true," he said eventually. "We all live in fear of our lives."

"But we did what you needed us to do. We got the letter to Austin," Andrew said. He felt amazed and honored they had done something to genuinely help the War of Independence.

"Yes. You did," Robert said, quietly. "And by now, the letter should be on its way to Connecticut and Benjamin Tallmadge. Tallmadge will get the letter to General Washington, so I hope we can save the French fleet."

Robert smiled and affectionately ruffled Andrew's hair, just like his Grandpa George would. Andrew beamed with pride.

The mill grew quiet as everyone paused in thought. Robert walked toward the door, to check no one was spying on the spies. Outside, it was a still and peaceful night. The moon lay lazily on its crescent back and tickled the millpond with its gentle light.

"I need to ask you a question," Andrew said. "Who had dinner with you tonight?"

Robert gave Andrew's question some thought, wondering if the young boy and his friends could genuinely be trusted. He took a long time before he eventually gave them an answer.

"Major John Andre," Robert said. "He's in New York from Philadelphia, and he's here to see Colonel Simcoe."

"And the man who was with him?" Christian asked. "We saw two men leaving Raynham Hall when we got back. We couldn't tell who the second man was."

Robert smiled to himself. "The other man was a very strange gentleman, indeed. He said his name was Mr. Barnes."

The children stared at each other with alarmed faces.

"Was he well dressed?" asked Jacklyn.

"There wasn't a spot of dirt on him," said Robert, with a brief chuckle. "And he didn't seem like the type of man that could ever appear unruffled."

"And he carried a cane?" Christian asked. "With a wolf's head pommel?"

"Yes," said Robert, with a look of astonishment. "He seemed very pleasant and civil, but there was something about him that made me feel he shouldn't be trusted."

"It's Baines," Andrew said, in a hushed voice.

"Isn't that the man you said is trying to undo the Culper Ring?" Robert asked, as everyone drew nearer.

"Yes," Alysse said. "He's trying to stop General Washington from winning the War of Independence."

"Then it's no surprise he's with a British officer," Samuel said. "But why?"

No one could answer Samuel's question.

"Samuel said there was another person with you tonight. A woman?" Robert asked.

"That's Ms. Waverly," Jacklyn explained. "She helped save us from the specter. Without her, I'm not sure what would have happened."

"I would like to speak with her," Robert said. "You need to bring her here."

"It's not that easy," Andrew said. "We don't know where she is, and I don't know how to get in contact with her."

"Find a way," Robert eventually said. "I need to know her allegiance and if she can be trusted."

"She can be trusted," Christian said. "She knew our grandpa for a very long time."

Robert thought it through. "Bring her to me when you can. Now you had all better get some rest."

Bidding them all good night, Robert left with Samuel.

The children were drained. They found it hard to keep awake. Jacklyn and Alysse laid down and fell asleep almost immediately. Christian sat on a hay bale, looking at his brother sitting against one of the mill walls.

"So what do we do now?" Christian asked.

Andrew took a deep breath and said, with a disheartened voice, "I haven't got a clue. Do you feel anything? Can you sense the fissure opening?"

"No," Christian said, flatly. "I feel nothing but dog-tired."

"Ms. Waverly said it could be days, weeks, or months before we complete the trial. Just think of Grandpa George. He was stuck doing a trial for nearly forty-five years."

The boys were quiet.

"I miss Grandpa George," Christian said. He lay down, resting his head on a pillow made of straw. "I wish he was here to help us."

Andrew kept quiet. He thought back to the garden at Raynham Hall a few nights ago, and seeing Baines pushing his sword into his grandfather's chest. He had felt so helpless and angry.

"We need to be patient," Andrew said. "Remember how Grandpa George always told us how you can't eat an elephant in one go, but perhaps you could if you ate the elephant piece by piece. Well, maybe that's what we need to do now. Piece by piece, we have to get through this. We need to wait and see what happens next."

Christian thought about it for a little while and then asked:

"I wonder if elephant tastes like chicken?"

20

MAJOR JOHN ANDRE

They were all woken up early the next day by a cockerel crow-
ing. Its high-pitched squawk shattered the peaceful morning,
making it impossible for the children to sleep. The sun was
barely cresting the horizon, and damp dew glistened on the grass like
tiny teardrops. The heat was rising, and the air in the mill already felt
sticky from the humidity.

"Doesn't that thing have a snooze button?" Alysse said, in a weary
voice.

"I doubt it," Jacklyn said, as she turned on her side and cuddled
next to Macy.

Andrew raised himself up onto his elbow. Sunlight began streaming into the mill. Bits of dust shimmered and danced in the slants of
light. He was still tired from the night before; but now that he was
awake, he knew he wouldn't be able to sleep any longer. As he slowly
rubbed his eyes, he saw a very calm-looking Ms. Waverly sitting directly in front of him.

Andrew was startled, and as he scuttled backward like a crab, he
knocked against Christian's legs, causing his brother to grumble as
he dozed.

"Guys!" Andrew said. "You should wake up."

Slowly, Christian came around. Then Alysse and Jacklyn joined
him.

"It's about time," Ms. Waverly teased. "Don't you know we have a war to win?"

Just like the morning before, Ms. Waverly had brought them some breakfast, folded in a square sheet. Bread, butter, a few apples, and a big clay flagon of milk.

"Baines was here last night," Alysse said as she nibbled on an apple core. "He was here with some British officer, having dinner with Robert Townsend."

"Major John Andre," Christian reminded her.

Ms. Waverly looked at the children. "I knew Baines would be around here somewhere. Just didn't think he'd be in our own backyard."

"I wish we knew what he's up to," Andrew said. "At least then we'd know what to do next."

"But we don't," Ms. Waverly observed. "And there's not much more we can do until he makes the next move."

"How long will that take?" Alysse asked. "I miss home. I miss my mom and dad. I want my own bed."

A cloud of sadness had wrapped itself around Alysse again. Each morning, she hoped she would be at home; and each morning, she became upset when she realized she was still in 1780 Oyster Bay.

Ms. Waverly looked kindly at Alysse. "I wish I knew when we could all go home, but I don't know for sure. We're here for a reason. That's all I can tell you."

Everyone turned quiet as they thought about what Ms. Waverly had said.

"Robert Townsend wants to talk to you," Christian said eventually. "He needs to know if you're with the British or for independence."

"Aha," she said nodding, and then began to clean up. Alysse and Christian helped her put the leftover breakfast items into her basket.

"I don't believe it!" Jacklyn shouted. She stood in the corner of the mill, her hands on her hips. "My star. There it is again!"

Jacklyn rushed to the back of the mill. The throwing star was lying against the wall, between some old sacks. She scooped it up and held it in her hands. She gazed at it in admiration before quickly tucking it safely into a pocket.

"That talisman seems to have taken quite a liking to you," Ms. Waverly said, with a look of surprise. "I've never seen one keep returning like that before. It's most unusual."

Jacklyn felt the throwing star in the pocket of her dress. Her fingers traced its sharp edges and points, and the weight of it in her hand comforted her. "We have a very special understanding," she confirmed, nodding her head.

"But we still need to be careful," Ms. Waverly warned. "There are more specters out there working for Baines—and only one of you, Jacklyn. I don't want to lose you. Any of you!"

"So all the specters are after us?" Alysse asked.

"Yes," Ms. Waverly said without hesitation.

"I feel *so* special," Alysse said flatly.

"What did you use against the specter last night?" Christian asked Ms. Waverly. "Was that a talisman?"

"It was. A favorite of mine: the Dagger of Rostam. It was a knife used by an ancient Persian king to defeat an evil enemy many centuries ago. I'm upset I don't have it anymore, and I wish I had put it to better use."

"Did you find it lying around, like Jacklyn's star?"

"You could say that," Ms. Waverly said. "Although, I tend to think talismans find us for a purpose. Just like I believe Jacklyn's star keeps returning to her for a special reason."

"So what are these things? These talismans?" Alysse asked.

"I guess you could say they are gifts," Ms. Waverly replied, as she gazed at Jacklyn. "They're mystical things given to help people who take the trial. They can be weapons, jewelry, or even clothing. Talismans are everywhere, if you know where to look for them.

"Sometimes they can be owned by a family for a thousand years or more," she continued. "They get passed down from generation to generation. And sometimes they're found and used only once and then disappear." Ms. Waverly paused. "Like my dagger. But they aren't really lost. Talismans can't be destroyed. Instead, they sometimes re-appear in another time period, for someone else to find and use."

She paused, then turned to Andrew. "The copper-colored key your grandfather gave you has been in his family for many years. It's a sacred talisman, one of the most powerful. With the key, anyone can travel through time, and it's the one thing that Baines covets most of all. If he gets it, I dread to think what could happen. Just think what he could do if he could move the people he wanted through history."

"Do you think the cane Baines has is a talisman?" Christian asked.

"It's one of the most powerful of all talismans as well. It's the staff of Sun Wukong. It belonged to the Monkey King in ancient Chinese mythology. I don't know how Baines found it, but somehow he has corrupted it and made it even more powerful. Now he seems to be able to use the cane to bend time at will."

"Does it give him all his power?" Andrew asked.

Ms. Waverly nodded. "I think so."

"So if we want to stop Baines, we have to take away his cane?" Christian inferred.

This time, Ms. Waverly smiled. "Perhaps, but let's not think about that just yet. We have to complete the trial."

"But if we stop Baines, we stop the trial." Andrew put on a brave face. "We can use Baines's power against him. And then we can go home, and there'd be no more trials."

There was a long pause before Ms. Waverly spoke again.

"We tried that once already. Your grandfather and I. We fought him for over forty years, across every continent, trying to take away his power. And just when we thought we'd stopped Baines once and for all, he came back. He's too powerful. He would know what we were up to before we got anywhere near him. We wouldn't stand a chance."

"Then we have to find another way," Christian said. "There's al-ways a solution to a problem. That's what Grandpa George told us."

"And your Grandpa was a very wise man," Ms. Waverly agreed. "And one of the nicest people I have ever met." She walked over to the door and looked wistfully outside the mill. "I wish he was here. I could use his council right now."

Andrew slumped on a hay bale. "So you're saying Baines can't be defeated?"

Ms. Waverly released a deep sigh. "I have to go. Tell Robert Townsend I will be here tomorrow morning, and I will speak with him then."

"Are you just going to leave us again?" asked Alysse.

Ms. Waverly turned back to the children. "Yes, but not for long. I'm going to find out what Baines is up to. Perhaps you should do the same. Look around, but don't draw any suspicion to yourselves. Remember, you're not from this time." Then, she gave them all a reassuring smile. "I will come back as soon as I can."

"I could so do with a shower," Jacklyn said, after Ms. Waverly had gone. "I feel horrible. Do you think people had showers in seventeen eighty?"

"I could do with a good night's sleep." Christian massaged the small of his back. He felt every kink in his body from sleeping on the ground with nothing but a hay mattress.

Andrew sat quietly brooding in the corner of the mill. He had pulled his knees up to his chest and had wrapped his arms around his legs.

"What are you thinking about?" Alysse asked.

"What if Christian is right? What if we could get that cane from Baines? Without his power, Baines can't do anything." Talking about Mr. Baines made the anger well within Andrew again. He wanted nothing more than to avenge Grandpa George. His eyes blazed brightly, as if he'd come up with the answer to all their problems.

"But you heard Ms. Waverly," Alysse said. "Baines is too powerful. What can we do?"

"We have to find a diversion," Andrew suggested. "A way of getting the cane from him without him knowing."

"I'm sure that's easier said than done," Christian said.

"But not impossible," Andrew replied. "And I'm going to figure it out."

He picked himself up and walked out of the mill.

"Where are you going?" Christian called.

"To think," Andrew shouted as he walked toward the pond. "By myself."

Christian shrugged his shoulders and shook his head. He'd seen Andrew act like this before, whenever he was frustrated, and he knew it was best to leave him alone.

"I'm going to try and get some more sleep," Alysse said. 'I'm tired."

"Me too," Jacklyn said. "Killing specters is hard work!"

"Then I'm going to take Macy for a walk," Christian returned. "Perhaps I can see what's going on in the town."

Jacklyn yawned. "Be careful. I don't want to have to bail you out of trouble again!"

Christian left the mill with Macy and walked slowly toward the town. Macy seemed excited to be out in the morning sunlight: she jumped around Christian's legs, letting out short, quick barks of ex-hilaration. Christian stopped now and again to pet Macy's head and scratch her ears.

They walked along the main road into town, and within a few minutes they saw the outline of Raynham Hall. "We better be care-ful, Macy," Christian said. "We don't want to draw any attention to ourselves."

They quickly walked past the old house and rushed toward the area of present-day South Street.

From out of the trees on the side of the road a rabbit hopped into view. It stopped and stared at Macy with startled eyes, knowing it had just made a fatal mistake. Before Christian could react, Macy bolted. The rabbit turned and quickly weaved along the road, run-ning as fast as its legs would carry it. Macy chased with all her might, and just when it seemed she might catch the rabbit, it turned sharply and switched direction, leaving Macy to start chasing it all over again.

Christian began to race after them, frantically shouting for Macy, but within seconds, both Macy and the rabbit were gone.

Christian ran as fast as he could along the road, trying to find Macy. As he rushed around a sharp bend in the road, he crashed headlong into a tall, lean man wearing a British uniform. He fell backward, stunned, and landed flat on the ground in a heap. He felt as if he'd just run into a brick wall. All the wind had been knocked from him, and he lay gasping for air in the dust.

The startled man rushed to help Christian. "Do you need assistance?"

Christian was dazed. He wasn't quite sure what was happening. He saw the man's hand dangling in front of him, and heard the voice of the British soldier. The English accent reminded Christian of Grandpa George, and he did a double take, to make sure the man standing in front of him wasn't his grandfather.

"I'm okay," Christian said, taking hold of the man's hand. Gently, the soldier hoisted Christian onto his feet.

"You took quite the tumble there," said the soldier. "Were you perhaps chasing that dog that just ran through here?"

"Yes," Christian replied, brushing dirt from his pants and his shirt. "Did you see her? Do you know where she went?"

The soldier pointed toward the harbor. "I believe your dog went that way, chasing a rather fast rabbit."

Christian let out a big sigh and looked to the sky. "I'm in so much trouble. I can't lose Macy. The girls will be so upset."

"Perhaps I can help?" the soldier said, with a friendly smile. "I do feel somewhat responsible. If you hadn't run into me, I'm sure you would have caught your dog."

Christian smiled, too. "I'm not so sure about that. I think she had me beat."

The soldier held out his hand as he formally introduced himself. "My name is Major John Andre."

Christian's eyes grew wide with astonishment. Out of all the people he could have bumped into, he had somehow managed to find the man who had dined with Robert Townsend the night before, and who was probably friends with Mr. Baines. Gaping, Christian stammered his name.

"Pleased to make your acquaintance, Master Christian." '

Christian shook the major's hand as firmly as he could, just like Grandpa George had taught him.

"Right then. Let's do what we can to find your dog, shall we? Her name is Macy? I heard you shouting for her." Major John Andre winked at Christian with encouragement. "It's a very charming name."

They walked toward the harbor. Some townsfolk had begun to mingle around their houses, starting their daily chores. A group of men were walking toward the fields, laughing at their own jokes. Three slaves walked behind the men, carrying tools across their shoulders. The slaves walked in silence, looking at the ground. British soldiers passed them, and they energetically saluted Major Andre, who nodded to them in return.

"So, do you live here?" the major asked.

"Yes," Christian said. "On Kellogg Street."

"Where?" the major said.

Christian realized he had made a mistake. A cold knot of fear tightened in his stomach. As calmly as he could, he pointed over toward Raynham Hall. "It's what my grandpa used to call the street," said Christian. "Silly family tradition."

"I see." Major John Andre smiled. "So you live with your grandfather?"

Christian was on high alert. He didn't want to say anything further that would raise any suspicion.

"My grandfather died, so I live with my uncle."

"I'm sorry to hear that," the major said. "Was he a nice man? Your grandfather?"

"Yes," Christian answered. He looked at the ground, trying not to think of Grandpa George and how much he missed him. The last thing he wanted was to appear upset in front of Major John Andre.

"Ah, I understand," the major said. "Best we change the subject."

"He was from England," Christian offered. "My Grandpa George. He often said how beautiful it was there."

"Yes indeed, it is beautiful," the major said, reminiscing. "And I can't wait for this silly war to be over, so I can go back home and we can all live in peace again."

Christian was surprised. "So you didn't want the war?"

"Heavens, no!" Major Andre said, with a distressed look on his face. "Only a fool likes war. And cruel men, of course. If I had it my way, we'd all come to some agreement over a cup of tea, and then we could go back to our homes as friends. I can't wait to see London again. A more wonderful city there is not."

Christian smiled. "Sounds just like something Grandpa George would say. He was born in Staffordshire. And then he moved to London. He said he liked London very much."

"What's there not to like in London?"

The major seemed excited before sighing to himself, remembering a dream that wasn't real.

They walked toward the area of present day Ships Point Lane, but there was no sight of Macy or the rabbit. Both Christian and the major called for her. Their voices echoed one another as they walked.

"Seems as if your dog has other things on her mind than being obedient," Major Andre joked. "What breed is she? She looked like a French Pointer."

"That's right," Christian said, surprised the major had guessed correctly. "It's my cousin's dog, and if I lose her, I don't know what I'll do with myself."

"She looked like an exquisite dog." Major Andre paused. "I like bulldogs myself. There's something about their fat, ugly faces that is so appealing to me. Used to have two of them when I was a boy about your age. I called one Romulus and the other Remus. They got into all kinds of terrible trouble! But they were the best friends I ever had."

Christian laughed as if a huge weight had suddenly been lifted from his shoulders. He felt relaxed around the major. He had an honesty and calm that made it easy for Christian to like him instantly. Major Andre was young, handsome, and charismatic. He had compassionate eyes and a sincere smile. He spoke softly and kindly. Despite the bright red coat of the enemy, John Andre seemed like an ordinary person to Christian.

"We'll find her," said the major, resting his hand on Christian's shoulder, like a big brother would. "Never give up hope, young Master Christian. One must always have a sense of optimism."

Christian looked at the major. "Thanks for helping me."

"The pleasure is mine," said a smiling Major John Andre. "I'm just glad to be of service. Now, where on this great earth could Macy be?"

After about fifteen minutes of searching, they heard a rustling in the trees. "Over there," said Major Andre, turning quickly and pointing toward the sound.

Christian looked hopefully as Macy slowly made her way out of a small coppice in front of them. She trotted up to them and sat in front of Christian with a guilty look on her face. She bowed her head toward the ground, accepting that she was in trouble.

"Macy!" exclaimed Christian. "You had me worried there!"

Major Andre looked relieved, too. "So all's well that ends well," he said joyfully, before giving Christian a big pat on the back, almost knocking him over.

Christian rubbed Macy's head and ears and then scratched her back and tummy as she rolled over.

Major Andre, too, squatted next to Christian and petted Macy vigorously. Christian watched him curiously. "You're not like the other British soldiers," Christian said. "I mean, people have told me some British soldiers have been mean to them and taken away their houses and food. You don't seem like that kind of guy."

Major Andre suddenly looked sad. He stood up and tugged on his jacket then straightened the sword at his waist. When he spoke, the Major sounded downhearted, as though he were confessing to a crime.

"Sometimes, we do things in groups that we don't believe in as individuals. And sometimes individuals do things that don't represent the beliefs of the many."

Christian rose to his feet. Macy bounded around his legs, excited at the prospect of continuing their walk.

Major Andre took out his pocket watch. "Heavens, is that the time?" He looked at Christian. "Unfortunately, I have to go. I have something rather important to take care of."

Christian was saddened to hear that Major Andre was leaving. Despite the fear of losing Macy, the time spent with Major Andre had been fun. "Perhaps I will see you around town?"

"Perhaps," Major Andre said, cheerfully. "And perhaps not. I'm expecting an old friend of mine to turn up any day now. You may know him, as he lived in Raynham Hall for some time. His name is Colonel John Simcoe."

Christian's stomach went cold, as if he'd just eaten a block of ice cream. "I've heard the name," he stammered.

"Yes," said the Major, looking wistfully up at the clouds. "With any luck, we can hatch a cunning plan together to win this war, and then maybe I will get to see London again."

Major Andre looked cautiously at Christian. "Don't go telling anyone what I just said," he whispered, tapping his nose. "It's supposed to be a secret!"

The major briskly shook Christian's hand. "It was very nice indeed to have met you, Master Christian." Macy stared at the Major and offered up a paw. The major laughed in delight. "And it was a pleasure meeting you, too, Macy!"

The major gave Christian one last smile, and then he was gone.

21

SIMCOE'S DINNER

When Christian got back to the mill, he was out of breath. Even Macy looked exhausted.

"How was the walk, Christian?" Alysse asked. "You were gone a long time. We were beginning to get worried."

"We need to speak to Robert," Christian spluttered. "I think the trial is going to happen soon." As he spoke, Christian felt something familiar in his tummy. A gentle tickle, followed by a faint pulse.

"What about the trial?" Andrew asked.

"I'm not sure," Christian replied, his eyes bright with excitement. "But I can feel the fissure. It's not strong, but at least I can feel it now."

The children all sat bolt-upright and gathered around Christian. Just the thought of completing the trial and going home to their families thrilled them.

"I was walking through town, and I bumped, literally, into Major John Andre."

"How did that happen?" asked Jacklyn.

"It's a long story that you can thank Macy for later." Christian sighed. "But Major John Andre told me he's expecting Colonel Simcoe to arrive any day now. He said Simcoe had a secret plan to win the war."

Andrew could feel the copper-colored key in his pocket suddenly grow warmer. He took it out, and it seemed to shimmer and sparkle in the daylight, like never before.

"This could be it," Andrew said, showing his brother the key. "Perhaps the trial is connected to the plan being cooked up between Simcoe and Major Andre."

The girls were smiling. "Does that mean we get to go home?" Alysse asked.

"I think there's still a lot for us to do before that can happen," Andrew answered. "We still don't know what we have to do, but hopefully it means we can go home soon."

Jacklyn quietly clapped her hands, with a huge grin on her face. Alysse also looked relieved.

Just then, there was a gentle knock at the door. The four children sharply turned around, scared that someone had found their hiding place, but were put at ease as Samuel opened the door.

"I've got something to tell you," Samuel said urgently.

"So do we," Christian replied.

"Colonel Simcoe has just returned to Oyster Bay." Samuel's face was animated, as if this were the news of the century.

"And he's going to hatch a secret plan with Major John Andre to try and win the war," Christian finished. "And that's something we have to stop."

"Baines is behind it, I'm sure," Andrew said, with a clenched expression.

The mill turned silent as everyone digested what had just been said.

Alysse turned to Samuel. "We have to talk to your uncle. We need to tell him what's happening."

"He said he'd meet you all here before dinner. He's leaving Oyster Bay because of Simcoe, and he's not happy."

"Where will he go?" Jacklyn asked.

"Caleb Brewster is in town," Samuel said. "He's one of Uncle Robert's closest friends. He's agreed to sail Uncle back to New York City. Uncle thinks it's best for him to leave as soon as possible with Simcoe being here. It's too dangerous for him to be around."

"But he can't go yet!" Andrew cried. "Something's going to happen. *Tonight.* He has to stay here for just a little while longer."

The children looked at one another. Without Robert Townsend's help, there was a strong possibility that things would not go well. They needed Robert to stay in Oyster Bay more than anything else, if they were going to complete the trial.

"You'll have to talk to him yourself," Samuel said. "Perhaps you can persuade him differently."

Andrew continued to feel the warmth of the copper-colored key after Samuel had left to go back to Raynham Hall. Something important was going to happen tonight—something that would shape the fate of the trial. He could feel it brewing like a storm.

"I wonder if Baines will be here tonight," Andrew said. "If we could distract Baines long enough, we could take his cane and use it against him."

"You heard Ms. Waverly. It's too dangerous," Alysse said. "We have to complete the trial so that we can go home."

"But don't you see?" Andrew pleaded. "Take the power from Baines, and we end this. Forever."

"If we can, we will," Christian said. "I promise. But for now, we need to do our best to complete the trial."

Andrew sighed. He was frustrated. He didn't just want to complete the trial. He wanted to take power away from Mr. Baines, so that no one would ever again have to do a trial. He wanted revenge for what Mr. Baines had done to Grandpa George. He felt his hand tightly grip the copper-colored key, making his knuckles turn white. The hatred for Mr. Baines burned in his mind.

The afternoon dawdled by.

The children poked around the mill. The day was hot and humid, making it almost impossible to even move. Hundreds of small, black water striders darted on the pond's surface. Seagulls circled the sky above, screeched, and then flew away. The children looked for flat stones, after Andrew suggested having another skimming competition, but no one was really interested. Even Jacklyn was exhausted by the heat.

As the afternoon wore on, the children went into the mill and rested in the shade. Macy slept. Andrew carefully flipped the copper-colored key in his fingers, studying every detail. Alysse and Jacklyn talked about the summer holiday they had taken to the Grand Canyon with their mom and dad the year before. Christian looked outside now and again, to see if anyone was coming.

It wasn't until the sun began to dip and the sky had started to darken that Christian saw Robert Townsend walking along the road to the mill, a large leather messenger bag thrown over his shoulder.

"He's coming," Christian quietly said to his brother.

"At last," Andrew said, relieved. "Is Samuel with him?'

"Yes."

As Robert Townsend entered the mill, they could all see he wasn't happy. He dumped his bag on the ground. Then, he paced around for a few minutes, kicking at the sawdust without saying a word. The children watched, slightly alarmed at what he might do or say next. Even Samuel said nothing to upset his uncle.

"They took my home," he muttered through clenched teeth. "They pushed my family out. They cut down my father's apple orchard. They take all of our food. They act with impunity. And then they tell me they are here to protect us against the rebels."

None of the children knew what to say. No one wanted to say anything that could further anger Robert Townsend. Eventually, Andrew asked, as politely as he could, "Is Simcoe at Raynham Hall?"

"Yes," said Robert, rounding on Andrew. "And tonight he expects to use my house to entertain his longtime friend, Major John Andre."

Andrew smiled, and Robert looked at him fiercely. "You think what I'm saying is funny, Master Andrew?"

Andrew shook his head. "No. Not at all."

Alysse explained: "We think Simcoe and Colonel Andre have a secret plan to win the war. We don't know how, but they're in this together.

"And we think that Baines is going to do everything he can to make it happen," said Christian.

Robert Townsend looked as if he were about to explode. His face was flush-red. He clenched his fists. "What plan?" he hissed.

Alysse went up to Robert and put her hand on his elbow. "I can't imagine how horrible this is for you and your family, Mr. Townsend. But we need your help if we're ever going to get home."

Robert looked at Alysse. He saw the fear in her eyes and paused. He began to relax. The color in his cheeks returned to normal as he took a deep, cleansing breath. "I understand, Miss Alysse," he said eventually.

Then, Robert looked at the boys. "How do you know this?"

"Major Andre told me today," Christian said. "When I was in town, walking Macy. But I don't think he meant to say anything. It just slipped out."

Christian continued: "Major Andre is a good man. He helped me find Macy, and I think he just wants the war to end and go home, like we all do."

"He is a civil man," Robert agreed. "If we were not enemies in war, I would welcome his company at my dinner table anytime. But with this war, people take sides whether they want to or not." Robert looked dejected. "So, Master Christian. What's their plan?"

Christian shook his head. "I have no idea," he admitted. "We have to find that out."

"And how do you propose we do that?" Robert asked. "I can't go near the house. If I'm seen or caught talking to anyone now that Simcoe's here, it could prove disastrous."

Robert and the children thought quietly for a moment, trying to think how best to find out what was going to happen over dinner at Raynham Hall.

"We'll go and listen," Andrew said eventually.

"What?" asked Robert.

"We could help serve the food."

"Too dangerous," Robert said. "They don't know who you are. They won't trust you. Nothing will be said in front of you."

Andrew held the copper-colored key in his hands.

"It's hot outside, right?" he asked.

"Yes," Robert said. "Almost as hot as hell itself today."

"So they will have the windows open?"

"Most likely."

"Then we'll listen from outside. By the dining room window. We can hide outside and listen to what Simcoe and Andre are planning."

"There will be guards," Robert said.

"Then we need to make sure we don't get caught," Jacklyn replied.

Robert Townsend looked at the children and smiled. Then, he began to laugh. "You are brave," he said, proudly. "I will give you that."

"Brave or not, we have to find out what's happening, or we don't go home," Alysse said. "We have to do this."

"I can help," Samuel put in eagerly. "I will get the servants to leave early and ensure Aunt Sally is in bed. Then I'll let you know when it's safe."

Andrew looked at Samuel with sincere gratitude and held his hand up for a high five. Samuel looked at him with a curious expression, wondering what Andrew was expecting. Andrew, with a sheepish smile, said, "Never mind," and instead gave Samuel a friendly punch on the arm.

The air was growing murky outside. Samuel had gone back to Raynham Hall. In the mill, shadows had hidden away most of the sunlight. The air felt a little cooler. Clouds formed in the sky. Robert Townsend said he thought it might rain. "One of those violent August storms," he said. "Short, but potentially devastating." To which Christian commented, "Just like Jacklyn." Everyone laughed, except for Jacklyn, who stood proudly, as if she had just been given the best of all possible compliments.

"Dinner is set for seven o'clock," said Robert. "It's nearly time. I will wait here. Do what you can. Stay strong and whatever you do, don't get caught!"

With fear tingling in their stomachs, the four children started to walk toward Raynham Hall. They had left Macy with Robert Townsend. Samuel would try his best to keep the coast clear once he was home. The sky was darkening. Gray, rain-filled clouds blotted out any sign of blue. The gentlest of breezes swirled about them, flicking their hair. They walked quietly, in single file: Andrew in front, then Jacklyn, then Christian, chewing on a piece of straw, followed by Alysse. They passed the millpond and picked up the dirt road into town.

"So, how are we going to do this? Alysse asked.

"Jacklyn and I will crawl around Raynham Hall and sit outside the window," Andrew said. "You and Christian keep guard. If anyone comes around, warn us."

"How?" Alysse replied.

"I don't know, make a barking noise or an owl hoot," Andrew suggested.

Alysse thought for a moment. "I'm pretty bad at that stuff."

Christian cupped his hands, and, blowing against his thumbs, made what sounded like a mellow warble. "How about that?" he asked.

"Works for me," said Jacklyn.

"Worst comes to worst, we can always shout 'run for your lives,' " Alysse recommended, with a shrug of her shoulders.

"That works also," Andrew said, with a wry smile.

"Let's wait at the barns over by the house until it gets a bit darker. Don't want to draw too much attention to ourselves," said Christian.

They sat by one of the outhouses and watched the road into town to see if there was any sign of Major Andre or Mr. Baines. They could see the fields, some cattle swishing their tails against the bugs, and hens scratching and pecking in the dirt for seeds. No one knew what time it was or how long they had waited when Christian saw the now familiar form of Major John Andre, slowly striding along the road.

"Do you see Baines?" Andrew asked.

"No," Christian said. "Only the major. Perhaps Baines is already in the house?"

"Let's hide," Alysse suggested.

The children made themselves inconspicuous behind a stout, gray barn. They could just about see Major John Andre the entire way, even as he walked up to the front door of Raynham Hall and knocked. They watched as the door opened, and they heard the distant, soft voices of two men welcoming each other like old friends.

"Let's give them a while to settle," Andrew said.

They waited as evening grew darker around them. The mosquitoes began to bite. Now and again, the children slapped at a leg, or at their own neck, but no one spoke. After a few minutes, they heard a noise, as if one of the back doors of Raynham Hall had slammed; then, the familiar voice of Samuel gently called for Andrew. The children stood up and waved Samuel over to the barn.

"They're here," he said. "They've just sat down for dinner."

"Is Baines there?" Andrew asked.

"No. Just Simcoe and Andre."

Andrew wondered where Mr. Baines could be. It seemed strange that he wasn't at the dinner party. He let out a deep sigh. "Keep your eyes open. Baines isn't inside, but he's going to do everything he can to stop us."

"No one should bother you," Samuel said. "I've told everyone to go to bed. Only Simcoe and Andre are up. And Marta."

"Who's Marta?"

"One of the servants."

"Okay. Let's go."

Samuel told them where the dining room was. Andrew looked at Jacklyn, who nodded her head, telling him she was ready. Looking at Christian and Alysse, Andrew pointed to opposite parts of the road. "Go and hide over there." Christian and Alysse nodded and scrambled to their positions. "Keep your eyes open," Andrew warned.

Samuel went back to the house and entered through the side door. Andrew and Jacklyn followed him as far as they could. They could hear him talk to someone briefly and then run upstairs. Andrew and Jacklyn crawled on their hands and knees along the back wall of

Raynham Hall, finding their way to the dining room window. They could feel the cool grass and dirt brush and scrape their hands and knees as they crept silently through the oncoming darkness.

They sat on either side of the open window and rested their backs against the house. Jacklyn did everything she could to slow her breathing and stop her panicked panting. Her heart was racing, and her hands were shaking as though she were cold. She looked at Andrew, who smiled back at her as best he could. But he, too, was scared, and was trying his hardest to resist the temptation to bolt for safety.

From their positions by the window, they could hear the two deep voices of the British officers: the booming voice of Colonel Simcoe and the more mellow and genial voice of Major Andre. As the conversation progressed, they tried their hardest to hear what was being said, even as the wind blew gently in the trees, and the chorus of crickets sang loudly in the darkening night....

"My intelligence source has assured me the American is willing to betray his country and help us win the war," Simcoe said, raising a glass of wine to his lips. "I believe you met my source and had dinner with him last night. His name is Mr. Barnes."

The room was empty apart from the two men. Candles flickered on the table, and a dim gloom filled the room, casting shadows against the walls.

"I did, indeed," said Major Andre. "I'm not sure I like the fellow. Can this Barnes be trusted?"

Colonel Simcoe laughed sarcastically. "Of course not. But I believe what he's told me is true, and that's why we are here today."

Major Andre looked at his friend. "And I thought it was to enjoy the pleasure of my company."

Colonel Simcoe gave Major Andre a wry smile before sipping his wine.

"So what would you like for me to do in all of this?" Major Andre asked.

"We need you to go behind enemy lines and contact the American traitor and help him," Simcoe said. "We have arranged a ship to sail you in secret, up the Hudson. When you meet the traitor, you need to ensure our plan to win the war is a success."

"So you want me to be a spy?" said Andre. "I'm not sure I'm comfortable with doing that. It's beneath me."

Simcoe pondered. "I know you are a man of dignity and honor, John. But you're the only person I can trust with this. And if it means we can win the war, isn't that a noble cause?"

Major Andre was silent. He stared out the window, looking at the stars beginning to form in the evening sky. At last, he turned to his old friend with a determined look and said, "I will do it. For our King and to win the war."

Colonel Simcoe smiled with relief and gratitude. Raising his glass, he toasted Major Andre: "To Great Britain," he said, "and King George the Third."

Both men sipped their wine and then resumed eating their dinner.

"There's something else," said Simcoe. "Our American traitor has told us the old fox himself, General Washington, will be visiting the fort. It's the ideal chance to capture him and make sure we end all this nonsense once and for all."

Major Andre's eyes lit up. "George Washington will be at West Point?"

"Indeed," said Simcoe. "Not only will the American traitor, Benedict Arnold, deliver us West Point but also General Washington himself." Simcoe sat smugly back in his chair.

"And Mr. Barnes has been the one who told you all of this?" Major Andre asked.

"Mr. Barnes is a man of many talents," said Colonel Simcoe. "A most powerful ally, if you know how to manipulate him."

"But there's just something about him," Major Andre returned. "I can't quite put my finger on it, but I can't bring myself to like him."

"Neither can I," Colonel Simcoe said. "He's a most despicable man—but no matter. He has given us what we need. Now we just have to spring the trap."

Major Andre poured himself more wine and took a large, nervous gulp.

"Did you know," said Colonel Simcoe, "that General Washington's favorite drink is Madeira wine?"

"I did not," Major Andre said, dabbing his mouth with a napkin.

"Funny," said Colonel Simcoe. "As we sit here drinking George Washington's favorite drink we are slowly planning his ultimate demise." The Colonel beamed with pride.

"You will need an alias," Colonel Simcoe said at last. "We need to let the traitor Benedict Arnold know you are coming. It would be a shame for you to travel all that way to be accidently shot as the enemy!"

Major Andre considered Colonel Simcoe's request for a few moments. "I don't know. This is all rather unseemly," he complained. "But if it must be something, let it be 'John Anderson.' "

"It's settled then," Colonel Simcoe cooed. "John Anderson, it is your fate to capture West Point and General Washington, and win the war!"

Major Andre slumped back in his chair as if a huge weight were crushing him. A troubled look filled his eyes as he gazed again into the dark night. The room had grown silent. The candles on the table were flickering as a cool sea breeze fanned the room. Abruptly, Major Andre stood up. "Well, it's time for me to go. Colonel Simcoe, it has been my honor, but I must leave you and start the preparations for my mission."

"Of course," Colonel Simcoe said, rising to his feet. The two men shook hands and wished each other a good evening.

Then, Major Andre quickly left.

2

Andrew stared at Jacklyn. He knew they had to withdraw without being seen. He nodded toward the direction of the mill. Jacklyn began to crawl through the grass, and then Andrew followed her. When they got to the stout, gray barn, they both stood up. Andrew could barely see Alysse. Christian was crouched between some bushes, behind a tree, out of sight.

"What was that all about?" Jacklyn asked.

"I'm not sure," Andrew said. "Sounds as if the British have a plan to capture General Washington. We have to tell Robert. We have to warn them."

Suddenly, they heard a low warbling cut through the humid night air. Andrew looked up and saw Christian crouching behind the bush, blowing frantically into his cupped hands. Then, he looked in the direction of the town. The moon had risen; he could make out shapes and movements. Boldly walking up the road was Mr. Baines. He was taking slow, deliberate steps, and his cane was swishing in an exaggerated arc.

Andrew pushed Jacklyn backward. Alysse had ducked behind the undergrowth and could hardly be seen. Christian, too, had disappeared.

"Little piggies! Little piggies!" sang Mr. Baines. He twirled the cane in his hands as if he were auditioning for a musical. "Come out, come out, wherever you are!"

"We have to get out of here," Andrew whispered, ducking out of sight.

Jacklyn had a terrified look on her face. "How does he know we're here?"

"I don't know, but we can't let Baines win now. We have to get back to the mill."

They quietly walked around the barn and crouched down again. Then, as best they could, Andrew and Jacklyn sneaked through the field along the side of the road, trying their hardest not to be seen. After a few minutes, Raynham Hall was out of sight, and they could see the empty road to the mill.

Jacklyn looked around. "Where's Alysse?" she asked, in a panicked voice. "I don't see her."

"And I don't see Christian," Andrew said. "We got split up."

"We have to go back."

"We can't," Andrew said, grabbing Jacklyn's arm. "We could get caught."

A rustling came from the trees by the side of the road, and Christian emerged from out of the woods beside them. Andrew looked relieved and gave his brother a hug. Then, within minutes, they saw Alysse running up the side of the road, taking time now and again to look behind her, to see if she was being followed.

"Are you okay?" Andrew asked as Alysse drew near. "Did you see what happened?"

"Baines met up with Simcoe and Andre at Raynham Hall," Alysse said, panting. "Andre had already left, but Baines persuaded him to return. Then he told them something, but I couldn't quite hear what he said. But then Simcoe started shouting inside the house, and I could see soldiers start to rush around the town."

"We have to get back to the mill," Andrew said again. "Something's wrong. Baines is up to something."

"Did you see Samuel?" Jacklyn asked.

"No," Alysse said. "We've got to hide."

Andrew and Christian nodded.

As the moon began to shine a brilliant, full white in the ink-black sky, the children jogged the last few hundred yards to the mill. Questions were buzzing around Andrew's mind. And if anyone could give him any answers, it would be Robert Townsend.

22

THE BRITISH ARE COMING

When they got back to the mill, Robert Townsend was writing a letter on a makeshift desk he had created with some hay bales and an old piece of wooden shingle. He stopped and looked up in wonder as the four children rushed through the door. The mill was filled with gentle candlelight. Robert was holding a quill pen, its gray–black feather long and elegant. Black ink stained his fingers and hand. Robert's careful and deliberate penmanship filled half of a very small piece of paper, although it was impossible for the children to see what was written.

The children shut the door carefully behind them. They were out of breath from running and soon fell on the floor, exhausted by their adventure. Macy was excited to see them all and bounced around them, her stubby tail wagging joyfully. Jacklyn cupped Macy's ears and gave her a big kiss.

"We heard them," Andrew said, in between gulps of air as he caught his breath.

"Who?" Robert asked, eagerly.

"Simcoe and Andre," Jacklyn said.

"What did they say?"

Robert gently put down the quill pen and turned his full attention to the children.

"I'm not sure," Andrew said. "There was stuff they were talking about that I just didn't understand."

"We were hoping you could tell us," Jacklyn said.

"Tell me," Robert said. "And don't leave out even the smallest detail. What may seem insignificant could be essential."

"They said they had an American traitor who was going to help them," Jacklyn blurted. "Some guy called Arnold."

"Benedict Arnold," Andrew emphasized.

"Yes, Benedict Arnold, who's at West Point," Jacklyn continued. "And they were going to give it to the British."

Robert's eyes widened with wonder. He stood up and walked to the door. "That's impossible." He seemed to be gasping, like someone had slapped him. "Impossible. General Arnold is an American patriot. He's one of the best soldiers in the Continental Army. Arnold won the battle of Saratoga. He won the battle at Fort Ticonderoga. He's one of our bravest men. A favorite of General Washington. Arnold can't be a traitor for the British."

"I'm just saying!" Jacklyn's nose began twitching. It bothered her that Robert Townsend didn't believe them after everything they had risked to discover the information.

"But Arnold has proven himself a hundred times or more on the battlefield," Robert said, trying to convince the children of Benedict Arnold's loyalty. "He is a man of valor and honor. I simply can't believe he would be a turncoat."

"A what-a-coat?" Jacklyn asked.

"A spy," a woman's voice said.

Ms. Waverly entered the mill as quietly as moonlight and was now staring at a bemused Robert Townsend.

"You must be Ms. Waverly," Robert said, trying not to sound too surprised. He stood up as tall as he could to look at the woman standing in the shadows in front of him. Ms. Waverly nodded her head in acknowledgment and then walked into the faint glow of the candlelight.

"I know you," said Robert. "I've seen you around here before."

Again, Ms. Waverly nodded.

Christian felt the taste of candied apples as Ms. Waverly looked at the children and smiled. "Tell the rest of your story, please," she said in a quiet voice.

Andrew looked at Ms. Waverly and then at Robert Townsend. He cleared his throat before speaking. "Simcoe stated that Arnold was going to give West Point to the British. He said that Major Andre was to go to West Point to make sure it happened. And they gave Major Andre a secret code name. John Anderson."

Robert stared into the dark. He was struggling to believe what he was being told. Eventually, he sat back on his stool. "I simply can't believe it," he said. "Arnold is a true hero."

"One who has been turned," said Ms. Waverly. "And one who has probably been paid handsomely to do so and promised things that General Washington could never deliver."

Robert Townsend's face began to grow angry. His eyes darkened. Even in the gloom of the candlelight, the children could see he had flushed beet red.

"There's something else," Jacklyn said. "They talked about capturing General Washington."

Robert looked intently at Jacklyn, who stared back at him with open, honest eyes.

"They said General Washington was planning to visit West Point and they would be able to capture him. They called him a sly old fox, or something."

"Scoundrel!" Robert Townsend shouted. "He has the heart of the blackest knave." He slammed his fist on the makeshift table and sent the wooden shingle flying. Alysse was caught by surprise. Seeing Robert Townsend so angry made her scared.

"With West Point lost and General Washington captured, it would certainly mean the end of the war for the Americans," Ms. Waverly said. "With the river Hudson under their command, the British will have won."

"And everything we have sacrificed will be lost, and for nothing," Robert said. "Me, Abraham Woodhull, Anna Strong, Caleb Brewster, Ben Tallmadge. Everyone."

"So what do we do?" Ms. Waverly asked, as she looked at the children.

The mill was cloaked in silence.

"Mr. Townsend," Christian eventually said. "Samuel told us your friend Mr. Brewster was in town. Is that right?"

"It is, Master Christian," Robert said. "He's staying with the Youngs by the cove."

"Then we can ask Mr. Brewster to take a letter to Major Tallmadge and then to the general himself," Christian continued, as if completing a 1,000-piece jigsaw puzzle.

Robert looked at Christian and smiled. "If we get the note to Tallmadge in time, perhaps we can stop this."

"Exactly. Andrew was suddenly very excited.

Robert hurried to find his leather messenger bag. "We need to write a letter." He turned back to the hay bale and put the wooden shingle back into place to re-form the table. From his pocket, he brought out a small, green glass vial. Alysse couldn't see what was in the vial, but Robert Townsend smiled as he held it with his forefinger and thumb. "Invisible ink!" he pronounced at last. "I will use the last of my invisible ink to write the letter. That should make sure the note doesn't betray us all."

Robert got to work. Using the same piece of paper he had written on earlier, he began to write carefully, dipping the tip of the quill pen into the vial of invisible ink, then carefully scrawling in the spaces between the lines he had already written.

"The general knows we secretly send him messages using this invisible ink. When he gets the letter, he will use a reagent to reveal what has been written."

Alysse was amazed. "You're just like James Bond," she said.

"Who?" Robert Townsend asked, barely looking up from the desk.

"Never mind," said Alysse, and left Robert to do what he needed to do.

Andrew motioned to Ms. Waverly to come outside with him. She did so, and all the children followed.

"I don't get it," Andrew said. "How come Baines let us know what he's planned?"

Ms. Waverly smiled. "Baines couldn't stop Andre and Simcoe from talking. He needed them to do so. Otherwise, the plan he concocted wouldn't work. Baines also guessed it would be overheard, but he couldn't stop that from happening or else he'd risk Andre and Simcoe never meeting. Now he has to stop you from getting the message to Tallmadge. That's what he wanted all along."

"I guess he doesn't like us," Alysse said.

"We're his enemy," Ms. Waverly said. "Just like we see him as our enemy. We're trying to stop him, he wants to stop us. The only problem is, if we don't win, then life won't be the same when—and if—you get back home."

"I want to go home," Alysse pleaded. "I just want to see my mom and dad."

"We all want this to end," Christian said.

Ms. Waverly looked carefully at Christian. "Do you feel it?"

"Yes," Christian said. The gentle pulsating he had felt earlier had gradually grown stronger as it reached up and down his body. Christian hoped the trial was drawing to an end. Now that Ms. Waverly felt it too, he was even more hopeful.

"Is the fissure opening then?" Jacklyn asked.

"It seems to be," Ms. Waverly said, with a grin. "But let's not build our hopes up too much. There's still a lot we need to do to complete the trial."

"So what's next?" Andrew asked.

"I think Christian is right," Ms. Waverly replied. "We need to get the letter to Major Tallmadge, get back, and then hope for the best."

"And Baines will be chasing us?" Christian asked.

"You can be certain of it," Ms. Waverly said. "He has only one thing on his mind, and that's to stop us from succeeding—and if at all possible, steal the copper-colored key for himself."

They heard the faintest of rustling coming from the bushes. Ms. Waverly looked over her shoulder to see two tall men step out from the trees. They were young, no more than eighteen or nineteen years old. They were dressed in what looked to be nothing but a pair of loose leather pants and simple shoes. Above their waists, they were bare-chested. Their faces were as tough and angular as their bodies were taut and muscular. The look in their dark eyes was stern. The hair on the sides of their heads had been shaved. Only a thin line of black hair traveled down the center of their heads; it looked shiny, as if greased. One of the young men carried a small, slim axe and held his other hand to the hilt of a knife lodged inside the belt of his pants. The other held a bow in one hand; a quiver of arrows was slung over one shoulder.

Ms. Waverly did not look scared. Instead, she smiled as the two men cautiously walked toward her.

The children stepped back. After everything that had happened that night, the appearance of the two young men was an unexpected surprise. Alysse couldn't take her eyes from the angry axe blade. It was as small as an oyster shell and glinted brightly in the full moon light.

"It's okay," Ms. Waverly reassured the children. "These are my friends."

She then began talking to the two strange men in a language the children couldn't understand. Andrew looked at Ms. Waverly in awe as she beckoned the two men to come closer. Of everyone present, the two men seemed to be the most frightened.

"Children, this is Towis." Ms. Waverly opened her hand to politely gesture to the young man with the bow. "And this is Sauan," she continued, looking at the young man with the axe. "They are here to help us."

"Can they speak English?" Andrew asked, looking at Ms. Waverly.

"We can," said Towis, in a deep, resonant voice. The young man's eyes locked onto Andrew's, as if trying to read his mind. Sauan stood beside Towis, sounding offended when he said, "We have worked among the people here since we were children."

"I'm sorry," Andrew said. "I didn't mean to be rude."

Andrew's cheeks flushed purple with embarrassment. This was the first time he'd met a Native American, and he felt it hadn't got off to the best of starts.

"Towis and Sauan are the ones who gave me the food for you to eat," Ms. Waverly explained. "They are of the Matinecock tribe, and have been very generous and kind."

Alysse walked up to the two young men. "Thank you for helping us," she said then reached out to shake hands.

The two young men looked at each other, smiled, and then looked at Alysse.

"You are welcome," Towis said, taking Alysse's hand. She felt the roughness of his skin and the strength of his fingers. Sauan also shook Alysse's hand, but he never let go of the axe, which hung with menace by his side.

The two young men now looked at Andrew. Their eyes softened, and each, in turn, rubbed Andrew's head, like Grandpa George would do.

"Don't be scared, little man," said Sauan. "We know people who are ruder than you could ever be."

Andrew looked at Towis and Sauan. He smiled shyly, glad to have made two new friends. He thought the two men were magnificent. Scary but friendly at the same time. Polite yet strong.

"I've been thinking about what you said," Ms. Waverly told Andrew. "About how you told me you wanted to stop Baines and take away his cane." She looked at Towis and Sauan. "Perhaps these two men can help you."

Andrew looked surprised. He thought Ms. Waverly had not liked his plan to stop Mr. Baines, but now he was secretly glad she was considering it. "How?"

"Sometimes you fight fire with fire," Ms. Waverly said. "I'd never thought about it before you mentioned it, but perhaps the only way we can beat Baines is to have a stronger power than he has."

"I'm not sure I'm following," Jacklyn said.

"Towis and Sauan have something they want to show us. Perhaps it can help us defeat Baines." Ms. Waverly smiled warmly at the two men.

The next moment, Robert Townsend appeared from out of the mill. Towis and Sauan at once assumed a defensive stance, firmly gripping their weapons. They seemed to crouch, as if ready to strike at a moment's notice. Sauan gripped his axe tightly and raised it slightly in his hand. His other hand pulled the knife halfway from its sheath.

Ms. Waverly quickly moved between the two young men and Robert Townsend, and then spread her arms to diffuse the tension. Christian was surprised to see that Robert looked scared. Towis and Sauan also looked scared. No one knew what to say, but Alysse stepped toward Towis and Sauan.

"Mr. Townsend is our friend," she said quietly. "I promise he won't hurt you."

The two young men looked at Alysse and saw that she was telling the truth. Robert stood still, scared he might do something to make the situation worse. The two young men began to relax. Sauan slid the knife back into its sheath and deliberately lowered the axe blade to his waist.

Alysse smiled, although her heart was beating a thousand times a minute. Her eyes beamed bright and sharp. She looked at Towis and Sauan, and they steadily gazed at her in return. Robert showed the palms of his hands as a gesture of peace, and the two young men nodded and smiled.

"Okay then," Ms. Waverly said, with a big sigh. "I'm glad to see we're all friends here. Shame we don't have a guitar. We could all sing 'Kumbayah.' "

Alysse walked up to Sauan. She took his hand from the hilt of the knife and led him to Robert Townsend. "Sauan," she said, politely, "this is Mr. Robert Townsend."

Robert extended his hand, and Sauan gingerly shook it. "And this is Towis," Alysse said, and Towis did the same.

The mood relaxed. Everyone smiled, even Towis and Sauan. Alysse thought both men looked handsome when they smiled. The cicadas strung their songs in the trees, glow bugs shone brightly for a few brief seconds and then disappeared into the black night. No one knew quite what to say, and that's when Samuel appeared.

Towis and Sauan immediately went on guard again. Alysse rolled her eyes. "Not again," she said, to herself. Looking at Towis and Sauan, she said, "You guys have got to chill. He's on our side!"

Samuel stood gawping at his uncle, his friends, Ms. Waverly, and the two men. For a moment, he wondered why he was there, and then he suddenly remembered. "They know about us. They know we're here. The British. They know about the spies."

Robert grabbed his nephew by his arms. In a quiet, authoritative voice, he asked, "What do you mean, Son?"

"That man, Mr. Barnes or Mr. Baines, he told Simcoe about us. He said we were spies. He also said you were a spy, Uncle Robert. The soldiers are searching the houses. They know we are here!"

"Did anyone follow you?" asked Robert.

"No," Samuel replied. "I didn't take the road. I came through the fields. That's why it took me so long."

Robert began breathing hard. All the color seeped from his face, leaving behind a haggard look of fear. His hands were trembling, but when he spoke, he seemed calm. "We need to leave. As soon as we can."

"Yes," said Ms. Waverly. "That would be wise."

"Have you written the letter, Mr. Townsend?" Andrew asked.

Robert looked distracted for a moment, but then, collecting himself, said, "Yes. It's written as best as I could. It will tell General Washington what he needs to know."

"So we have to escape and deliver the letter?" Jacklyn asked.

"That's about the long and the short of it." Ms. Waverly smiled.

"You can go to Caleb," Samuel suggested. "He will get you to Connecticut so you can deliver the letter to Major Tallmadge."

"It's too dangerous," Robert said. "The Redcoats will be swarming all over Oyster Bay. We can't lead the enemy to Caleb, or they will hang us all. We have to hide. At least for now. And then we will have to find a way to get to him."

"We will hide you," said Sauan, walking toward Robert. "You come with us. We will make sure you are not found."

Robert looked at Sauan, trying to judge if what he said was true. Sauan stood resolutely holding Robert's gaze, reinforcing his promise.

Robert nodded and held Sauan's arm. "Thank you," he said. "Thank you for all your help."

"We'd better go," Ms. Waverly said.

The shouts of men were getting stronger a short distance down the road; the sound of boots on the road was building like a rainstorm. He couldn't see what was happening, but he could tell the men were getting closer. Voices were clear in the night air. "Over there!" someone shouted from the road. "The mill."

Fear surrounded the children like a lasso. "Get the letter and make sure you have it safe," Ms. Waverly instructed to Robert. "Andrew, take your brother and the girls and follow Sauan."

Andrew was more scared than he thought possible. The sound of the soldiers grew even closer. He could hear the rattle of swords against the hips of men and the clatter of muskets being loaded.

Christian grabbed Andrew's shoulder. "It's time to go," he implored. "Jacklyn, get Macy and let's get out of here."

Robert dove back into the mill. Within a minute, he returned, his leather bag over his shoulder. "I have the letter," he said to Ms. Waverly. She nodded and pushed him toward Towis and Sauan.

"Samuel, go home," Robert commanded. "Hide as best as you can and make sure your Aunt Sally is safe."

Samuel nodded, said goodbye, and dashed off toward the beach.

"I want to leave now," Alysse said, to no one in particular. Her face was full of dread.

"We're going, Alysse," Ms. Waverly said. "I promise I will keep you safe." Her eyes looked completely at peace, as if being chased by the British Army were an everyday occurrence for her.

Sauan looked at the children. "Follow us," he commanded. "Do as we say or you will die."

With incredible speed, the two men rushed into the trees beside the millpond. Robert started to trot and then run, holding onto his leather bag. Ms. Waverly followed. Christian looked at his brother and then at the girls. "Let's roll," he ordered, and they began to run as quickly as they could, with Macy dashing ahead of them.

As the children made for the trees, the soldiers came into view. Jacklyn stopped for a brief moment, to look back. A half dozen soldiers were trotting toward the mill. By the full light of the moon, Jacklyn could see that they were all dressed in bright red coats, white breeches, and black boots. She could see the soldiers raise their muskets up to their shoulders and pull back the flintlocks. She started to run again. She had never been so terrified as she scrambled toward the trees and up the hill leading to Mill Neck.

Within a few seconds, they all heard the *pop! pop! pop!* of the muskets firing. The bark of the trees shattered as the musket balls crashed into them. Smoke from the guns bellowed out like an angry exclamation. Shouts were heard: "Over there. In the trees," British soldiers were pulling gunpowder horns from their sides and filling up their muskets for another volley.

The children ran. They ran as hard as they could, until their lungs were burning. They ran up the hill, falling over now and again, before scrambling back to their feet. At the top of the hill, they saw Towis, wildly waving them on. "This way!" he shouted. In the distance, they could hear dogs barking from the town. *Bloodhounds,* Andrew thought.

Towis notched an arrow. His strong arms pulled the bow back easily. But then he relaxed, as though he had not seen any target worth hitting, and he looked to ensure the children were following him. Then, he ran on.

They raced as fast as they could. Branches hit their faces as they pushed through the undergrowth. Bushes clipped their shins. They scrabbled through as best they could. Christian fell and clawed the damp earth with his hands, to pull himself upright. There was another volley of whizzing musket shots and the *spat! spat! spat!* of the iron balls hitting the trees.

"Really?" Andrew shouted, covering his head with his arms. "Are they shooting at us?"

"Go!" Ms. Waverly shouted as she turned to look at the oncoming soldiers. "Run!" she ordered.

Alysse stopped to take a breath. She watched as Ms. Waverly closed her eyes and spread her hands in front of her. Then, Ms. Waverly took the deepest of breaths. Alysse felt the hair on the back of her neck stand on end. In the sky, the clouds began to tumble and roll, shielding the moon. Ms. Waverly stood statue-still: the first crack of lightning struck the mill. The British soldiers looked for cover. They fell and stumbled over one another in the grass. Lightning scissored through the black, paper sky again, and then the rain began to fall.

As the first drops of rain hit the ground, so did Ms. Waverly. It seemed as if all life had left her, and she lay limply on the dirty ground.

Alysse shouted as loudly as she could: "Sauan!"

The young man stopped, looking toward Alysse and Ms. Waverly. Then, he quickly ran back down the hill. Branches broke instantly as he ran through them with ease. It seemed as if nothing would stop him. He raced as fast as he could, past Alysse, almost pushing her out of the way, then ran down to where Ms. Waverly lay. The soldiers saw Sauan....and Sauan saw the soldiers. The rain fell, but the lightning had gone. In one swift movement, Sauan pulled Ms. Waverly up onto his shoulder and then ran back up the hill. Alysse, followed him; Jacklyn, Andrew, and Christian joined her as she came up to them. But still, Sauan was faster. He ran as if the very wind were carrying him. The rain was beginning to fall in sheets; it cascaded down onto the ground, but nothing seemed to stop Sauan. He ran past

Towis, who had notched his bow again, looking for a target. Only after Robert, the children, and Macy had passed him, did Towis drop his guard and turn to follow.

They ran through the trees and down the other side of the hill. There was no path, but Towis and Sauan knew the way. They were sprinting much faster than the children thought possible. The sound of them all breaking through the undergrowth was deafening. Leaves and branches crashed. The rain fell like a waterfall as they fled, but the sounds of the soldiers and the hounds began to diminish. Struggling for breath, the children ran after the two young men. No one knew exactly how far they had gone or for how long they ran. They crossed a stream, their feet slipping on the water's muddy bed. They ran through thickets, along rocks, and beside maple trees. Towis and Sauan did not stop. They forged onward, up and down hills, never dropping the pace despite Sauan carrying Ms. Waverly. Even Macy was tired…but still, they ran. They ran until everything in their beings begged them to stop. And only then did they slow down and eventually rest.

23

THE WENDIGO AMULET

O ut of breath from the long chase, they came to what looked like a long barn. It was built from wood. Layers of cut tree trunks were stacked horizontally upon one another and in neat angles, forming sturdy walls. The roof was simple thatch. The area around the longhouse had been cleared of trees and brush and formed a broad, open space. Other Matinecock men, resembling Towis and Sauan in their strength and physical appearance, were standing outside the longhouse. Two or three at most. A small boy hid behind his father's legs as Sauan, carrying Ms. Waverly, emerged out of the woods. Robert, the children, and Macy followed. Some quick words in a language that Jacklyn couldn't understand were shared between Towis and one of the men standing in front of the longhouse. Within moments, they were hurriedly ushered inside.

Sauan gently lay Ms. Waverly on a straw bed at the far end of the longhouse. A small fire burned at the other end. The building was dark, and the smell of wood smoke and cooked meat filled the air. Some women tended Ms. Waverly. They brought water and cloths and did what they could to make Ms. Waverly comfortable. The children were dazed, and even Robert Townsend seemed daunted about what they had done and where they were now standing.

"She will be safe here," Sauan said, as he slowly regained his strength.

Andrew looked at Ms. Waverly. She lay motionless, like a wax doll. He couldn't believe she had sacrificed herself so they could escape the British soldiers. Without Sauan's help, Andrew wasn't sure what would have happened to her. He watched helplessly as the women dabbed Ms. Waverly's head with damp cloths. And at that moment, Andrew thought again of Grandpa George and the sacrifice he had made so they could escape from Mr. Baines. Suddenly, he felt inadequate, almost guilty, that the life he so thoroughly enjoyed was only given to him by the grace of others.

"Will she live?" Alysse asked.

One of the women who had wrapped a blanket around Ms. Waverly looked up at her. Her eyes were expressionless as she spoke: "It will be difficult to tell."

"Come," said Towis. "There is nothing we can do here. Only time can tell what will happen next. We have to be patient."

The children slowly walked toward the fire at the other end of the longhouse. Macy was whining and looking back at Ms. Waverly. Jacklyn did everything she could to calm her, but still, Macy whined.

"Where are we?" Robert asked. It had taken him some time to regain his breath, but as his eyes grew accustomed to the dark, he began to feel himself again.

"We are at my home," said Towis. "This is where my family lives." He looked at a man standing in the corner. "That is my father. Over there, with the princess, is my mother," he said, pointing to a woman sitting beside Ms. Waverly.

"Princess?" asked Jacklyn.

"She is our princess," Towis said, pointing at Ms. Waverly. "Anna is what we named her. In our language, Anna means 'mother.' " He looked sad, almost bashful. "It was Anna that helped us find this land which is our home. It was Anna that told us what we should do when our lands were sold."

Andrew looked at Ms. Waverly. There was so much he had to ask, so much he needed to know.... A ball of fear gripped his stomach as he wondered if he would ever have the chance to ask Ms. Waverly the questions burning in his mind.

"It's late," said Sauan. "The Redcoats won't find us now," he said, reassuringly, his hand clenching the axe. "Eat something. Then sleep. We will talk in the morning."

Two young girls brought food to Robert and the children. They sat on the floor and ate with their fingers. For Alysse, it was the best food she had ever tasted.

They ate in silence. And when they were done, they slept.

In the morning, the air was clear. The humidity that had oppressively covered the children like a dirty blanket over the last few days had lifted, and a freshness had eased into the longhouse.

Andrew was awake before the others. He got stiffly to his feet and looked at his arms and legs. They were covered in red, angry scratch marks from running through the undergrowth. Only now did he feel sore. He tiptoed to where Ms. Waverly was resting. She lay completely still, and Andrew couldn't tell if she was breathing or not. He bent down and touched her arm, letting his hand linger against her skin. "Come back to us," he whispered.

Others began to stir. Light came through the gaps in the walls and doors. The fire had long ago gone out, but the smell of wood smoke was strong.

Andrew saw Christian get up. He looked tired and rubbed his eyes, yawning. The girls were still sleeping. So was Robert Townsend. Macy quietly walked over and licked Andrew's hand. Then, she curled herself beside Ms. Waverly, resting against her hip.

"Is this really happening?" Christian asked.

Andrew pinched himself as hard as he could. White whelp marks appeared on his arm like deep scars as he looked at his brother. "I'm not waking up."

"What are we going to do?"

Andrew sighed. "I have absolutely no idea."

"I wish Grandpa George was here," Christian said.

"So do I," Andrew replied.

They ate breakfast. One of the women stoked the fire. The men shared bits of cornbread and smoked meats with Robert and the children. The sun gained strength in the sky, and the children walked outside. From where they stood, they could see only forestland. The Matinecocks had planted crops around the longhouse; there was also a small pen of goats, and a chicken coop.

"It's nice here," Jacklyn said. "It's like a farm."

Towis looked at her and smiled. "It was always nice here on the island," he said. "Until we gave up the land. And now we hide here."

Jacklyn looked at the ground, wondering what to say next. She said the only thing that came to mind: "I'm sorry."

Towis laughed. "It's not your fault, little girl." He looked at her sincerely. "We gave up our land for some wampum, a few rifles, and some empty promises. We were lied to. But we believed the lies. So who is to blame?"

One of the young girls from the longhouse came out and spoke some brief words to Towis.

"The princess has woken." Towis smiled, and his eyes danced with excitement.

They all rushed into the longhouse. Ms. Waverly was sitting upright. She still looked dazed, but they could see her strength was returning. She smiled as the girls rushed up and wrapped their arms around her. Andrew couldn't help but laugh, and then he felt a lump in his throat. Christian stared at the floor, unsure of what to say or do, but grateful Ms. Waverly was awake.

"I guess I lost it for a moment there," Ms. Waverly said. One of the women handed her a bowl of hot broth. "Conjuring storms is more exhausting than I thought."

Outside, Robert Townsend was pacing fitfully. The boys, Sauan and Towis, watched as he swirled in place, kicking up dust. Robert held the small, square piece of paper in his hand. "We need to get this letter to Caleb," he stressed to Andrew and Christian. "We have to get it to him today."

"How do we do that?" Andrew asked. "British soldiers are searching every part of Long Island for us right now. We'll get caught as soon as we're seen in Oyster Bay."

"We can help," said Sauan. "We can get you to where you need to be. We know these woods and fields better than anyone."

Robert looked gratefully at Sauan and Towis. "Thank you," he said, humbly. "I don't know what we would have done without you."

"We will leave later today. When the sun sets," said Towis. "For now, the best thing we can do is rest and gather our strength."

The day floated by. The fresh air was comforting. The children sat outside and watched Sauan, Towis, and their family go about their daily chores. Andrew was surprised to see some of the young children playing lacrosse. The children laughed as they ran around the field, throwing the ball effortlessly.

The same young woman who had spoken with Towis earlier came from out of the longhouse and spoke with him again. They exchanged a few words, and Towis nodded.

"The princess needs to talk to us," he told the children with a solemn voice. "We should go inside."

Ms. Waverly looked much stronger than before. She was sitting upright, talking to some of the women. A look of confidence had returned to her eyes, and her hands rested steadily on her knees. The four children circled her and sat on the floor. Robert Townsend kept his distance and stood against one wall of the longhouse. Macy walked over to the group and sat at Ms. Waverly's feet.

"My sisters have an idea," Ms. Waverly said, nodding to the women standing beside her. "Do you know what a wendigo is?" She looked at the children as she asked the question.

Christian shrugged his shoulders, and Andrew shook his head.

Towis answered: "It is an evil spirit. A cruel ghost. Something that wants to harm others. Something that eats other people."

Jacklyn looked horrified. "Like a cannibal?"

"The evil spirit turns ordinary people into monsters. It means they are no longer human." Sauan's hand tightened on the handle of his axe as he spoke.

"Sound familiar?" Ms. Waverly asked.

"You think the specters are the same things as wendigos?" Alysse said.

Ms. Waverly nodded. "Perhaps."

"Or Baines," Andrew suggested.

"To fight fire, sometimes you use fire." Ms. Waverly opened her hand to reveal a small necklace. It was made of leather, with a silver pendant about the size of a coin. Carved into the silver was the face of a dog that looked eerily similar to Macy. "This is an ancient amulet that has been in the protection of Towis and Sauan's family for many generations. It protects the wearer of the amulet against the evil spirit of a wendigo."

"It's beautiful," Jacklyn said.

Sauan looked at Macy, who was still sitting beside Ms. Waverly. "There is a legend among my people that dogs were given to us by the spirits to guard us against wendigos. Who knows if the legend is true."

"Come to me, Alysse," said Ms. Waverly.

Alysse got to her feet and did as she was asked. Ms. Waverly looked at her with a stern countenance. "I believe you are here for a reason, Alysse, even though you never wanted to come." Ms. Waverly placed the amulet in Alysse's hand and shut it tightly with her own. "Use it wisely, Alysse. Trust your instincts."

For a moment, Jacklyn thought her sister was about to cry. Alysse struggled to say anything and eventually mumbled, "Thank you." She looked up and saw Towis and Sauan smiling, and then she returned to sit next to Jacklyn.

"I have something else," said Sauan, pulling the long, sheathed knife from his waistband. "You may need this in the dark night when

I'm not there to protect you." Sauan gave the knife to Christian. "Look after your brother like my brother looks out for me."

Christian held the knife in his hand. "Are you sure?" he stammered.

"I'm sure, my strong little friend." Sauan smiled and gave Christian a playful shove. "Besides, my brother here gave me a bigger knife!" Sauan pulled out a much larger, newer, sheathed knife. He showed it to Christian, much to Towis's amusement. Everyone laughed, and then Christian carefully put the knife into the waistband of his trousers, wearing it the way Sauan had.

As the late afternoon merged into early evening, Robert became increasingly anxious. He had hardly sat still all day. Now, he seemed to be working himself into a frenzy. As the sun began to hide against the horizon, Ms. Waverly came out of the longhouse. "It's time for us to go," she murmured to them all.

Sauan checked his new knife and hooked his axe against his belt. Towis checked his quiver for arrows and tested the string on his bow. The children watched as Robert put on his hat and slipped the strap of his leather bag over his shoulder.

"We can only take you as far as Cove Neck," Ms. Waverly said. "After that, I don't know what help we can give. Baines and his specters will try to stop us. They'll know what we will be trying to do. They will want to ambush us. Remember, we have to get the letter across the sound to Connecticut at all costs."

"Let them try to stop us," Robert challenged, his face resolute.

Ms. Waverly smiled weakly and nodded. "If Baines comes, you will need to run. I don't have the strength to fight him anymore."

"The wendigo is a powerful spirit," said Sauan, looking at the children. "We will do what we can to protect you, but we cannot promise you anything else."

They started to walk. Sauan led the way. He walked swiftly, his feet confidently finding their way through the forest. They all followed in single file, with Ms. Waverly bringing up the rear. At times, they walked through clearings and skirted plowed fields. Now and again, they would have to cross a stream, either walking through the cool water or jumping from bank to bank. Sometimes the children stumbled, and when they did, Towis or Robert helped them up. Only Macy could keep up with Sauan, who would pat her head affectionately in reward.

Darkness began to set in. Alysse was unsure of where she was. All she could see were endless trees and the thick undergrowth that scratched her shins. They hadn't seen anyone on the roads, which she guessed was a good thing, but she felt tired. Her legs grew heavy and sore. The last few days had been exhausting. She just wished she could go to sleep in her own bed.

"We're nearly there," Sauan whispered. "Over the ridge, we can find a small path that will lead us down to the water."

Robert nodded. He knew the area and could tell where he was. "Caleb will be waiting for us," Robert reassured everyone. "He won't leave us. I promise."

"Let's hope not," said Andrew.

In the distance, they could see the Youngs' house. A small swirl of smoke eased from the chimney. Through the windows, the children could see dots of candlelight. From time to time, they could even see the shadows of people walking in the house.

They all crouched down in the undergrowth and looked at the road by the house, to see if anyone was coming. Everything was still and silent. Only the cicadas' rash rattle could be heard, a constant drumbeat in the night.

"Caleb will have his boat hidden down towards the inlet, about a half mile away," Robert said. "The Youngs have always been Patriots. This has been a safe harbor for us during the war."

"How do we get there?" Andrew asked.

"We can circle around the house," said Sauan. "And then we should be clear."

Robert took a deep breath. "We should go."

They quietly walked toward the road, anxiously looking for any Redcoats, but no one could be seen. Treading softly, they easily walked past the house and found their way down toward the inlet.

"Not much farther," said Robert. He was smiling. Despite the odds, he could tell they were nearly there.

The smell of the sea was powerful. The moon was now full and high, its reflection shimmering in the water like a face. They stood in the tall grass. Sauan had his hand on his axe. Towis stared into the dark, as if trying to see the invisible. Robert took off his hat. "He will be here," he promised. "Let's just wait."

The night wore on. The sky seemed to grow darker. Andrew wasn't sure what time it was, but he wanted to sleep. Christian sat next to him. Andrew nudged him. Christian gave a weak smile.

Just when Robert thought they had made a huge mistake in coming to the cove, a big man could be seen in the darkness, making his way toward them. As he drew closer, they saw the smile on the big man's face was as broad as his shoulders. Towis and Sauan withdrew into the tall grass as Robert walked up to his old friend, Caleb Brewster.

"I didn't think you would come," Robert scolded.

"And miss helping you?" Caleb teased. "How are you doing, my old friend?"

The two men embraced, patting each other on the back and laughing.

"I've been better," Robert replied.

Andrew stood close by, with Christian, Alysse, and Jacklyn just within eyesight.

"And who are your friends?" Caleb said sternly.

"You can trust them as you can trust me. We've been through quite a bit together over the last few days."

Caleb looked carefully at the children. He then turned and saw Ms. Waverly, Sauan, and Towis, standing just to the side.

"Your friends as well?" he asked casually.

Robert nodded. "The best of friends."

Caleb Brewster smiled. "For you to have friends at all, Robert, is quite a thing. I know all about that! And I guess we'll take all the friends we can in these dark days."

"There's a problem," Robert said. "We need to get this letter to Tallmadge. We think Benedict Arnold is going to betray our cause and capture His Excellency General Washington."

Caleb took a deep, sharp breath, as if he were sucking the bad news through a straw. His eyes glinted in the dark. "Sounds like my type of problem," he hissed at last.

"And the British know about me," Robert said, with a desperate expression.

Caleb Brewster stopped smiling. "What will you do?"

"It doesn't matter now. We need to get the letter to Tallmadge, and we can determine what happens after that. Where's your boat?"

"Up there. About a few hundred feet." He pointed along the cove.

"We need to go," Robert urged.

As the children joined Robert and Caleb and headed toward the boat, Macy suddenly began to growl. Her eyes were focused toward the Youngs' house. Andrew could see Towis holding up his bow, notching an arrow. Sauan pulled the axe from his belt in one hand, his knife in the other, and silently ran toward the road.

"It's Baines," Ms. Waverly said, gazing at the boys with a resigned look. "You have to go with Robert."

Andrew looked confused. He wasn't quite sure what Ms. Waverly was implying.

"We will hold them here for as long as we can," she said. "Make sure the letter gets delivered, Andrew. That is your trial; you can't fail it. My trial is here."

Andrew paused, trying to determine the right course of action. The next moment, he became aware of the copper-colored key in his pocket. The key was getting hotter. He pulled it out and saw its reassuring glow, shining in the darkness.

"Go," Ms. Waverly urged. "Get the letter to Tallmadge. Don't stop until you do."

Andrew felt himself being pulled by Robert Townsend as he watched Ms. Waverly give him one final smile. Then, she calmly walked through the tall grass, toward the road.

24

ACROSS THE DEVIL'S BELT

The children bundled themselves into Caleb Brewster's whale-boat, which lay hidden in the tall grass. Macy jumped onto Jacklyn's lap. Robert and Caleb pushed the boat into the sea, running through the water's edge before leaping on board.

Caleb rushed to the oars and began rowing. He looked excited, happy. It was obvious to Christian the thrill of the chase was something Caleb enjoyed.

"What can we do to help?" Alysse asked, trying to get her balance in the rocking boat.

"Keep out of my way, young lady," Caleb barked sharply. "And maybe then we'll get out of this with our lives."

Caleb heaved on the oars, as if wrestling two mighty snakes. Andrew heard the slap of the water against the boat and the sound of wood creaking against the oarlocks as he stared into the black sea. Caleb was breathing hard. As he pulled the boat through the water, he would groan, as if each row of the oars were a stabbing pain.

Christian looked back to the beach. He could hear shouting in the distance but couldn't make out anyone specific on the shoreline. He was terrified for Ms. Waverly, Towis, and Sauan. He couldn't believe they had just left them to face Mr. Baines and the specters by themselves, and he felt ashamed he and the others were safe on the boat, heading for Connecticut.

"We have to go back and get them," Christian said.

"We can't." Andrew's voice was flat and emotionless. "We have to get the letter to General Washington."

"But they can't beat Baines by themselves," Christian pleaded. "He'll kill them, just like he killed Grandpa George."

"They sacrificed themselves so we could complete the trial." Andrew felt numb. "We have to deliver the letter, Christian. That's what we must do, and that's what we're going to do."

"I will unfurl the sail soon," Caleb told them. "We'll be across the Devil's Belt in a couple of hours."

"Devil's Belt?" Alysse grew alarmed.

"Just another name for the Long Island Sound, is all." Caleb smiled. "One I'm very fond of, to be honest."

Robert Townsend looked across the water. The wind was up and filled the sail, pushing them forward. Now and again, Robert felt the cold flicker of sea spray as the waves lapped against the side of the boat. The moon was full and bright and shone like a lighthouse across Long Island Sound. "Bad night for smuggling," Robert said to Caleb.

"Aye, that it is," Caleb returned. "But we do what we have to, don't we?"

"Thanks for saving us," Robert murmured, but Caleb just nodded.

The children felt the rise and fall of the whaleboat as it cut through the water. Caleb manned the rudder. Robert sat next to him, clutching his leather bag tightly, frightened to let go.

"You see over there?" Caleb shouted above the wind, pointing toward Oyster Bay.

Everyone looked. Jacklyn squinted as best she could, but at first she couldn't see anything. Then, as if from nowhere, she saw what looked like the sail of a boat in the distance.

"We have company." Caleb laughed. Andrew gently half-stood in the boat, trying to keep himself balanced. He glimpsed a sail billowing in the wind. "They were waiting for us, all right," shouted Caleb. "Hold on tight, it's going to be a bumpy ride."

Caleb Brewster sailed the whaleboat as effortlessly as most people breathed. It came naturally to him. He could feel the wind and the water, as though it were part of his skin. He sensed the strength of the tide, the push of the breeze, and, with the skill only a few can master, he raced the boat faster and faster.

"They will have some work to do to catch me!" Caleb whooped, looking back at the chasing sailboat. "The British may have the best navy in the world, but I'm the best sailor."

Robert Townsend laughed. "Modest till the end, Caleb."

The boat undulated in the water as the sail, catching the wind, drove them forward. Caleb worked the boat, his hand on the rudder, feeling his way across the sound in the moonlight. Time seemed to pass quickly. Within a little while, they could all see the shoreline of Connecticut.

Robert stared back into the distance. "I don't want to dent your ego, but they are gaining on us, Caleb."

Caleb looked around. "Impossible," he challenged in disgust. But the ship following them had gained pace. The distance between them was shrinking. "Good thing we're nearly there," he screamed. "Seems as if they have the devil's breath behind them!"

Caleb rammed the whaleboat against the shore. The children were startled by the sudden jolt as the boat hit the dry land. Macy whimpered as she fell from Jacklyn's lap. Andrew held onto Christian to steady himself.

"Time to go," Caleb urged. "We have about five or ten minutes on them."

The children jumped into the shallow water and ran up onto the beach. Macy followed. Caleb and Robert pulled the boat as far as they could onto the shore to keep it from drifting away.

"In the boat, Robert," Caleb shouted. "Two muskets under the sackcloth. Get them."

Robert jumped back into the boat, took hold of the muskets, and jumped back out again.

They stood on the beach. The British ship was closing, looming larger as it came into view.

Caleb took the muskets from Robert. After quickly checking them both, he handed one back to Robert. From his bag, he gave Robert a powder horn and a packet of paper-wrapped musket balls. "One for you, and one for me." Caleb smiled. "Been a while since you held a musket in your hand rather than a quill pen."

"But I can still shoot better than you," Robert warned.

"So you would like to think." Caleb smiled, slinging his musket over his shoulder.

"Where are we going?" Jacklyn asked.

"Up there." Caleb pointed. "And then down the road a little. And then we wait for Ben."

"Major Tallmadge?" Alysse asked.

"That jumped-up little scoundrel will always be Ben to me." Caleb laughed. "Major Tallmadge! Ha! You should have seen him when he was a little boy. Never cared about anything but adventure. Always getting into trouble, that boy. And I wasn't far behind, if I'm honest." Caleb chuckled to himself as he remembered his past. Again, Alysse could see the glint in Caleb's eye. He was enjoying himself. She wondered if he saw this as anything more than just a game, or if he simply had no fear.

They set off on the beach. The British ship was close enough, now, for Andrew to see people on board. Christian looked for Mr. Baines but couldn't make him out among the chaos.

"Up here!" shouted Caleb. "We can hide in the field over there."

The children did what they were told. Running as fast as they could, they raced across a dirt road into the forest and threw themselves into the undergrowth. As they hid, Andrew smelled the pungent earth as he gasped for breath.

"How come we always seem to end up in a bush?" Jacklyn asked. "Are you kidding me?"

Andrew smiled. "You should see my scratch marks," he said. "I'm covered head to foot."

"And the mosquito bites," Christian complained, scratching at his legs. "They're driving me nuts!"

"Where's Ben?" Robert asked, looking at Caleb.

"He'll be here," Caleb promised. "We can trust Ben."

"And if he isn't?" Robert asked.

"Well, you've always been the brains of the group," Caleb said, looking at Robert with a wry smile, "so I hope you will figure something out."

Macy began to growl. The children looked at one another silently. "That's not okay," Jacklyn warned. "The specters are here." She took hold of her throwing star. It seemed eager to be in her hand ready to fight.

"We have to be quiet," Andrew warned. "They're here."

Robert prepared the musket by pouring gunpowder into the barrel, pushing the metal ball, and then tamping it with the ramming stick. Caleb did the same. Christian pulled out the knife that Sauan had given him. The sharp, dark blade looked large in his hand.

Andrew looked at Alysse and started gaping like a fish. Around her neck, the wendigo amulet was shining a dim pale blue. Alysse held the pendant in her hand, as if it were from an alien world. "What's going on?" she said.

"I'm not sure," said Andrew. "Whatever happens, stay close to me." He took her hand. "We'll be okay. I promise."

They could hear the rattle of men walking up the road. In the forest, the children crouched as low as they could, willing themselves invisible. Through the trees, they saw four soldiers. *Redcoats.* They walked cautiously along the road, their muskets pointing in front of them. A tall man brought up the rear. He wore a black cloak that reached the ground. On his head, he sported a hat that covered his face in shadow, but Andrew knew immediately, it was the specter from the garden at Raynham Hall, Mr. Mud.

Andrew turned to Christian, who nodded.

Next to Mr. Mud walked another dark figure. She also wore a black cloak, but her head was bare: she bore no hat. Instead, long, reddish hair curled around her neck like dancing serpents.

Behind them was Mr. Baines. He strutted along the road and was carrying the wolf's head cane. Christian noticed that the pommel was glowing a broody red. Mr. Baines had an eager smile on his face. He seemed euphoric, as if this was the time he had been longing for.

Caleb cocked his musket. The sound seemed deafening to the children.

Mr. Baines stopped. He tilted his head back and forth, as though trying to locate the sound. Then, he began to sniff. Large, exaggerated snorts of air, coursing through his long, thin nose. "Fe, fi, fo, fum. I smell the blood of a couple boyish pups. Be they alive or be they dead, I'll grind their bones to make my bread." Mr. Baines started to laugh. The two specters turned to him for orders. "Mr. Mud, Lady Matilda. Find them," commanded Mr. Baines.

The specters began walking along the road and then turned to the forest. They moved with a supernatural swiftness; within a few moments, they had disappeared into the gloom of the trees.

"We have to go!" Andrew snapped to Caleb.

"Go where?" Caleb responded, looking at Andrew. "This is it, young man. We stand, or we fall."

Andrew was dumbstruck.

"Robert," Caleb hissed. "You take the Redcoat on the left, I'll take the one on the right. Load and repeat. You understand?"

Robert looked at Caleb and slowly nodded. He pushed the musket up to his shoulder and pointed the barrel at one of the British soldiers.

For a moment, Andrew couldn't breathe. The air felt thick, like oily water. He gulped and gulped, but still, he felt suffocated. Everything slowed. He looked at Christian, then at the girls, and wondered what to do next.

The next moment, there was a puff of smoke, the smell of sulfur, and the crack of musket fire. Alysse covered her ears and screamed.

"And again!" Caleb ordered Robert, before the smoke had cleared. "We'll give them a run for their money before the night is done!"

Robert frantically prepared the musket. Caleb did the same. The soldiers on the road scattered. Only Mr. Baines stood firm, as though without a care in the world. He was laughing, as if someone had just pranked him.

"It ends here," shouted Mr. Baines, as he twirled the wolf's head cane. "Tonight. Your good General Washington will lose the war."

Another crack of muskets. Smoke filled the air again as Christian shook his head, trying to rid himself of the thunderous ringing in his ears. Macy crouched on the ground. She growled, her teeth sharp and threatening.

"Run!" Robert ordered as he quickly passed the letter to Andrew. "Get out of here. Find Tallmadge. Get the letter to him, or this will be for nothing."

Caleb Brewster looked at Andrew and winked. "Run, boy. Take your friends. It's time for the big boys to fight!"

Andrew looked at his brother, Alysse, and Jacklyn. Then, he watched Caleb and Robert reload the muskets. Andrew knew what he had to do, but he was rooted to the ground in fear. So many people had given so much for the trial that he felt he couldn't ask anyone else to do anymore.

Alysse, seeing the indecision on Andrew's face, stood up. The amulet around her neck was shining more brightly than ever. "Let's go," she commanded. "You heard what they said."

Standing amid the undergrowth, Alysse walked calmly to the road. Christian and Andrew blindly followed her, as if they had been charmed by a spell. Jacklyn looked at Robert and Caleb and then looked at her sister and the boys. "Go!" she shouted, holding onto Macy. "I'll stay here and help them."

Alysse nodded and stepped onto the road. Andrew and Christian ran behind her. In the distance, they saw Mr. Baines walking toward them, his wolf's head cane tightly gripped in his hand. He didn't seem concerned the children might escape him, and, as they turned to look down the road, they understood why. The two specters, Mr. Mud and Lady Matilda, stood in front of them, like two closed gates.

Andrew, Christian, and Alysse came to a sudden halt. They were trapped. Mr. Baines was to the west of them, the specters to the east.

The children looked around frantically, wondering what to do next. They could try and make a run for it through the undergrowth, but they knew they wouldn't get too far by themselves, and the specters would be upon them soon enough.

"The game is up," Mr. Baines cooed, drawing close to them, with a look of contentment, "and you played an admirable hand!"

Christian watched the wolf's head pommel. It had turned blood-shot red in the moonlight. Mr. Baines stood his ground. The specters lazily shuffled closer.

"Before we end this charade, you have something I want," Mr. Baines said. "The key."

Andrew clenched the copper-colored key in his pocket. He could feel it, pulsing. Everything they had done was now in jeopardy. He turned to look at the ugly smiles of the specters. Their eyes were thin, orange flecks, like tiger stripes. Their teeth were jagged and sharp. Their complexion was swarthy. Mr. Mud towered over Lady Matilda, but she looked just as fierce and just as threatening.

Christian held the knife Sauan had given him; even so, he was terrified. He felt more scared than he'd ever felt in his life, and wished he could be back home with Grandpa George.

As Andrew wondered what to do next, Alysse started walking to Mr. Baines. At first, the boys didn't realize what she was doing. But as they turned their attention from the specters, they watched Alysse striding forward.

"Alysse!" Andrew cried. "What are you doing?"

Alysse did not seem to hear Andrew. She pulled the amulet from her neck, breaking the leather strap. The amulet glowed daylight blue and bathed Alysse in a bold brightness. She held the amulet directly in front of her as she walked closer to Mr. Baines. In a commanding voice, she screamed:

"Leave us alone!"

Mr. Baines shrieked and drew backward. A look of pain and fear shot across his face. For a moment, he looked older. His skin became grooved and etched, like a reptile's tail. His eyes turned glassy, and his snarling lips revealed teeth that were decayed and frail.

"That thing," Mr. Baines howled in horror. "Get that thing away from me," he ordered the specters.

Both specters flew past the boys, rushing as fast as they could to obey their master's order. Christian desperately swiped at Mr. Mud with his knife, but missed. Andrew fell backward as Lady Matilda lightly set a hand on his shoulder and pushed him out of the way with a mere turn of her wrist.

"Run, Alysse!" Christian shouted.

Andrew struggled to his feet. Alysse turned as the specters rushed toward her. She raised the amulet as a warning. They stopped about six feet short of Alysse and warily eyed her.

"What's up, pretty girl?" Lady Matilda teased.

"Stay away from me," ordered Alysse. The amulet glowed in front of her.

Mr. Mud began to laugh. But Lady Matilda twiddled her hair around a long finger. "My, my, aren't you the tough little girl."

Mr. Baines had staggered back to his feet. He lifted the wolf's head cane and tried to pull the blade free from the scabbard, but it wouldn't come out. He suddenly looked flabbergasted. No matter how much he pulled on the pommel, the sword wouldn't budge.

"The amulet," he hissed again. "Get rid of the amulet and the girl."

Mr. Mud started to walk forward. Alysse eyed him cautiously. "Give me that," the specter commanded, putting his hand out, inviting Alysse to drop the wendigo amulet into his palm.

"Get away!" Alysse ordered, with a low growl. She raised the amulet. The pendant cast her whole body in blue. She took a step toward Mr. Baines, who let out another loud howl.

"Make her stop it!" Mr. Baines shouted. He doubled over and dropped the wolf's head cane onto the ground. Then, he covered his head with his hands. A look of intense pain made him grimace like a jack-o'-lantern.

"Andrew!" Christian cried. "Grab the cane!"

Andrew reached out to steal the cane. But Lady Matilda rushed forward and blocked him, protecting the wolf's head cane and allowing her master to grab it. Andrew couldn't believe it! One moment, the specter was behind him...but the next moment, she had moved with lightning speed and was standing a full two or three paces in front of him.

"Not so fast, little boy." Lady Matilda smirked.

Andrew backed away, a look of anguish on his face. He had nearly stolen the cane, and could have ended Mr. Baines's power for good.

Mr. Mud knocked Christian away then darted his hand at Alysse, trying to reach her and snatch the amulet away. Alysse stood her ground, not even bothering to look back at the specter. With fierce determination, she took another step toward Mr. Baines. Her hand held the amulet steadily in front of her. It hung straight down from its leather necklace, never quivering.

"Get it now, or I will cast you both into pain for a thousand years!" Mr. Baines furiously commanded the specters. He looked even older, more decrepit. His stature was shorter, his back hunched and bony. The suit that had fitted him so well was now too big for him. His hair was thinning, revealing a bald scalp, and the skin on his face peeled, as if sunburnt.

Mr. Mud stepped closer to Alysse. He let out a bear growl, but just as he stretched for the amulet again, a crashing came from the undergrowth.

Andrew looked up. Standing directly in front of him was Jacklyn, the throwing star in her hand. Macy stood by her side.

"You leave my sister alone!" Jacklyn shouted above the din. Andrew watched in amazement as Jacklyn pulled her hand back and, in one effortless movement, threw the star.

The throwing star spun free from her fingers. It buzzed through the air. Mr. Mud watched as it cut toward him, but he had little time to do anything about it. The throwing star hit him with a dull thud. Mr. Mud's eyes bulged wide, and he let out an ear-piercing shriek.

Andrew stared open-mouthed. The throwing star had hit the specter directly in the heart. Mr. Mud reached out and began to clutch at it, but there was nothing he could do. The tall specter fell to his knees and let out a long, agonizing moan that echoed through the forest. Gasping for his last breath of air, Mr. Mud threw back his head and shouted one last time at the sky in frustration. And then he began to crumble like a knocked-over sand castle. Within seconds, he was gone forever.

"*Shedazzle!*" shouted Jacklyn. She crossed her arms in front of her and beamed in delight.

Lady Matilda darted toward Alysse.

"Run, Alysse!" Andrew shouted.

But the next moment, Macy sprinted forward, galloping effortlessly through the grass. She leaped at Lady Matilda, sinking her teeth into the specter's ankle. Then, she shook her head wildly. Lady Matilda let out a high-pitched yell, forcing everyone to cover their ears. She gave Macy a quick kick to the stomach. Macy fell backward and yelped as she landed on the ground.

Alysse began to run. She slid the amulet into her pocket and sprinted to Jacklyn. Lady Matilda saw her chance and rushed to intercept Alysse before she could get to her sister. Grabbing Alysse by the arm, Lady Matilda pulled her around, until they looked each other face to face. Lady Matilda smiled at Alysse with jagged teeth, and then lowered her head and gently bit Alysse on the shoulder. Alysse screamed. Andrew and Christian could do nothing more than watch in horror.

The loud *pop!* of musket fire again came from up the hill. Andrew first saw the burst of smoke, then heard the *whizz* of the iron ball. Christian watched as Caleb Brewster lowered his musket. Then, Christian saw Lady Matilda swirl around, falling to the ground while letting out another high-pitched scream. Alysse, freed from Lady Matilda's grip, slumped listlessly onto the ground.

"Alysse!" Jacklyn shouted, running to her sister. Andrew and Christian followed.

Recovering his strength, Baines gingerly got to his feet, using the wolf's head cane to stand up. Unshackled from the glow of the wendigo amulet, he was looking more like himself, but he was still not quite the same man. Gone were the signs of age that had made him seem so weak and vulnerable. Instead, Baines looked dazed and woozy, as if he'd just walked off a terrifying roller coaster. He went to pull the sword from the wolf's head cane, but still, it wouldn't come out. It was jammed, as if melted into place by the amulet. He looked disgusted, and he stared at the four children with dripping hatred.

Caleb reloaded his musket and began to walk down the hill. He raised it up to his shoulder, ready to fire. Lady Matilda had stopped screaming. She was crouched on the ground, holding her injured arm. A steady stream of blood flowed between her skinny fingers like sticky molasses.

"I don't know what evil you have brought here tonight," Caleb shouted at Mr. Baines, "but it's nothing a musket ball through the heart won't cure."

Baines turned to stare at Caleb. For the first time, there was a look of uncertainty in Mr. Baines's eyes as he tried to understand what was happening. He turned to look at Lady Matilda, who was hissing in pain, making a sound like a punctured tire.

Then, the ground began to shudder. In the near distance, Jacklyn heard the voices of men and the pounding of horse's hoofs. It reminded her of the encounter with Mr. Sandy Voice on the Huntington Road, but this time she could tell more horses and men were approaching.

Caleb Brewster grinned wildly. The sound of horses, the voices of men, and the rattle of swords became even more distinct. "Thank Goodness for Ben Tallmadge!" Caleb whispered to himself. "Even if he's a scoundrel."

Alysse lay on the ground, moaning. Her sister tended to her, along with Andrew and Christian.

While the children were preoccupied, Baines gazed along the road. Lady Matilda, limping and holding her arm, slowly made her way over to her master. The look of loathing on Baines's face magnified. He looked desperately around him, deciding what to do next. His eyes found those of Andrew's. For the briefest of moments, Andrew felt the hate and the pain of Mr. Baines, as if he were being touched by a devil's hand. It lasted no longer than an instant, before Mr. Baines started smiling again. The shield of impenetrability had returned as Mr. Baines fully regained his strength. Holding Lady Matilda next to him, he spoke with the calmest of voices: "See you again soon, my young pup."

Then, retreating into the forest, Mr. Baines and Lady Matilda suddenly disappeared, like nighttime after daybreak.

25

JOURNEY'S END

J acklyn crouched next to her sister. Alysse still lay on the ground, quietly moaning in pain.

"Are you okay?" Jacklyn's eyes were full tears.

"It hurts," was all Alysse could say.

Macy licked Alysse's hand and whimpered softly. The boys began to lift her up. "It will be okay," Andrew said. "We'll get you some help."

"I don't want to turn into one of them," Alysse insisted, through muffled sobs. "Please, don't let me turn into a specter."

Caleb and Robert ran down the hill as the troop of horses rounded the road. There were four men dressed in dusty-blue uniforms with white trim. They wore bright silver helmets with white plume feathers. This was the Second Continental Light Dragoons, one of the most distinguished regiments in General Washington's Continental Army. Major Ben Tallmadge rode in front. He rode over to Caleb, who was striding purposefully along the road to meet his old friend.

"Am I glad to see you." Caleb laughed with relief.

"First I've ever heard you say that," said Major Ben Tallmadge. "Usually, you tell me off for being late!"

He dismounted his horse then walked up to Caleb and warmly shook the hand of his oldest comrade.

"So, who are your new friends?"

Ben looked at the four children and then turned to look at Robert.

"This man here," said Caleb, "is Robert Townsend. But you know him as Culper Junior."

A look of astonishment crossed Ben's face as he stared at Robert Townsend. "You shouldn't be here," he said at last. "You have compromised your safety, sir."

Robert gently nodded his head. "I'm afraid we had no option," he said. "We had to get an important piece of intelligence to His Excellency George Washington, and, well, things didn't go as planned."

"I see that," said Ben, and then he turned to look at the children.

Caleb, as if sensing the next question, gently coughed. "Well, you see, it's a long story. But without these children, we wouldn't have got the message across the sound for you to take to Washington."

Ben looked at his old friend sympathetically. "When we have dinner in more peaceful times, you can tell me the whole story."

Robert called for Andrew, who ran over to him. "Have you got the letter, son?"

Andrew pulled the small, square piece of paper from his pocket and gave it to Robert.

"This is for His Excellency George Washington. We have information that Benedict Arnold is going to betray his country and give up West Point to the British," said Robert.

Ben Tallmadge looked stunned.

"It's true, Ben," insisted Caleb. "We have to warn His Excellency. They also plan to capture Washington and hold him ransom."

"Well," said Ben, "perhaps you can tell him that yourself."

"What do you mean?" asked Robert.

"Washington is but two minutes down the road, with Alexander Hamilton. They were traveling with us before he was scheduled to go to West Point and meet General Arnold."

"General Washington is here?" asked Robert, with a twinge of fear.

"Indeed," Ben said. "In fact, I think I hear him coming now."

The rest of the children had walked over to stand by Robert and Caleb. Christian stood on one side of Alysse, doing his best to hold her up, while Jacklyn stood on the other side. Alysse was gently crying but trying hard not to be heard. The wound on her shoulder was small, but blood had beaded on her shirt like red rain. Macy was standing close to the children, and now and again licked her stomach, where Lady Matilda had kicked her.

The sound of horses grew louder. Andrew looked down the road, until, eventually, he could see a small group of men riding toward them. In the middle of the group, on a gray-dappled horse, rode General George Washington. He sat commandingly in his saddle and rode effortlessly through the night.

"Is that who I think it is?" asked Jacklyn, with an incredulous voice.

"I think so," Andrew replied.

"General George Washington," Christian stated. "Can you actually believe it?"

Even Alysse managed to ignore the pain to smile for the briefest of moments.

Once the group of riders had reached them, Ben walked up to General Washington, who sat silently on his horse. Christian watched the men talking, looks of shock and dismay slowly dawning on their faces as they heard the news. After what seemed like a long time, General Washington nudged his horse, commanding it to walk slowly over to the children.

Caleb and Robert bowed stiffly to General Washington. The four children copied the bows as best as they could, but somehow they didn't feel they had done it right.

"I want to thank you for your service," General Washington said. His voice was calm and full of authority. "You are a credit to yourself and to your country."

"Thank you, Your Excellency," said a bashful Robert.

Caleb grinned. "It's my pleasure, sir."

"The news you bring is alarming to me and will be for many others. I pray it's not true, but I fear it is. Whatever the truth, we will find it out, and we will bring the guilty to justice."

Then, General Washington looked at Andrew, Christian, Alysse, and Jacklyn.

"You have been incredibly brave for ones that are so young." The General smiled as he praised them. "I am indebted to you and your efforts."

"Thank you, sir," said Andrew, and he bowed awkwardly again.

General Washington took off his hat and nodded. "We must be off. There is work to do and treacherous plots to foil." He gave them a wink before putting his hat back on and returning to his men.

"We have to get Alysse back to Raynham Hall," Jacklyn urged Caleb. "Please, can you help us?"

Caleb smiled. "Of course I can." He then turned to Robert. "And what about you, my old friend? Are you going home?"

Robert looked glum. "I don't think I have a home to go back to. The British know who I am. They will be waiting for me."

Ben put his hand on Robert's arm. "Then come with us and work with the Continental Army," he invited. "We need loyal men like you. And once we've won this war, then you can go home."

Robert nodded and threw his bag over his shoulder. "I don't think I have much of an alternative."

Robert turned to the four children.

"I guess our time together has come to an end." A warmth came into Robert Townsend's eyes as he hugged each of the children in turn. "Let's hope we get to meet one another again, soon."

♈

They sailed back toward Long Island, the wind steadily pushing them homeward. Alysse looked pale. Her head was feverishly clammy, and her hair was lank. Despite the warmth of the night, she felt cold. Jacklyn hugged her sister as they sailed through the night. She rubbed Alysse's arms, trying to keep her warm.

"I feel very sleepy…" Alysse said.

"Don't go to sleep," Christian warned. "You have to stay awake. We have to get you back to the fissure."

"What happens then?" asked Jacklyn. Her face was clouded with fear.

"I'm not sure," Christian said. "But we have to get her home, to our Oyster Bay. That's the only thing I can think of."

"Can you feel it? The fissure?" Andrew asked.

"Yes. Loud and clear." Christian smiled. "I think we did what we had to do. Now we need to get back."

Andrew sensed the copper-colored key glowing in his pocket. Its gentle warmth made him smile to himself.

Caleb knew where best to moor the boat along the cove near Oyster Bay. The shoreline was dark, but the moon made the night seem much brighter, as if a giant beacon were showing them the way. Once they landed, they crept off the boat and walked into the tall grass. Macy jumped eagerly ashore while Christian and Jacklyn carried Alysse between them like a mannequin.

It was late, well past midnight, and no one was around.

"It's about a half mile from here to Raynham Hall," said Caleb. "Can she make it?"

Alysse was drifting in and out of consciousness. Her forehead was covered with sweat, and her face was paper white and hollow. She could barely stand by herself, and without the help of Christian and Jacklyn, she would have quickly crumpled to the floor. Now and again, she let out a soft moan.

"I don't understand," said Caleb. "It was only a small bite. I've had worse from an opossum."

"Trust me," Jacklyn said. Her eyes were red from crying. "You don't want to be bitten by one of those gnarly things!"

"I'll carry her."

In a swift movement, Caleb lifted Alysse into his burly arms, and they all walked to Raynham Hall.

The old saltbox house was quiet and dark as it came into view. The children and Caleb made their way to the garden, looking around anxiously, checking to see if they were being watched. But the British had apparently left the house abandoned.

Christian could feel the tingling in his stomach intensify as they drew closer. It was pulsing, like waves lapping the beach. "We're going home." He smiled excitedly to himself.

As they walked to the garden, they saw a figure standing in the dark shadows beside the barn. Everyone became tense until the figure stepped into the moonlight.

"Ms. Waverly." Andrew laughed.

"Shh!" Ms. Waverly urged as Andrew hugged her wildly. "I'm glad to see you, too."

"I can feel it, Ms. Waverly," Christian said, rubbing his stomach.

Ms. Waverly nodded. "So can I."

"How did you get here?" Christian asked. "We thought you were killed by Baines."

Ms. Waverly smiled as she looked at Christian. "Sometimes discretion is the better part of valor."

Christian had a puzzled look on his face. "What does that mean?"

Ms. Waverly paused. "Sometimes it's better to run away like a scaredy cat than to stand and fight like a lion. And we ran as fast as we could."

"And what about Towis and Sauan?" Andrew asked. He desperately wanted to see the two young men and thank them for all their help.

"They ran faster than me!" Ms. Waverly smiled. "They would have done anything to stop Baines, but we knew it was useless. As long as we caused enough of a diversion for you to get away, everything was good. They are safe at home now."

Then, Ms. Waverly saw Alysse.

"She was bitten by Lady Matilda," Jacklyn said. "There was nothing we could do about it."

Ms. Waverly looked at Alysse and put her hand on her brow. "We have to get her home," she said. "There's nothing we can do for her here. We have to get her through the fissure. Only the fissure can save her."

They looked at the garden beside Raynham Hall. It was dark and quiet, and, to the ordinary eye, there was nothing unusual to perceive. The trees stood still. Only their leaves fluttered gently in the breeze.

"Can you see it?" asked Ms. Waverly of Christian. "The fissure?"

Christian stared hard. At first, he couldn't see anything, but then he saw a faint shimmer of light. It lit up briefly, then melted back into the night. The fissure was there, it was open. Christian's whole being felt a glow of warmth as the fissure revealed itself again to him for a brief second.

Andrew walked up to Caleb and held out his hand. "It's time for us to go."

"Go where?" Caleb asked, shaking Andrew's hand with a look of puzzlement on his face.

"To where we belong," said Andrew.

"You mean it's not here?" Caleb was more confused than ever.

"Not quite," said Andrew. "But it's very close to here. Sort of."

Caleb embraced Andrew in a bear hug, his forearms almost squeezing all the air from him. "You take care of yourself, Master Andrew, and make sure you get Miss Alysse the help she needs."

Andrew nodded. "We will."

Caleb looked at Ms. Waverly, who smiled back. "Don't worry," she said. "Robert will be all right."

Caleb looked reassured and tipped his finger to his forehead. Within a few seconds, he was gone.

Ms. Waverly lifted Alysse with all her strength.

"Are we going home?" Alysse asked in a thin voice.

"We are," Ms. Waverly comforted her. "Just a few more minutes and we'll all be back to your Oyster Bay."

Macy came beside them, and they all stood beside the fissure. In the right light, the children could see its edges rippling like silver, moon-lit water.

"It's beautiful," remarked Jacklyn. "It didn't look like this when we came through the other side."

When they were ready, Andrew took hold of his brother's hand. Christian reached out to Jacklyn, who firmly held onto Macy. Ms. Waverly still had Alysse in her arms.

"It's time," said Christian.

Andrew held the copper-colored key in his hand as they walked into the fissure. Christian felt it open, welcoming them in. His stomach somersaulted as he felt the edges of the fissure wrap around his body and cover him like a warm duvet. He saw Andrew in front of him, Jacklyn beside him. A sudden sense of happiness began to envelop him, as if the fissure were happy to see them and welcome them home.

When he could see again, Andrew realized they were in the garden of Raynham Hall. The streetlights were flickering orange and then went off, as if broken. He could see the white picket fence, the familiar flowers and the blanket of grass. The garden was dark. His senses weren't quite back to normal when a huge flash of lightning blazed above him, making the air flicker and sizzle like a firework. He could see Ms. Waverly, carrying Alysse, and checked to see Christian, Jacklyn, and Macy.

Everyone was there. Everyone was safe.

Andrew's head hurt for a brief moment, but he shook it off like sleep. He was trying to get his bearings. What time was it? He wasn't sure. He watched as Ms. Waverly put Alysse down. When Andrew could see her, Alysse was smiling. She didn't look sick anymore, and Macy was excitedly jumping up and down on Jacklyn.

Andrew turned and saw Christian. "Are we home?" he asked.

Christian beamed. "I think so."

"But when?" Andrew said.

"Just after we entered the fissure," Ms. Waverly said, looking at them both. Her face was serious.

"Grandpa!"

Andrew ran to the fence and saw Grandpa George lying on his side in the street, the back of his head facing them. "Grandpa!" he shouted again, and hopped the fence. He raced into the road and wrapped his arms around his grandfather. Within a few seconds, Christian was there, too.

"Grandpa?" Andrew implored. "Grandpa, can you hear me?"

Sticky red blood covered his grandfather's shirt and pooled in the road; Andrew touched his grandfather's face. His skin felt cold, but Andrew was sure Grandpa George was still breathing.

"Grandpa!" Christian shouted. "Wake up!"

The old man's eyes flickered open, and he let out a dull moan.

"It's okay, Grandpa," Christian said, trying to keep calm. "We're here."

Andrew looked for help. He couldn't see anyone on the street.

Grandpa George began coughing, and then, in a voice barely audible, he asked, "Did you do it?"

Andrew choked back tears. "Yes, Grandpa. We finished the trial. We really did it."

Christian could see the glimmer of a smile on his grandfather's lips.

"The fissure," Grandpa George croaked. "I can feel it calling me."

Christian looked back to the garden. The fissure was still open, shimmering in the dark. He could also feel the fissure's pulse in his stomach—but, this time, it felt different. Stronger. Warmer.

"Get me to the fissure, my boys." Grandpa George's voice was guttural. He squinted at them through his glasses. The brilliant blue eyes were dimming. "Please boys," he begged. "Get me to the fissure."

The boys tried to pick up Grandpa George, but he was too heavy.

"Help us!" Andrew called.

Ms. Waverly, Alysse, and Jacklyn ran from the garden. Even Macy trotted over. Grandpa George whimpered in pain as Ms. Waverly and the children dragged him to the fissure.

Men and women began congregating at the end of West Main Street and South Street, now, looking at the tree that crossed the road, burning viciously from the lightning strike. Now and again, they would point and cover their mouths in shock. Andrew and Christian didn't see them. They heaved with all their might as they pulled their grandfather into the garden.

"Lay him down over there," Ms. Waverly suggested.

They pulled Grandpa George as close as they could to the entrance of the fissure. A deep sigh came from their grandfather as they gently rested him on the grass. He lay completely still. His eyes were hardly open, and all color had drained from his face. The boys couldn't believe what was happening.

"Step back," Ms. Waverly warned. She ushered Andrew and Christian back a few paces, over to where Jacklyn and Alysse were standing quietly with Macy.

They all stared at the fissure. It glowed a warm yellow, like sunlight, and was making a faint buzzing noise. It grew bigger and bigger, gathering closer to where Grandpa George lay on the ground. As soon as the fissure reached him, the light became brighter and more intense. The children squinted as the pulsating fissure began to fold itself over Grandpa George until, finally, it engulfed him completely. And then, Grandpa George and the fissure were gone.

Everything went dark again.

"What happened?" Andrew shouted. He turned to look at Ms. Waverly for an explanation.

Ms. Waverly stared back at him blankly. "I don't know," she confessed. "I've never seen anything like that before."

Andrew panicked. "Christian, can you feel the fissure?"

Christian shook his head with a look of disbelief. "It's gone. I can't feel anything."

The children heard the sounds of the fire engines as they rounded onto South Street and then drove up West Main Street. The townspeople ran down the road, pointing at the blazing tree and the fallen power lines that buzzed and flickered with sparks. People were shouting in confusion.

"We have to go," Ms. Waverly said. "There's nothing more we can do here."

"But what are we going to do about Grandpa George?" Christian asked.

"The fissure has closed. There's nothing I can do. I can't just summon it back."

Ms. Waverly looked desperate, and both boys could see she was telling the truth.

Andrew felt empty, as if someone had just pulled his insides out, like the stuffing from a teddy bear. For as long as he could remember, Grandpa George had been in his life. He felt he had lost him once, when they first went through the fissure. Now, he felt the same pain of loss . . .

"He can't be gone!" Christian cried, trying to hold back tears.

"We have to go," Ms. Waverly said again. "I can't give you any answers. Sometimes things just don't make sense."

She guided the children from the garden. Andrew and Christian blankly followed her, not knowing what else to do. Alysse and Jacklyn trailed quietly behind them, alongside Macy.

They could see the fire engines at the end of West Main Street. The firemen were hooking up the hoses to the hydrant. They were shouting orders to each other as they worked. The flashing of the sirens lit the street and houses with blue and red light. The noise was deafening.

As they stepped into the street, Christian stopped suddenly. In his stomach, he began to feel a familiar sensation—the warm, fluttering pulse of the fissure. He turned to look at Ms. Waverly. Their eyes met for the briefest of moments, before Christian ran back to the garden.

"What's going on?" Andrew cried, as he watched Christian racing back to Raynham Hall.

"The fissure!" Christian shouted back to his brother.

Andrew looked at Ms. Waverly, and they both ran, to follow Christian.

The fissure was open again in the garden of Raynham Hall. Its edges glowed gold and platinum. Christian stood a few feet in front of it. He could feel the light on his face and body, basking him in warmth. Andrew ran to stand beside him. Alysse, Jacklyn, and Ms. Waverly huddled close by, with Macy. The sounds of the fire engine, the shouts of the people, the wailing of the sirens, were all forgotten as the fissure grew in size.

At first, they saw a hand come through the fissure. It looked familiar. And then…an arm. Within a few seconds, they saw the outline of a shape, the form of a tall man. The fissure grew brighter and brighter, almost blinding them all. Christian and Andrew covered their eyes with their arms. Gold light gave way to a calm blue, shimmering before it dimmed, almost disappearing.

The boys uncovered their eyes and blinked in the dark. Standing before them like a vision was Grandpa George. But something was different. Instead of the familiar Grandpa George, they both knew so well, this Grandpa George seemed much younger, as if layers of age had been peeled away from him.

"Hello, my boys," Grandpa George beamed. "I'm back!"

The boys rushed up to him and folded Grandpa George in their arms. Grandpa George bent down, picked them both up, and hugged them back. "My boys. My beautiful boys."

Ms. Waverly stared at Grandpa George with a look of bewilderment. "There's something different about you," she stammered. "I can feel it."

Grandpa George looked at her with his big blue eyes. "It would seem so," he replied.

"Has the fissure made you a Watcher?" Ms. Waverly beamed with excitement.

Grandpa George nodded. "Don't ask me how and don't ask me why, because I don't know." He smiled. "All I know is I'm glad to be here, and I feel great…like, the best I've felt in years!"

Ms. Waverly laughed as she touched Grandpa George fondly on the arm. "You look so much younger."

Grandpa George nodded again.

Ms. Waverly looked at the fissure. It had begun to shimmer blue, slowly building in brightness. "I feel it calling me," she whispered.

Grandpa George held Ms. Waverly's hand. "I know," he said. "I saw some things when I was in the fissure. It needs you. Baines hasn't been defeated. I think the fissure wants us to stop Baines once and for all."

Ms. Waverly smiled at Grandpa George. Turning to Alysse and Jacklyn, she kissed each in turn and wished them a quiet goodbye. Then, she turned to Andrew and Christian and ruffled their hair. "I'll see you soon." The boys nodded, and then Christian rushed up to Ms. Waverly and embraced her. Andrew quickly followed suit.

Ms. Waverly looked at Grandpa George. Taking a quick step toward him, she gave him a soft kiss on the lips. "Don't keep me waiting this time," she said, and then quickly stepped into the fissure. It gleamed as if happy to welcome home an old friend, and then, it faded into the night.

Grandpa George stood silently for a few moments. He took a deep breath in sadness before turning to face the children and Macy.

"Nice to see you again, young ladies," Grandpa George said to Alysse and Jacklyn. "And you Macy!"

The girls smiled, and Macy wagged her stubby tail as Grandpa George petted her ears.

"And we're glad to see you," replied Jacklyn. "I defeated Mr. Mud."

"I know," said Grandpa George, with a grin. "I hoped you would."

"So what now?" Andrew asked. He stood close to Grandpa George, as if scared he might run away.

"Well, I'm sure you have plenty to tell me," said Grandpa George. "I know I have plenty to tell you. So why don't we go back to my house and have a nice cup of tea?"

EPILOGUE
FORT HILL CEMETERY

The next day was an unseasonable, chilly June day. A brisk breeze blew through the trees, and the sky was a clear, cool blue. It was the first day of the summer vacation. Andrew and Christian slept late, grateful they didn't have to go to school.

Grandpa George made breakfast, as usual. The boys stared at him in amazement. He seemed so much younger. His skin was smoother, his eyes brighter. He was slimmer, and he looked much stronger than before. He danced around the kitchen, making pancakes and frying eggs. As soon as he saw the boys walking sleepily up to the counter-top, he gave them both a strong, crushing hug.

"I'm so glad to see you, boys." Grandpa George laughed.

Andrew and Christian's mom and dad sat in the family room. As usual, their eyes were firmly attached to their laptops. Neither their mom nor their dad had noticed or commented about Grandpa George's sudden youth.

"I can't believe how different you look," Andrew remarked.

"I *feel* different," Grandpa George replied.

"What will you tell people?" Christian asked.

"I'll tell them that I've been going to the gym and drinking carrot juice." He giggled. "That should get them all wondering, or asking me where I buy my carrots."

"So, you're a Watcher now," Andrew said. "What does that mean?"

"I'm not sure," Grandpa George said. "At least, not yet. I saw things in the fissure that I don't understand. But I know I will, in time."

"How long were you in there?" Christian asked.

"Hours. Perhaps a day, at most. It was hard to tell. Time has no meaning in the fissure."

Christian eagerly ate his breakfast. "These are the best pancakes ever!" he declared.

"Didn't you like the bread and cheese that Ms. Waverly brought you?" Grandpa George asked.

"How did you know about that?" Andrew said.

"The fissure," Grandpa George answered. "It showed me everything you went through. You were very brave."

The boys smiled. "We had a lot of help from Alysse and Jacklyn," Andrew said.

"And Macy," Christian quipped.

"I knew there was a reason you all had to take the trial," Grandpa George said. "Even Macy."

The boys laughed.

"After breakfast, I want to show you something," Grandpa George added. "It's important."

The boys nodded.

They got dressed and left the house. Andrew and Christian were glad to be back in their Oyster Bay. They heard the bells of St. Dominic's, the leaf blowers, and the cars. Next door, they could hear Michael playing the trombone, and the boys up the street were bouncing a basketball and shooting hoops, laughing. Grandpa George seemed happy, and both boys were glad that he was still alive.

They walked down South Street, turned left onto Tooker, then rounded the corner and stopped.

"Look up," said Grandpa George. "Look at the street sign."

"Simcoe Street," Christian said in amazement.

"Strange, isn't it?" Grandpa George asked. "An enemy of General Washington has a street named after him in Oyster Bay!"

"He wasn't very nice," said Andrew.

"In war, there are good and bad guys on either side," Grandpa George remarked.

They walked up Simcoe Street. At the end of the road stood a row of trees. "Come on, boys," he said. "Follow me."

Andrew and Christian did as Grandpa George asked. As they walked through the trees, they came to a small cemetery. Aged gravestones, covered in moss and weathered by time, stood in the ground. Some were straight, some leaned a little to the side. Wild grass grew in places. A flag had been set on some of the gravestones.

"Where are we?" Andrew asked.

"This is Fort Hill Cemetery," Grandpa George said. "A lot of wonderful people were laid to rest here."

"Such as—?" Christian asked.

"Read the names," Grandpa George instructed. "See for yourself."

Andrew and Christian started to walk among the tombstones. Some of the graves were overgrown, but most were carefully looked after. Suddenly Christian stopped. He knelt down and rubbed his hands across the words engraved on the stone. "This gravestone says, 'Samuel Townsend.' " Christian looked at Grandpa George. "Is that the Samuel we know?"

"It is," Grandpa George confirmed. "Although when he died, he was an old man, and quite successful."

"And this one says 'Sarah Townsend,' " Andrew said. "Is that Samuel's Aunt?"

"That's right," Grandpa George replied. "This is the Townsend family graveyard. Most of the early Townsends are buried here."

The boys strolled over to one particular tombstone. They crouched down beside it and stroked the carved lettering with their fingertips. "This is Robert Townsend's grave," said Andrew solemnly.

Grandpa George nodded.

Andrew began to feel a tightening in his chest as he realized what he was seeing. "He died?" Andrew asked.

"He lived nearly two hundred and fifty years ago and was eighty-one when he passed away. Despite living a long life, he never told anyone he was Culper Junior, or that he helped General Washington win the War of Independence," .

"But we saw him only yesterday," Christian protested. He touched the gravestone and remembered the stern but friendly man who was Robert Townsend.

"And in some ways, he is still living," Grandpa George said. "We only see time in the present, but as you know, people exist in many different times." He smiled.

"Can you bend time, Grandpa, now that you're a Watcher?" Christian asked.

Grandpa George laughed. "I'm learning, but I haven't got it mastered yet. I may still need some help."

The boys looked at the graves.

"I'm going to miss them," Andrew said. "Samuel and Robert… Caleb…Towis…Sauan."

"I know," Grandpa George agreed.

"Whatever happened to Major Andre?" Christian asked.

Grandpa George stood silently for a while before answering. "As you know, John Andre was part of a secret plan with Benedict Arnold to give West Point to the British. The plan failed, thanks to your help and that of the Culper Spy Ring. Andre was eventually captured by the American Continental Army as he tried to escape back to New York, and unfortunately, they hung him as a spy."

Christian was stunned.

"But he was such a nice man. He helped me find Macy. He hurt nobody."

Christian felt a sharp stab of pain in his stomach. He had grown very fond of Major Andre; knowing that he had been executed made him feel incredibly upset.

"It was our fault that Major Andre died," Christian confessed.

"No," Grandpa George said, firmly. "What happened would have happened with or without us, if history was allowed to unfurl as usual. It was only because of Baines and the trial that an alternate history became possible. All you did was ensure history unfolded correctly and didn't get changed to serve what Baines wanted."

Christian still felt sad. He remembered Major John Andre's kindness, his cheerful voice, and how all he wanted was to return home, to London.

They stood in silence for a few minutes. The sun rose higher in the sky, but there was still a freshness in the air. Now and again, they heard birdsong.

"Do you feel it yet, Christian?" Grandpa George asked.

Christian looked at his grandfather, who winked at him.

"The fissure!" Christian said, smiling. "I can feel the faint pulse."

"We have to stop Baines," Grandpa George said. "Andrew, you were right. We have to take that wolf's head cane away from Baines. If we do that, Baines loses his power. But it's risky. Either he defeats us, or we defeat him. One of us has to win."

Andrew looked at his grandfather enthusiastically.

"Use that phone of yours and text Alysse and Jacklyn. We can't do this without them."

"Do what?" Andrew asked.

"Another trial?" Christian replied.

"Are you kidding me?" Andrew laughed.

"No," said Grandpa George. "I'm not kidding you. Only this time...I'm coming with you."

Made in the USA
Columbia, SC
09 February 2018